By Jesse Hill Ford

Novels

MOUNTAINS OF GILEAD

THE LIBERATION OF LORD BYRON JONES

THE FEAST OF SAINT BARNABAS

Play

THE CONVERSION OF BUSTER DRUMWRIGHT

Stories

FISHES, BIRDS AND SONS OF MEN

THE
FEAST
OF
SAINT
BARNABAS

THE
FEAST
OF
SAINT
BARNABAS

by JESSE HILL FORD

An Atlantic Monthly Press Book
LITTLE, BROWN AND COMPANY · BOSTON · TORONTO

A portion of this book appeared originally in the *Atlantic*.

ATLANTIC–LITTLE, BROWN BOOKS
ARE PUBLISHED BY
LITTLE, BROWN AND COMPANY
IN ASSOCIATION WITH
THE ATLANTIC MONTHLY PRESS

*Published simultaneously in Canada
by Little, Brown & Company (Canada) Limited*

PRINTED IN THE UNITED STATES OF AMERICA

To
PETER DAVISON

THE
FEAST
OF
SAINT
BARNABAS

1

THE WOODYARD

I t is still called Papa John's.

It was a grocery when the Woodyard had lumber stacked on
it, during the days of the last of the sailing ships when Ormund
City was a leading lumber port on the Florida west coast — a
condition that vanished like the sailing ships early in this century at which point in time the Woodyard became haven and
headquarters for Negro whiskey distillers and Cuban rum-
runners, Spanish Negroes and Catholic Negroes and part-In-
dian scrub Negroes who drifted into Ormund City from the
citrus groves inland and drank the rum and the Woodyard
whiskey. The Woodyard was the beginning of Ormund City's
central niggertown. The Woodyard became the gathering
place for Negro stevedores and railroad workers, by which time
the store was owned by a black Jamaican Catholic who called
himself Papa John.

Papa John sold charms and love potions. Hung by a leather
thong about his scrawny neck he wore a small gray bag, made,
it was said, from a mouse skin, and containing certain relics
which were said to place the wearer beyond death. Thus Papa
John's life was charmed and to prove it the black man walked
into the midst of knife fights. The little skin bag protected

him. It was rumored fire would not burn him, and it was a fact well known that each Friday midnight Papa John talked and conversed with the Devil.

The Woodyard was so much his kingdom that in time the neighborhood became known exclusively as Papa John's Woodyard. The grip of legend had grown so powerful that when Papa John finally died nobody could think what to do with him. One and all, they believed he was 150-years-old. Nobody would touch him.

A young midwife (who deviled crabs and peddled them in the neighborhood) was sent for, and the midwife, taking an ice pick, carefully raised one eyelid. She held a fragment of mirror a hairsbreadth from Papa John's nostrils. No eye movement; no breath. Satisfied Papa John was dead and not merely entranced, she hesitated, nonetheless. She was afraid.

A big Cuban stevedore who had been watching all this while, a huge fellow not supposed to be afraid of anything, fetched a pair of ice tongs. Hooking the tongs under the cheekbones he dragged the frail corpse. Out of the store he dragged it, and straight up the bright, sunny street and into the shade of a big water oak. Leaving the little corpse lie where it was the Cuban went back to the store for rope, seven fathoms of it. When he returned, with the rope worn in a coil over one of his powerful shoulders, he slowly explained that in all such cases the corpse must be hanged. Otherwise . . .

The corpse was duly hanged. Still no one touched it. The marks left by the tongs gave the fragile features of the dead man a dignity never possessed for them in life. The marks began to ooze. "Papa John shedding tears," said the Cuban. The very sign he had been waiting for, said he. And now he required a barrel.

A barrel was brought. The Cuban stationed it upright, directly below Papa John's bare, bony feet. The Cuban stood back then and eased off suddenly on the rope. Down came the corpse into the barrel. The Cuban jerked the remainder of the rope from the tree and a little gray billygoat beard of Spanish moss came down with the bitter end. The Cuban coiled the rope — all seven fathoms — and dropped it in the barrel. He tossed the ice tongs in, and finally, even the little beard of moss. He called for salt.

The little midwife fetched a bag of ice cream salt from the store. The Cuban shook his head. "The ignorance of people!" he seemed to be saying. "Wrong salt," he explained loudly. "*Fine* salt. *Table* salt! Eh? Quick!"

The young midwife nodded her head. Embarrassed, she went slowly back to the store toting the ice cream salt. Up the bright sandy street she went with everyone silently watching her. Her head tied in a red bandanna, her blue calico dress was swaying — barefoot she went, treading her own shadow barefoot in the white blazing sunlight, and above, the sky blazed with brassy heat. Flies troubled about the rim of the barrel.

She came slowly back to the shade of the great tree bringing a red box of table salt.

Taking the box the Cuban opened the metal spout with his thumbnail. He dropped a few grains in his hand. He tasted it. He nodded, looked all around, and spat. "Table salt," he said. And now at last, he began measuring salt into his huge hand. The white grains poured gently, a few at a time like sand in an hourglass. Each little white mound grew slowly in the Cuban's flat, steady palm.

Seven portions he poured, counting in Spanish. "*Uno, dos, tres, cuatro* . . ."

He carefully dumped each portion into the barrel as it was counted. ". . . *cinco* . . . *seis* . . . *siete!*"

This done, all seven measures, he handed the salt box to the midwife. "The rum!" he said. "Quick, now!"

The midwife brought a bottle. She poured for him. He held his hands over the barrel, washing them in rum. Then he took the bottle from her, raised it to his lips, took a swig and tossed the remainder, bottle and all, into the barrel. The midwife handed him a clean flour sack. He dried his hands.

"Nothing more now until after sundown," he said. The midwife picked up the round wooden lid. She put it carefully on the barrel.

"What day?" the Cuban asked. Loudly, wanting all to hear.

"Sunday," she replied. He nodded.

"What month?" He frowned.

"The month of June."

"What number of the month?"

"The eleventh day."

"What year — ?"

"It is 1933," she said.

He seemed satisfied.

"We will wait in the store," said the Cuban after a pause. "It will be safe in the store."

No one disputed him. They all went back and entered Papa John's store.

Some stood. Some leaned against the counters and the walls. Others sat awkwardly at the little tables. Now and again someone went cautiously to the door and looked up the street.

"A watched pot never boils — eh?" said the Cuban loudly. He laughed each time someone ventured to the porch and looked.

During the afternoon a storm came looming and drifting

[*6*]

eastward from the Gulf. Sheets of blind, warm rain whipped down to raise a roar on the metal roof; gusts swayed trees in the Woodyard. Limbs, leaves, and clumps of moss fell and floated in the sandy, flooded street. With his back to a corner the Cuban sat drinking rum, drinking tea, eating the little midwife's deviled crabs and now and then shouting above the roar of the rain. This, said he, this storm was just what he had expected. "I was sure of it!" he shouted.

During a lull in the rain the young midwife remarked that certain people of *her* acquaintance could kill a snake and by hanging the carcass a certain way, on a lime tree, could cause rain.

"Rain! *Rain!*" said the Cuban. He sat licking his fingers as though rain were nothing to him. "But how many mens you know can-a create storms?" he asked.

With the sky already so dark there was no telling when the sun went down. The wind came gusting. More rain rattled on the roaring tin roof. Lamps were lit. The rain stopped.

The Cuban wiped his mouth. The big fellow also carefully wiped the blade of his knife. Then he put the knife where he always carried it, strapped to his right leg with his trouser cuff rolled down to conceal it.

He had eaten a whole platter of crabs. Now the midwife brought him figs in a bowl. One after the other he slowly ate them. The bitten stems he placed on the table before him in a crescent, making the slender outline of a new moon. Finally he offered the last fig around to anyone who would have it. "No one? Nobody?" He laughed, as though to say "Nevermind!" He ate it himself. It was pitch black dark outside.

Rummaging around the store for a lantern the Cuban found one, finally. It refused to light. He called everyone to see. There was oil in it. The wick was clean, but would it burn? It would not. Touch the timid wick with a match flame and it only managed to flare a little.

"The wick, the lantern himself, she is frightened," the Cuban said. "See for yourself. Seven times I have tried to a light him with the kitchen matches."

The midwife meanwhile found another lantern. "Ha — ! Now a fearless one!" said the Cuban, for this one lit the very first try, the first match. With the battered, fearless old lantern swinging at his side the Cuban went out ahead of the others, making for the big water oak. He followed the very path he had made earlier in the heat of day, while dragging the corpse of Papa John with the ice tongs. Forty men, three women including the midwife, and a few children came following him.

When they reached the tree there was no sign of the barrel. Holding the lantern high the Cuban let everyone look for himself. Then lowering the light he made a cross in the sand with the bare heel of his left foot, marking the place where the barrel had been set. "The Devil has taken a him," said the Cuban. Anyone who doubted was free to search the Woodyard, he said.

Some of the braver men made as if to look round a little. They returned soon enough. It was true they said. There was no sign of the barrel. The Devil certainly had taken him.

It was discovered later that the store and the Woodyard had been willed to the Cuban by Papa John.

People said the Cuban was one of Papa John's many children. It was rumored that the Cuban drank blood. The midwife bore him a son. Her family name being Walker, the child therefore went by her name. She called his first name Purchase and he grew up playing in the Woodyard and running about the store. His mother read Bible stories to him. The Cuban taught him chords on the guitar. He went to the Negro school now and then off and on, but it came to him early that he was set apart. The teachers deferred to him. He was stronger than other children. He learned easily. The schools ended by boring him until at last he went his own way, fishing, hunting, reading — doing what he pleased.

When Purchase was sixteen Big Cuba died. Big Cuba was buried in the Negro cemetery.

"Now that your father is dead I must depend on you," Mary Sula Walker told him. "The store is yours — the Woodyard is yours," said Miss Sula, the midwife.

As big as his father had been, but darker, Purchase was as dark as any of his mother's people. To keep him out of the Army a hardship deferral was arranged. He was after all Miss Sula's sole support. Thereafter for four years Purchase ran the store selling groceries and rum and Woodyard whiskey until he was twenty-two years of age. Then he sold the business to a white man.

Purchase no sooner sold the store to Felton Watridge than the white man made an arrangement with the Ormund City police and the Meade County sheriff. Watridge ran the place as it had always been run — wide open. Before Watridge came to the Woodyard the law had been content to steer clear of the district and let it govern itself. Before Watridge every man was his own policeman, as the saying was.

Now suddenly the police moved in; sheriff's deputies no longer feared the Woodyard. Watridge, a strange man with a shady background, turned fancy. He bought a flamingo pink neon sign for the front of the store. WATRIDGE GROCERY COMPANY, but the sign presently took to flickering. Finally one evening it blinked out completely and turned a dull bone white and same as always the place was known as Papa John's. The rain fell, and the sun shone as before.

2

WATRIDGE

Nigger tales — Felton Watridge never knew whether to believe them or not. You know not what to believe.

God help him and wasn't the Woodyard full of tales? All of them wild, and perhaps sometimes calculated to *scare* a white man?

The one they told, for instance, about the Cuban's jealous girlfriend, Big Cuba's death, that after she had poisoned him with a slow poison and he was helpless she stuck an ice pick in his belly. Then with Big Cuba lying helpless and watching her all the while she melted a little pot of lead on the stove and poured it in his ears. If nigger tales could be halfway believed, Big Cuba died screaming like a wildcat.

Then he was "held out" two weeks while plans went forward for his enormous funeral. Goats and pigs to be barbecued, fish to be baked; the midwife smoked mullet and mackerel — the rum was on the house — and finally they put Big Cuba in the sandy ground. Then back they marched to Papa John's, did the cakewalk and the snake wiggle all the way from the cemetery with the band playing, and Spanish niggers beating and pounding the drums the way Big Cuba had liked to hear the drums and the music in life and him six feet underground at last and his ears stopped with lead, his eyes closed with twenty-dollar gold pieces. Back they came — all his friends — marching and dancing and so on with the barbecue and the fish, the deviled crabs and the rum, — soft drinks, knife fights, cock-fights, crap games:

> *Eyes of gold, ears of lead*
> *Rum on the house — !*
> *Big Cuba dead!*
> *Yah-yah!*
> *Big Cuba! Big Cuba!*

Let the Spanish niggers get about half drunk and they would sing it till Felton Watridge got a sick headache from all the racket. Drum it, sing it, chord it on the guitar, dance it. God, oh God.

Felton Watridge had come to know there was no point trying to understand niggers, for there was no telling what a nigger was thinking, and above all there was no sense trying to lump all niggers together under one single brand or label. There were too many different kinds and there was no agreement among them. For all Watridge cared let them live like they died, like savages. As for yourself bridle your tongue. Sit quiet, mind the cash register, pay the police, give the sheriff his little sweetening on time and if a white man were extra careful, if a white man didn't somehow foul up, then he might expect to live and do well.

Nigger tales about the Woodyard. *Papa John bounced three times a day — Little Papa John! Was in the midst of a bounce when he tranced his last and final time, in the one-hundred-fifty-first year of his life — Little Papa John!*

Little Papa John was just about as popular with them, about the same size as Jesus Christ, in Felton Watridge's opinion. Or maybe more so. Then they had Big Cuba to brag about.

Big Cuba! — he bounced seven times a day, seven different ways, with seven different womans!

Sometimes a man had to ask himself was this Meade County, Florida or was it Africa? He had to step himself outside the store and look around to be sure he hadn't been kidnapped — transported to the God damned Congo. Shanghaied.

It could be a great help sometimes either at dawn or at sunset just to step out of doors and witness the sky for a few minutes and to realize this was actually the United God damned States of America.

Long ago when first he came here coming south from the Georgia line where he had been born and raised — bred up in the roadhouse and honky-tonk business — he had been able to smell it, the special stench, the sickly sweetish odor of their blackness, like fishrot in the alleyways. All that remained did a man stay with it long enough was the eternal pressure of the heat come April and then down into May like a slow train, and finally into June and damnation. That's when it really started, in June, and by then every white man rich enough to afford bus fare or free enough to stick out his thumb by the roadside or strong enough to hop a freight, had long since cut out for someplace northern and cool. The rich who wintered in Bayside and over on the Island, had long since tooled out to the Ormund City Airport in their big black nigger chauffered limousines. They had long since flown away like a migration of the winter birds.

Felton Watridge and his kind — men with their money and

time and their whole life's investment tied up in some Central or Woodyard place of business — whites like Watridge had to stay with it, and even if after so many years you no longer particularly minded the stink, the heat was something else. The heat was always the neverending same. Such savage hot weather broke a man down so he didn't eat right and couldn't sleep good, and he didn't watch it and his mind would start to wander, his brain would get lost like a cow, or a young calf lost in the scrub. A man would find himself, wake up and see himself doing what never in the world would he otherwise have done. Acting crazy. Your brain could go soft as alligator pears.

Which as it happened, was the cause of the deed, the act, the crazy thing Felton Watridge did Saturday night, and here it was now Sunday morning and he could not wipe the stain of the foolishness out of his memory. Nothing made him drunk; nothing stopped his headache; nothing let his mind rest, relax, and quit thinking and remembering and yet didn't he *know* if he didn't get some kind of relief he would go insane and die?

His tomfoolery of last night. Tomfoolery. Such as made a man wonder were it possible for the Devil to jump inside his skin, take him over suddenly, make him raging blind and cause him to do those things he would not ever otherwise have done in his right mind, a thing that would not have happened if he had held a normal purchase on his senses. My tomfoolery of last night. And now it comes . . .

Sunday morning. That thing I done last night. Sunday morning, and why I done it. For I was not drunk. For I was sober. For I seen a hunerd thousand drunks the same way and never down acted so. Because the little officers come when I called, come right away because that is the reason they are paid and sweetened and paid off and is why they get things, pussy

and things free for the reason that they will come when they are
called and will not dangle and hesitate but will come on when
needed, and the other reason which is not the big one, that they
will leave you alone to run your business, to open and close and
run it as you see fit, but the big reason is so they *will* come. So I
called and they come right on. Saturday night and the heat like
a fester on my brain. Sunday morning.

And oh the torture of a worried mind. A Guilty Brain. God
help. And it gets worse. It don't get better. Anything will
always look worse at three o'clock in the morning, I say. The
whole God blessed world looks like cold grease at that hour
and being Sunday don't improve the son of a bitch either, being
Sunday don't help a bit. What I done last night after they
come, after they hancuffed him hands back of him and him
helpless.

Because the police they hire down here, I say. The police
they hire gets younger ever year that passes. Them two kids
hardly old enough to shave twice a week and they come when I
called just as you want them to come right on and they taken
the little nigger and the nigger was old and black as a prune
and drunk as three trailer trucks, they taken and handcuffed
him, hands back of him, nothing rough, just cuffed him and
grinned at me and I know they would have walked out of here
with him and that would of been the end of it but then something popped. Turn on a bulb, electric light and sometimes if it
already happens to be on the verge of blowing out it will pop, it
will flash, and something went that way in my brain and maybe
I was thinking the whole while that the boys would stop and
hold me back but they didn't and I says, I told 'em, I says it
wadn't enough he comes in here getting drunk and loud and
bothering the regular customers, this grove ape, I says, grape-

[14]

fruit picking grove ape, the little police boys grinning and I says if it wadn't enough that he come in here bothering and sassing people he come in with a sack and brought his own wine that he bought up at the Webster's Kutrate supermarket, I says, that he bought up there for less than I have to pay for it here and bragged about it, yes, by God, bragged it right to my face.

(Them little police boys holding him like a sack with two dogs in it between them laughing is maybe what done it the way the kids, the little police laughed at the idea of a God damned grove ape coming in town out of the scrub and buying his wine at the Kutrate and coming down here to the Woodyard to drink it right in my face, sitting in my chair, sitting at my table, getting drunk as a gopher and them having to drag him up and put the cuffs to him, holding him and laughing to hear me tell it.)

Next thing I know I've done kicked him down from between them. Down he goes and me taking my feet to him like you will sometimes dream about that you taken your feet to your enemy, I taken my feet to him and they done nothing but just watched and grinned until the girls that are niggers but have more sense than the children we hire on the force nowadays, the girls come from behind the bar and from the tables and they forced me back and held me off of him otherwise I would have killed the little bastard whereas now he is in the hospital and I have done it in front of God and a hundred witnesses. I have made my mistake, whereas in my brain someplace something must of popped, something went out after it flashed blue and I hardly knowed myself what it was before I had him down and was stomping and kicking and I could feel him give and the memory of it sickens and something goes down on me because when you

[*15*]

weigh 240 it looks a whole lot worse and if it had to be why not here in the back room instead of out where everybody in the Woodyard, everybody in Central, every nigger in Ormund City could watch me do it and him handcuffed.

And here it is Sunday already.

"Rap the tables," I says. "Lock up." And I started checking out the register. I lifted out the change tray after I had counted the hard money and took it back to the office and set it in the safe and I went back then and I counted the bills and put them in the sack and went back to the safe and my hip was hurting me where I broke it where the truck hit me when I was twelve doing a man's work already and it healed stiff, gimped me but you live with something that way, and it was also hurting from the way I stomped and kicked and the Guilty Brain come back on me so that maybe they all noticed it or maybe her in particular or maybe they draw straws but insofar as the bouncing, far as that goes I never started it and Purchase Walker said it himself when I bought the store, he said the policy around here is you work the prettiest snatch in the neighborhood, that's how the business operates, he told me, and the policy is Submit or Quit, so that way when you want yourself a bounce you have one. Submit or Quit.

From the look on my face they knew. They got the last customer out, got the chairs put up, got the floors mopped, wiped the bar and washed the glasses, took the hose from outdoors and went in with the scouring powder and the hard brooms and cleaned the toilets and hosed out the piss from the men's where I fixed it so you can use the hose that way and it just drips on out and drains out behind the store because otherwise when they get drunk and the amount they pee otherwise it could not be kept no other way, and when the hose was put up they started leaving, letting themselves out the doors on the night latch and the new one come back and I was already sitting on the daybed. The safe was closed and she was the delegation of one supposed to bring me out of it, this daze or whatever it was.

"Mint gin — get a pint out of stock," called another one that hadn't left yet. "He has it with Seven-Up," she says and this new one with her placket already unzipped, the new one goes out and comes back with the ice and the glasses and the mint gin and the Seven-Up.

"What you think you're doing?" I says.

"She said mint gin. Didn't she say mint gin, Mister Feltons?"

"Go get me two headache powders," I says. "And tell Leona or whoever the hell it is still out there she can go home but don't forget tell her we open again at one p.m. not one-by-God-thirty, tell her."

She went out and I heard her. "He say we opens next at one. Don't be just a little bit late."

"Uh-huh." I could tell it was Leona. "Okay, girl. Good luck — "

"Why — what you mean by that?"

"Just good luck, that's all."

"Girl, don't worry about me. Hear?"

"Good luck," Leona says. The door slams on the night latch.

She came back to the office with the headache powders. She made a couple of Mint Gin & Sevens. I put the powders on my tongue.

"Now I'm gonna make you feel better," she says.

She peeled herself like a banana, me thinking and you don't bounce 'em and they will get the idea your grip is lost and you

[*17*]

don't wipe their plate clean and they will get the idea they're boss, so I kicked my shoes off and she taken them both. "Blood," she says.

"It will wash," I says.

"Clean 'em? *Now*, Mister Feltons?" She grins, kidding me.

"Come here," I says. And I start and she helps until I'm shucked naked as four ears of corn.

"My," says she. "So hairy. No wonder you rich. So much hair all over you. My oh my!"

I made a grab and caught her the way you handle a horse. She gave a yip. "Daddy like rough house," she says. "Huh?" Maybe she was scared. Her eyes looked wrong.

"Fight," I says. "I won't kill you. Try me. Go ahead!"

So she dodged and bumped the safe and I caught her again getting the vision of her backside and in catching her I hit the light hanging above and it started to sway the room. I put her down. She was strong and she kept fighting, moving and dodging under me like a God damn mink.

"Don't over do it," I says.

"You ain't big enough to bounce me!" she says in a whisper whereupon as it was too much to take something popped again like it will sometimes that way and I was in her and all over her, in and out of her such that for the while it lasted maybe if I didn't forget anyhow perhaps I was eased a little and the light kept the room rocking, very slow now, back and back and forth.

A while later then and it happened. Then it happened again and she got up and the light wasn't swinging anymore. She poured two more Mint Sevens and I watched to make sure she didn't get our glasses mixed up. She didn't. She was careful and by that alone I knew she was all right. By that I knew she knew I wouldn't care to drink after a nigger, that I wouldn't have it. She kept the glasses straight and I waited until mine was cold before I drank it. All along I kept asking her what time it was and she kept getting up and going to look at the clock out over the bar that is lighted up, the beer company clock and she coming back and it was only an excuse to see her go and come back and forth and finally I handled her again but luck wouldn't have it because halfway along, about as I would guess exactly half way, I seen the shoes where that she had set them under the greencloth covered chromeleg armchair at the desk, beside of my desk and what I done started going down on me again, crawling down and I was like a man on a runaway horse then, like somebody trying to run away to eternity and under me all the while I felt her go from wondering to amazement and then fear on her and it pushed her off the edge of herself inside and she started to squirm and struggle saying she couldn't take the crushing and the pounding no more but it wasn't no way to stop once I seen the shoes for I could feel him under me again under my feet and the thing I done until her fingernails went down my sides like rake tines, until she screamed and went into a fit or a faint and just as quick it was over, for then I spent myself. My check was cashed — but it was not no help. I wet a bar towel in the ice and wiped her face, cooled and wiped until she come around and roused up a little and I told her I says: "Sometimes it goes that way and I'm sorry but that's just how it will happen sometimes for I never meant it to go that way or happen like it did."

"I feel like I laid down in front of two automobiles, like two sheens passed over and killed me. Like some army tank hooked up to a meat grinder — "

"Get dressed," I says.

"When you get hongry for it you strictly famished, ain't you?"

"It will go that way sometimes," I says. I pulled on my

clothes, feeling lousier, lower — feeling worse than ever about what I done and asking myself what besides a nigger could be lower in this world than me. Here it was the Lord's Day.

I went outside where if it was a little cooler for being so early, still and all it was damp, very damp and heavy and I could feel it on my skin how it would be pretty soon and I looked and saw where the sky already was getting pale and across the street, across Woodyard, there was a drunk nigger with one hand leaned against the porch post, against one of Purchase Walker's rent houses. He was peeing a puddle in the sand and two buildings away on the corner in the nigger rooming house a radio was going up loud as it would because the nigger owns it is deaf and lost his hearing for having worked all his life in the roundhouses and around the rail yards fixing heavy railroad equipment so now the way to know when it's Sunday you don't even have to think because you can hear Smith's radio blasting and blaring and carrying on that way, playing all the gospel programs dawn till dusk — the singing, the preaching, the praying.

And Smith, black as he is, will probably go to heaven whereas I won't go, I'm thinking. And so standing and hearing the radio and watching the West Florida sky brighten some bit by bit up behind the store and above the trees, seeing the trees as they began to make the dark green outline, I could not decide. So I went around then to the porch and finally sat down on the bench next to the wall near the kerosene pump smelling the kerosene and the birds began to jump and chirrup in the trees and the bushes and the old man's radio and me wondering what I ought to do, what I better do, whereas the fellow says and the little boy allows, whereas the fat's in the fire. What I done. I will go to hell and will not be mourned.

It finally got light enough and I could see my shoes and I could see what was on them and it went down on me again, like seven pounds of lead it went down and rested there weighting down the inside my stomach.

If I just had never down bought this place, if that nigger had just not sold it to me whereas I thought at the time it was such a good deal and no sooner bought it than it seemed the Kutrate started up selling everything for less than I could buy it and the nigger, Purchase Walker, got rich, got the bag from the Eye-talian with what he got when he sold to the government housing whereas in my belief it was dumb of him ever to sell off anything but he did and the government housing didn't bother so much as a hair of his rent houses, his rent houses stayed full and then he bought both taxicab companies and somehow bought out the Eye-talian who was old anyhow, got the whole bag from bolita to the black and tans, got rich as God whereas before I was thinking what a fool thing it was he done when he sold the store to me — all of it down there in my stomach on top of what I done.

So I taken off my shoes. I throwed them in the bushes. Then I walked back into the store barefooted and hunted my boots out of the closet back of the safe and put them on and laced them but it still didn't feel no better, not very much nohow. My headache come back and I laid down on the daybed but it wasn't no use because I could smell her and the smell by itself was enough to keep me wide awake, over and over remembering and I wished I had not sent her home and it come to me how memory is the torture of a Guilty Brain . . . it come to me if only I had not done it.

If only I had not.

3

FATHER NED

FATHER Ned helped himself to another spoon of peanut butter and considered the dawn.

Perhaps the world will always be a world of separate races, he thought. Perhaps it was intended by God from the beginning that the world should be thus divided. Here was a cistern whereon the Negro clerics of the United States could break their pitchers if they so chose. The Black Muslims, meanwhile, came sweeping in like a tide of barbarian invaders intent upon tearing down the walls that for so long had protected the citadels of Christ.

Hate the white man. The message was getting through and the Muslim voice was only one in a chorus of many.

Steal Whitey's goods; burn his places of business; murder his peace officers; rape his women. Get Whitey.

Predictable as sunup, Whitey responded. His bad police and deputies got worse. Jittery officers and sadistic officers got more and more trigger-happy. Black Rastus, the Negro Everyman, as unpredictable as Africa itself, found his mind set fire to by the thundering of visionary war drums —

Weird interpretations of the Christian message.

New religions compounded like sausages, from age-old, long-spoiled ingredients.

The strange doctrine that let every man decide for himself what was lawful.

The promise of Christ predicating the promise of anarchy — freedom without responsibility.

The meaning of love somehow twisted into a new term — hate.

Father Ned finished the last swallow of orange soda. He belched and sighed. There was so much else to think about. The Bi-racial Committee, for example. He was named to it. In a special room at City Hall the Committee met. All and sundry drank black coffee. Homemade fudge from the kitchen of the mayor's wife was passed. Reports were read in a monotone . . .

Noteworthy victories for the Committee came when chairs and tables, removed from the Ormund City public libraries when the courts ordered them opened to Negroes, were returned so that people could sit on furniture instead of sitting on the library floors or leaning against the library walls. "Chair-and-table" victories, they came to be called.

The Ormund City schools hired a Negro teacher who went about from school to school leading students in the singing of songs. She was termed the Director of Music Education, and it was claimed that every white child in Ormund City had at least one Negro teacher, as a result.

Without being prodded, one of the downtown department stores hired a Negro salesgirl.

The Negro hospital had its designation changed. It was declared an integral and non-racial component of the Ormund City hospital system. Still none but Negro patients applied there for admission. The secondary infection and death rate remained so high that patients entered only as a last resort. Privately and somewhat jokingly it was spoken of, in Negro circles, as ". . . someplace to go die in peace."

Meanwhile the real powers had no connection with the Committee and the Committee found itself wrestling with one impossible premise after another.

Example: "All men are brothers; ergo, why are all men not brothers?"

Example: "Negroes are no more criminal than whites; ergo, why is the Negro crime rate higher in Ormund City than the white crime rate?"

Example: "The police are not brutal; ergo, why are the police brutal?"

Example: "Narcotics, prostitution and illegal gambling do not exist in Ormund City which is a clean city; ergo, why is there so much dope peddling, prostitution and illegal gambling in Ormund City?"

Example: "There is no price discrimination in Ormund City; ergo, why must the Negro pay more for food, clothing, shelter, borrowed money, whiskey, beer, wine than the white people in Ormund City?"

Each conundrum received the meticulously involved consideration it did not deserve. Once shoved into the collective Mind of the Committee, a monumentally labyrinthine organ of inexplicability, worthy, in its higher moments, of comparison to the United Nations, nothing ever was settled; nothing ever was decided. Mrs. Paco Perrone, the wife of the mayor, furnished the fudge. The city furnished the coffee. The newspaper sometimes furnished a young reporter who yawned, smoked a pipe, and took an occasional note. Editorials appeared nearly every week decrying racial violence in other cities and explaining why

such as that could not happen in Ormund City because it would
not happen in Ormund City because the harmony between the
races in Ormund City was such that it soared, a shining obelisk
of purity and piety and example and progress as hand in hand
the black and the white went forward toward a new day of
progress and prosperity . . .

Because it could not happen and because it would not happen and because . . .

All the while everyone knew it would happen.

The city was a caldron. Any instant the seething pot could
boil over.

Because everyone with any knowledge of the situation knew
this to be true, everyone made all the more effort to say in a
louder and louder tone of voice that it was *not* true.

"Myself included," the priest told himself.

Thus dismayed, he took his rusty pail across the street to the
service station and filled it from a faucet beside the gasoline
pumps. He recrossed the street to the house again, lit the gas
stove in the kitchen, and set on the water to boil. He opened the
refrigerator and got out his shaving things. A random issue of
the *Reader's Digest* caught his attention. He took it up, opened
it, and began reading the little jokes at the end of each article.
He sat down on the piano bench. Someone was knocking at the
front screen. Still reading he wandered to the door. "Yes?"

A huge white man stood on the porch. For a moment, although the face was certainly a familiar one, Father Ned could
not decide who the man was. Then it came to him that he had
never seen him except at the cash register in the combination
saloon-whorehouse-grocery. The man was Felton Watridge.

"Come in, Mister Watridge," said the priest.

Watridge entered. Father Ned went back to the piano bench

and sat down. He had just happened upon the "Life in These United States" feature. He was finding it more engrossing than he had imagined it could be, for he had read the same magazine many times before. Just how many times over he could not count or even estimate, yet the same little ideas tickled him again. The accounts were so human.

The white storekeeper, whoremaster, whiskey seller or whatever he could be called, stood about awkwardly, peering with a sort of wonderment at the compaction of boxes and newspapers and books and magazines.

"I done a pretty terrible thang," he was saying. "Don't Purchase Walker and his gal attend over to your church?"

"Yes," Father Ned replied. "They've been regular for some months."

"I was wonderin if you was busy," Watridge said.

"Composing my sermon," Father Ned replied, not looking up. He was listening in fact for a simmering from the pail on the stove in the kitchen.

"Why say, that's very interestin," Watridge said. "What was you thinkin you'd preach on today?"

"Today?" The priest looked up from his magazine and scratched his head. I must remember to get a haircut, he thought with one portion of his mind. Now he regarded Watridge as though for the first time. The man looked a mess. His face was bloated, his eyes were bloodshot, his hands tremulous. "Today happens to be the Feast of St. Barnabas — Eleven June," said the priest, pondering.

"Why say, that's real interestin," the white man said. "Saint what?"

"Barnabas," Father Ned replied.

"Barnaby," said Watridge, staring vaguely towards the

[26]

door leading to the kitchen. "What was you aimin to say about him? I suppose he's in the Bible ain't he?"

"Oh, yes. He was companion to St. Paul."

"Paul — oh sure. That's interestin so as it might be said I caught you at a busy time."

"No," said the priest. "I'm never busy. I was busy as a young man. Old men have all the time in the world."

"So you're preachin on *Paul*," the white man said in a forced voice, a voice so obviously the opposite of what the man felt that the priest knew some favor would be wanted of him.

"No, Barnabas. The meaning of the feast, which is a feast of love, of course, is that although St. Barnabas was not a great leader like Paul, he nevertheless did his part. He served faithfully in the ranks of — well, the Christian communion. He was a part of the evangelical — ah, explosion!"

"How wonderful," Watridge said in a tired voice. "You say you'll see Purchase this mornin and maybe have a few words with him?"

"Yes," the priest replied, impatiently now, for he was warming to his subject. "Just sit down why don't you?"

"I believe somethin is bilin in yonder on the stove," Watridge said. He sat down wearily on a box.

"Nevermind," said the priest. "Could I offer you some peanut butter? Or a can of tuna?"

"Why no — ah. I come up this way wonderin if you'd be up this early."

"What about a magazine?" Father Ned opened the refrigerator.

"I was gonna say that if you was gonna see Purchase you might tell him — ah, ask him a favor for me on account of last night. I got so drunk I didn't know what I was doin if you know

[27]

what I mean. The fellow says I got downright blind. Slips up on a man that way now and then."

"I'll tell him you were drunk," Father Ned replied. He went to the kitchen and returned with the pail, holding the wire bail with a sock he had found on the floor beside the stove. He put the pail on the piano and adjusted his little shaving mirror. "If you want to make me a note. I have so much on my mind these days sometimes I forget. Write down what it is you want to tell him. Walker's quite a powerful man, isn't he?"

"He's a stud buck. He owns this town," Watridge agreed. "You got a piece of writin paper?"

"On top of the refrigerator," the priest said. He dipped a cloth into the water. He let it cool a moment before he steamed his face.

"I'm sure obliged for this," Watridge said. He got a piece of tablet paper and sat back down on the box. "Number one, tell him I did not mean to do it. Number two, tell him I am sorry about it. Number three, tell him that it won't happen again. Number four, tell him I need help if he don't mind because . . . let's see." Watridge was writing.

"Yes, Purchase and Miss Ton-Ton have been very regular." It came to Father Ned that he might somehow work the gist of the message Watridge wanted delivered into the body of the sermon itself. "What was it you did?" the priest asked.

"Stomped a nigger," Watridge replied in a sleepy voice.

Father Ned covered his gray stubble of whiskers with a white beard of lathery soap. He picked up the safety razor.

"Tell me about it," he said gently. Leaning forward, he commenced to shave.

For thinking about his sermon Father Ned found it hard to listen to Felton Watridge. Apparently the white man had done something fairly awful and his fear and his guilt were such that he needed to tell someone. The priest shaved very slowly, working carefully and nodding now and then as though listening to Watridge. The true direction of his thoughts, however, wandered toward the composition of his sermon. It was sometimes best, he had found, to decide first what his people could not be told and to proceed from there.

There was no help in the Collect nor any evidence anywhere in the Scriptures that *Barnabas* was anything special. Father Ned had checked the Biblical references. He had turned to a verse in the Acts of the Apostles.

"And Joses, who by the apostles was surnamed Barnabas (which is, being interpreted, The son of consolation,) a Levite, and of the country of Cyprus, Having land sold it, and brought the money, and laid it at the apostles' feet."

Again no help. Just last Sunday Father Ned had preached on giving. Another money sermon this soon would be wholly out of order. Any wonder he had put *this* one off until the last minute — subconsciously no doubt? He smiled.

Thinking: *Now that "Son of Consolation" could be a race-horse. The kind of bangtail that always comes in last.*

As for St. Barnabas himself, the man had done a lot of traveling with Paul. He was Paul's buddy, so to speak? A reformed rich man to boot, who ". . . Having land sold it, and brought the money, and laid it at the apostles' feet . . ." at a time when the Resurrection was being preached by the apostles.

The kingdom was close at hand back in those days. The money was suddenly rolling in; the Church was now on its way to power and wealth, on the road to Rome and from Rome into the provinces and the possessions of the Empire, and finally even to Britain, into the hands of an English king who would

want a divorce and being denied it would denounce the Pope
and blackmail his English bishops. King Henry wouldn't hold
still for anything short of a Church of England, of his own,
and the years of Our Lord would roll down and lo, one Father
Ned Matthews, Negro, would open the Bible and Prayer Book
just at daylight on Eleven June and wonder how in the Sam
Hill an Episcopal priest, being a Negro to boot, could reach his
flock? Such as it was? Located as it was, so to speak, in the
asshole of Florida? Which was therefore (again so to speak)
doubtless the asshole of the United States and thereafter perhaps the Christian world? How to relate this to anything at all
in the least pertaining to somebody called Joses who happened
to have been nicknamed Barnabas, Son of Consolation, by the
apostles when the apostles were just then all getting rich off the
Blood of Jesus Christ?

Yeah, man. Reaping profits from the Resurrection. This
here, this Son of Consolation was one of the very earliest to
buy his way into their graces. Sold his land and handed the
cash over to the Big Twelve. Laid the loot at their feet and then
they decided the Son of a Levite might be just possibly kosher
after all? So they gave him a surname, Barnabas, and a few
mentions in the Bible. And a feast day.

Big deal.

A little reading *between* the lines made it fairly plain that
Barnabas, through his powers of persuasion, had helped convince the other apostles that Paul, formerly Saul, was possibly
okay and *ought* to be accepted.

Barnabas championed Paul who in turn invented and in-
culcated into the scriptures and therefore into "Christianity"
any number of his own inspired prejudices — against sex;
against marriage, against divorce. Paul had been a straitlaced,

[30]

intolerant, bloodthirsty Pharisee. Whereas at first he had worked his guts out to suppress Jesus of Nazareth, whereas he really got his licks in against the followers of Jesus, as Paul himself told it before Agrippa:

". . . and many of the saints did I shut up in prison, having received authority from the chief priests; and when they were put to death, I gave my voice against *them*."

So would it be any wonder therefore that the apostles found Paul Baby a little hard to take when he all of a sudden pulled the switcheroo on the road to Damascus? When he went blind and decided he wanted to come over to the other side?

Barnabas proved to be the transistor Paul needed when obviously hard-nosed, straitlaced Paul *was* requiring something electronic even for back then, something slightly faster than a miracle if he was going to make his vision and his conversion and all his jazz on the road to Damascus, hold water.

And perhaps because it was so unbelievable; perhaps because of the obstacles instead of them, Paul went on to become one of the greatest. He became the biggest preacher of intolerance in the Book.

Christianity paid the going price for Paul when the old Pharisee strictness, the old wrathful Pharisee intolerance, began to come out in his writings and rantings wherein he rediscovered and revamped and restated the Old Testament wrath — the uncleanness of men; Paul deciding on his own what was "natural use of the woman," and what was unnatural. Paul, singlehandedly, rediscovering in humankind all the queers, the backbiters, the haters of God, the proud boasters, covenant breakers and such like. After raving and ranting on and on about these unclean ones, practically in the next breath, he calls on his dearly beloved ". . . not to avenge yourselves,

[*31*]

but rather to give place unto wrath: for it is written Vengeance is mine; I will repay, saith the Lord," saith Paul. Don't think like me, folks. Think like I tell you *you* should think.

Whereas the Lord Jesus during his life, passion and death takes the soul of a felon with him to paradise; defends an adulteress; goes straight up Gethsemane carrying his cross to tell the world that God loves all mankind, and then, with Christ ascended, along comes Paul, writing, to wit:

"Be not deceived: neither fornicators, nor idolators, nor adulterers, nor effeminate, nor abusers of themselves with mankind, Nor thieves, nor covetous, nor drunkards, nor revilers, nor extortioners, shall inherit the Kingdom of God."

He also said:

"He that is unmarried careth for the things that belong to the Lord, how he may please the Lord: But he that is married careth for the things that are of the world, how he may please *his* wife."

Paul applied the same heavy rule of thumb to women. The married ones would only be thinking how to please their husbands, he said, so his notion was that in the ideal church the men and women would all be virgins; hold hands, perhaps, but that would be the outside limit. When a man and woman were too old to mate — then they could marry — no harm then!

All this in the very face of Jesus of Nazareth's unbounded love for children — little children?

Conclusion: Paul must have had it in for children like he had it in for everybody else? Heaven is going to be *Paul's* exclusive country club?

The gravest, the most devastating likelihood was that Paul probably would have had something going against niggers, that Paul would, had it ever dawned on him, really hit him, that the world was going to last long enough for any number of

black folk to begin meeting together and calling themselves
Christians and expecting, in the same breath, to be allowed into
Saint Paul's All-Virgin Anti-Masturbation League of True
Believers, the awful likelihood has to be that Paul would have
segregated his church?

And we've got Barnabas to thank for Paul.

"Or I only and Barnabas, have not we power to forebear
working?"

Such that you begin to wonder just who Paul thought he
was, and just why he had to fight so hard to keep his body
under subjection, and how much of what he said in the name of
Jesus Christ was really the gospel according to anyone besides
Paul himself, the great original white Mister Exclusive Christian, Saint Perfect.

For no — Paul might not always have been right; but he was
never wrong.

Or take it another way, if you could think your way back
through the Biblical and historical brierpatch to Brother Barnabas; if it hadn't been for Barnabas then perhaps Paul
couldn't have got himself accepted so that *one* way to look at it,
if you especially cared on Eleven June, just at sunrise, to do so,
with your sermon unprepared and sweat running, soaking
down your arms — one way to look at it, Barnabas was you
might say responsible for the founding of the Church of
England.

In one sense anyway. For Barnabas predicated King Henry,
the Eighth wonder, the Man, who caused everything to happen
and thereby turned the tide against the close followers of Paul,
those hoarding Holy Roman Money Men with their monaster-
ies and their nunneries, their huge estates, their vineyards, wine
cellars, and homosexual jealousies.

Had it not been for Barnabas perhaps a black priest with a

Mission Church in Central, Ormund City — Florida's rankest niggertown — breezeless on this Sunday, like one big stinking outdoor steambath of sand, asphalt, brick and concrete and burgeoning, rotting vegetation — a certain middle-aged black priest, Ned Matthews, might not this day face his flock of black people, among them fornicators, adulterers, backbiters, whores, a murderer, several drunkards—might not face them and preach the Gospel of Jesus Christ? To wit:

God loves you. Even you. Even me?

"I don't know if I ought to cut out and leave everything and head for Georgia before Purchase Walker sends after me," Watridge said in a worried voice.

"Nevermind such haste," the priest said gently, automatically; but the train of his thought was interrupted, and he was reminded as so often happened in his low moments, of the winter cornfields back home in North Carolina. He would see again the hard frozen earth, the dead orange of oak trees in the distance, white pockets of ice marking the frozen puddles . . .

In his exile the heat was like a pressure at the back of his brain. Early morning was often a bad time for him. Memories rustled the dead leaves of his past. Last night he had dreamed his wife was alive; he had dreamed his daughter was home and unmarried; he had dreamed that he served a church where men of all races came to a common altar to feed upon the body of God.

Not even waking to the damp reality of Ormund City had served to put away the spell. For a time he had lain awake, still locked in the pleasant thrall. He dreamed often.

With his wife dead and his daughter living in West Germany with her soldiering husband; with the one buried and the other taken care of, the notion of death which came often came

[34]

to him just upon waking, brought a pleasant, even a thrilling sensation. He felt himself to be at the top of a slide on the edge of a precipice and one day soon he would move quickly down that smooth incline gathering speed, plummeting endlessly faster and faster. What once frightened him now left him ecstatic. Of late his weary body pulled him, stiff-jointed, from his lonely bed. He would much rather remain prone to sleep, to dream . . .

Early morning could also be a bad time for the sick at the Negro hospital. Bleakly ashen faces would be turned toward that slowly graduating mauve beyond windows looking like a backward glance into a world which the dying, without really knowing why, longed to re-enter.

After services would he go there today, to the Negro hospital, which, like everything else, the heat made worse? The damp corridors would stink. His own body would leap inside, frightened by odors of ether and strong antiseptic. The body had a mind of its own. No brain, however rational, could convince the body otherwise of what it knew instinctively. Here, by the very odor, was a place of suffering and death. Other bodies transmitted the vaulting fear. His impulse always was to turn and run out of the hospital.

Pondering the sixteen years he had served the Negro Episcopal Mission Church in Ormund City, he fretted on toward composition of a sermon. He had a great store of brilliant ones perfected in times past. As a younger man he had served a church in Washington, D.C. He had been *the* prominent Negro of the Episcopal Church, U.S.A. As such he had been what the white Christian world so desperately wanted to believe and embrace. Not only had he been brilliant, clean, sharp-witted and good-humored; he had been dependable, temperate, and rational. Although a Negro, he had been a gentleman, and white Episcopalians had adored him.

In moments of weakness, back then, he had wondered if he might someday, somehow, rise to the office of bishop.

Then his wife died. It was as though she had run away with another man.

Her lingering illness served to tear him apart with emotions of jealousy; with hatred for this heartless *thing* that was taking her away permanently.

Every bedside vigil found him pleading with her not to desert him. He begged her to come home to him. Each time the look he received in return was the look of a woman who has taken a strange lover in the place of the man she once happily lived with; the look was a distant gaze that told him without words that his cause was hopeless. He began asking himself strange questions.

"Why did I love her in the first place? What did I ever see in her? What is death but a passing? How then can I be so upset? What have I done that she should love me so little as to leave me now?"

He had prayed silly prayers. "Give her back to me! Not my will but thine; but consider our child! O God, who art the creator . . ."

He remonstrated with her doctors. Like gentle-eyed judges they had pronounced her sentence. They awarded her to another party when plainly it was he, the man who had married her, the man who loved her, the man who had fathered their child; he it was who had first claim and right to her.

How was it then that doctors could bring themselves to pass her over into the bony arms of Death? What right had Death to a man's wife if her husband had remained faithful to her?

"I was faithful in the face of every temptation," he had told himself.

The injustice of her illness began so to bear down on him that the doctors gave him medications to make him sleep.

On his own he began drinking a little. Drugs and drink, he found, had the power to pull everything into focus, at least temporarily. Drunk and drugged he could consider her mordant infidelity almost coolly. He could deliver a brilliant sermon, given three or four cocktails and a dose of phenobarbital.

He was assured by medical personages that the need for sedation would pass. Meanwhile he must make the best of it. She *was* going to die. There *was* no cure. The best course for a faithful man and wife meanwhile, was to accept the awful fact — by ignoring it.

He had bought an elaborate manicure set. As long as she was physically able, she had manicured his nails a couple of times a week. It had given her a sense of usefulness. It had restored his old dependence on her. She read picture-book stories to the little girl. Then very quietly on a Sunday in December one day after Christmas, when snow was falling into the listless Potomac, she died.

It was the end of him. His child, growing up, had gotten scholarships to schools far more fashionable than he could afford. She had married a Negro Army lieutenant, a fine young man from a wealthy Baltimore family.

Father Ned, meanwhile, slowly split at the seams. First one parish and then another had need of him only to discover after a few months that they hadn't needed him after all. He passed from diocese to diocese. There was no question of his brilliance. It burned, it shone from his handsome face and reflected itself in his peerless language. The sermons remained as brilliant as before, but the priest was a hemorrhaging spirit — a secret drinker who suffered from blackouts; a drug addict.

As a last resort they had sentenced him to Florida, to the West Coast, the hell hole — Ormund City, where his drinking and doping, his whoring even, would blend with the scenery. Ormund City had the one Mission Church in the United States, insofar as the episcopacy was aware, that was, totally, without a single saving grace. Ormund City's Woodyard Mission had ruined a procession of young priests. White and black they had gone there and always the heat or the whiskey or the girls, the gambling, the dope — or a combination of it all, perhaps, served to bring them to ruin.

Therefore they sentenced Father Ned, who was already ruined. Surprise! The heat dried him out; the open traffic in drugs turned him against narcotics; the lascivious women transported him to a lonely island of abstaining righteousness.

The word got out. Father Ned, by what miracle no one in the church could fathom, had given up his predilection for the world and the flesh and was become clean and chaste.

He knew he would die here. He loathed the place so, he fought it so with every sinew of his spirit that there was no slightest chance the bishop would move him.

The alteration he underwent in Ormund City was that he suddenly became quite ordinary. Friends who had known him in Washington stopped in frequently at first, expecting, as always before, to find him brimming with conversation and brilliant ideas.

They found instead a threadbare old Negro living in a house stuck like an infected thumb in the midst of a stark, Negro slum. In the living room — that out-of-tune baby grand piano. Those years of old magazines and boxes of books obviously never unpacked, piled so that the piano looked as though it might collapse. The floor shook when it was walked across. The joists in the building were rotten and termite infested.

The priest's sleeping room had an iron bed with a bare mattress. There was a reading lamp and a broken easy chair. The window shades were kept drawn. There were no curtains.

The upstairs rooms were also stacked with junk. There were broken card tables, old innertubes and empty corrugated boxes. One room was packed with secondhand lumber.

Father Ned's study had a bookshelf on one wall. There were no books on it. There was a chair and a plain wooden table by the window.

The single bathroom was not used any more. The priest had ordered the water cut off years back because the pipes, here and there, had rusted through, and he had never gotten around to having them repaired. The ramshackled service station across the street served his needs for ablution. Twice or three times a week, late at night, he dragged the water hose around in back of the station, stripped off his clothes, wired the nozzle to a convenient tree with a coathanger, and took a showerbath in pitch darkness.

For sustenance he ate canned foods — mostly tuna fish and sardines, and mayonnaise which he bought in small jars. When the refrigerator burned out in 1963 (he had penciled the date and the time of that calamity on the plaster wall beside it) he converted the box to a library for old copies of the *Reader's Digest* which members of his flock passed on to him from time to time. It had been one of his pleasures for a time thereafter, to open the refrigerator door late at night, after a showerbath, and to remove a copy of the magazine and read from it by the light inside the refrigerator. In time, however, the bulb burned out and for years now he had intended to replace that light-bulb. He had never got around to it. And after all, he reasoned, two bulbs sufficed — one in his bedroom and another upstairs in the study.

Every month or so he played the piano for a few minutes — old tunes that he had relished back when his wife was living and his daughter was a small child, "Tea for Two," "In the Still of the Night," "Only Make Believe," and certain movements from "Rhapsody in Blue."

Afterwards in pitch darkness he would fold his hands and his head would come down over them above the keyboard and he would weep. Bitter visions would flash through his mind.

Scenes from his childhood, the faces of people who had been kind to him, memories of his wife, certain gestures and expressions of hers, and lazy mornings when the child would come crawl in bed between them and snuggle while he dozed and dreamed and plotted what brilliant thesis he would set forth that coming Sunday. Mercifully, his daughter never wrote him letters. She had never set foot in the State of Florida, and the priest had never laid eyes on his grandchildren. It was not intended, he supposed, that he should see his daughter again or ever look upon the faces of his grandchildren.

His days were taken up anyhow — with various things. He dried his face and opening the jar, helped himself to another heaping spoon of peanut butter.

"I will speak to Purchase Walker in your behalf," he told Watridge, speaking in a muffled tone of voice, chewing. He began removing his old green shirt. He had cut the sleeves off some time ago. Stripped to the waist the priest began to sponge himself, taking care to wash under both arms. He wore paint-spattered linen trousers and a pair of comfortable army surplus sneakers.

Still mulling the lump of peanut butter around in his mouth he took an orange soda from the carton on the piano bench and opened it. The bottle cap fell and rolled. Father Ned took a swig to loosen the peanut butter and wash it down.

Daylight having now been made manifest beyond the front windows by a salmon evanescence rousing above the thick foliage of the trees, the priest was reminded that given a few years of abandonment the city would revert to the vegetable kingdom.

It would be just as before, thought the priest, looking at Watridge. *Before the freebooters,* he thought.

"Sure you won't have something to eat?" Father Ned asked.

The white man shook his head. "I've had it. I know I've had it," he was saying. "What made me come to this roach town in the first place?"

The priest nodded and smiled. This much he could understand.

4

THE BLACK AND THE GREEN

Because he was someone born to rule, the Woodyard people rarely had a chance to glimpse Purchase Walker. There was hardly a way ever to see Purchase or Ton-Ton either, aside from going to church; but come Sunday and rain or shine Purchase and Ton-Ton, Sunday mornings appeared at the shabby little Episcopal Mission Church, located in the black heart of Central, not far from the Woodyard. Promptly at 9:15 on the dot, Maco, their driver, eased Purchase Walker's black Lincoln limousine alongside the curb in front of the little church. Maco leaped out to open the curb door for Ton-Ton, who emerged first, and he held the door then for Purchase, a giant beside Ton-Ton.

Walker's Sunday clothes were always black — black suit, black shoes, black silk handkerchief showing in the breast pocket of the suit; cuffless trousers; black tie showing only a stripe, sometimes, of darkest viridian; black enamel tie clasp with a single small ruby in its center, like the eye of a snake.

Ton-Ton's colors were green to contrast the cream-coffee brilliance of her complexion.

Together they made the Black and the Green. She wore

simple jewelry; tiny emerald rings for her pierced ears; no rings on her fingers because her hands were so perfect, so small and tapering; sometimes she wore a gold bracelet of charms on her left wrist and her wrists were slender and her legs were long delicate columns of beauty; she was proud as a greyhound and her face was modeled on small bones; her nostrils were narrow and Egyptian and nothing escaped the vision of her dark eyes with their soft, slender lashes.

A tiny mother-of-pearl cross was hung from her neck by a delicate gold chain — the cross glowed just above the visible cleft of her breasts, twin melons in their perfection.

After the fashion of her kind, Ton-Ton wore no brassiere. Purchase didn't approve of harness. No kind of harness for his women, no kind of harness for him, said he.

When they sat down in their pew what people saw then was the massive quality of his head, close cropped; the width of his powerful neck; the leonine mask of his intelligent face. During prayer his face was impassive, he intoned the responses in a singular monotone that was still somehow melodious but not possessed of the same rhythm of speech usually heard in Central, for the tongue he spoke was curiously closer to British, and was flavored with the sea island lingo, and cadenced with occasional echoes of Cuba.

During the sermon his brow wrinkled into a frown. He was always intent; always listening. When the choir sang his eyes filled. By this it was known that like many another king, music was his weakness, and how beautiful a weakness, how strong a weakness, that the exquisitely trained, that the expertly tuned and cultivated voices of his own people could create tears like diamonds on this young man's handsome cheeks. By this mark alone they knew. He loved them.

Any member of the congregation here present; any black citizen of the whole district of Central, of Ormund City colored town from the Woodyard to the banks of the River Meade (that dark artery meandering, bleeding eternally westward towards the green tideflats and salt fusion of the Gulf), any one of the people gladly would have died for him.

For them as for Ton-Ton, Purchase was both a symbol and a cause.

"Amen!" boomed a voice at the rear of the church. The artillery of response, a sure sign that the message was getting through, and Father Ned, apparently encouraged, reached for the handkerchief tucked in his sleeve and wiped the flowing sweat that enveloped him.

"The Feast of Saint Barnabas, a Christian feast set aside in the calendar of the Christian year and scheduled for every June eleventh, rain or shine!"

"Amen!"

"Here that day dawns today upon a Sunday, my sisters and brethren in the Lord. That day gleams here with the golden sunshine of salvation. It shines upon us with the love of God for all mankind. My belovéd, God loves you. He invites us to take part in the feast of love, to love one another.

"Now out of excess of worship there comes an evil. Some worship the sun and that is *heliolatry;* others worship fire and that is *pyrolatry.* Others are so bound up by the inner and outer workings of the church temporal that they worship the method and the form and the men, the priests, and they are guilty of *ecclesiolatry;* others are so tied up in their study of the Bible and in their enslavement to books that they worship these and they are guilty of *bibliolatry.*

"But we have in our midst something worse than all of this,

[44]

because it is planted in ignorance, cultivated in darkness and
harvested in fear. You know what I'm talking about and I don't
even have to name it but I will name it, I will call it out in the
open. I'm talking about voodoo and hoodoo; about obeah and
the practice of conjure and spell-casting. The man with the
rabbit's foot in his pocket and the woman with the wishbone in
her purse and the people that still pray to the devil and go to
fortune tellers and listen to mumbo jumbo and need charms and
potions and poisons in order to make their way through life.
They believe in good luck and bad luck, hex, the evil eye and
they worship the spirits of the dead and the dread of life is in
them. They go by signs and they let signs tell them what they
will do. They let signs make important decisions for them.
They say if I see a bird fly over the river this evenin in a
certain some such direction then I will marry, or I won't marry.
I knew a man once that if he met a funeral procession on the
road he said that was his lucky day and anything that day he
did would succeed. And he believed it. The power of decision is
thereby removed and taken away and people don't have to decide for themselves if they will steal or rob or take away the life
of another or lay out drunk because they let the direction that
a bird flies or a spider crawls decide it all for them and then they
don't feel any guilt."

"Amen!"

"Now Barnabas was a young man and without the help of
birds, without the help of animals, without the help of the sun
or the moon or the stars or a lot of delving in books he made a
decision. That decision was to sell his property and to take the
money and to lay it at the feet of the leaders, the disciples who
had followed Christ. And after that Barnabas made another
decision, and that was to go with Paul and tote for Paul and

[45]

make a way for Paul and to serve Paul on his travels. To comfort Paul in prison, to look after him on the road, to be with
him right to the end and help him carry the good news about
the love of God for mankind, into many and various foreign
lands.

"Barnabas didn't have to carry a rabbit's foot. He didn't
need a bag of bones to cast out on the ground and tell him what
he must do. He didn't have to pray to the devil!"

"Amen!"

"Now I hear it said that there is something new in the world.
Perversion and adultery and drunkenness and sloth — laziness
— and taking drugs. People walk up to me and tell me that's
all new and that we got a new generation but let me tell you
here and now that none of it is new. Not perversion, not
adultery, not prostitution, not drugs nor drunkenness. That's
all old as mankind. That's so old it's out of date. That went out
of style with Sodom. If that is the only answer the young people
we depend on have to offer, if that's what they believe is new, if
this old fade, this old copout is their new road to salvation,
then somebody needs to tell them they are walking up a blind
alley. They've started up a dead end street. They have chosen
for themselves the Skid Row of history. They are going to turn
on and lose themselves inside themselves and sprawl in the alleyways and stagger down that street named Marijuana, past
Heroin Alley to LSD Boulevard."

"Amen!"

"All of that is old as hell. All that happens to be what
Barnabas gave up in the First Century."

"Amen!"

"Last night a terrible thing happened. One man who is a
member of the white race, a businessman in this community and

neighborhood, a man most all of you know and are acquainted with, did a very wrong thing. He attacked his fellow man. He took his feet to a man who was already chained, already manacled, already taken prisoner by the police who were about to take him away to jail. And the handcuffed man, who was drunk and out of place and out of order, was defenseless. The police stood by and watched the white businessman take his feet to the helpless drunk and when the white man was finished they didn't have to drive to the police station. No, they drove to the hospital with their prisoner for he was in no condition to be placed in a cell and locked up to bleed and die."

Instead of an 'Amen' there was a profound silence. The priest looked about, pausing.

"That white man would like to be forgiven. He came to me this morning to tell me of his sorrow and grief and remorse. He said the devil must have gotten into him to make him behave so toward an innocent man. Have we forgiveness in our hearts?"

"No!" came a voice.

"Think again!" the priest said.

Another silence greeted him.

Ton-Ton fanned herself and she fanned Purchase with one of the fans to be found with the hymnals and the prayerbooks in every pew. The little mission church was deathly hot.

"Think again." The priest spoke quietly this time, and then he turned toward the altar.

5

THE POLICEMAN

SUNDAY, and Carter would be coming by for him in a moment. Carter was usually late. The policeman stood on the walk in front of the rooming house and pondered the string of circumstances that had set him here this day, on this sidewalk.

Perhaps it was somehow wrapped up in the direction he had taken. The direction he had taken, young as he was, had been south and downriver from Arkansas. Downriver to New Orleans.

East then along the rim of the Gulf, Dempsey Mack Morton, nicknamed Dimple, made his way. Something pulled him always southward. He hated cities, put up with towns, was happiest in the woods. Now and again he got picked up for there being about him a feral quality. Dimple gave police and deputies an uneasy feeling.

Jailed he was like a cat. He took it calmly. Let loose he was still like a cat. He walked on his way. He had a proud step. His yellow eyes drew him into the countryside and ever east and south along the Gulf rim shore.

If no one offered to feed him free of charge he would wash

dishes, mow grass, pick up hay bales. He would work on a charter boat, cutting bait, opening Coca-Colas, icing down the red snappers and observing that usually there would be two people seasick and four sunburned. And at least one drunk.

When he could work it Dimple would borrow a week's wages in advance or he would borrow ten dollars or five dollars, anything. "To send my mother. She's down sick." Or: "My sister's just had a baby and she owes the hospital and I'm trying to help her." Or: "I want to make a downpayment on a suit of clothes so I'll look decent enough to go to church."

One excuse or another usually got the money. Then Dimple was gone again. Borrowed money was travel money. Like another man would get drunk or spend it on women, Dimple used borrowed dollars to move on — to New Orleans to Mobile to Pensacola where he worked for a land developer clearing building lots back in the scrub. The developer took a shine to Dimple. For one thing Dimple had a feeling for how a lot should be cleared. He knew good trees from trash trees.

"I want to make a downpayment on a car," Dimple told the man. "So I can get to and from church on Sundays."

"Don't go buying some heap of junk," said the developer.

It was the opening Dimple needed. He hit the developer for five hundred dollars and that very evening he moved. On down the coast. Down past Cedar Key. On south into the citrus belt, until he struck Ormund City with money to burn and cash to spare.

The money evaporated. Meanwhile Dimple met Evan Sanchez.

Sanchez kept a dictionary in his room. He was a talker, always on the lookout for big words. He also needed a partner.

Dimple agreed to work with him. Sanchez had a list of

names, addresses, and phone numbers. He had taken pains, he said, to develop the list. He had stood around in one bank and then another, watching for the antiques to come in and make deposits. He would move in beside the old customer and get the name. Then he would look up the name in the phone book and get the address.

Now all he had to do was start working on the list.

"All you do is answer the phone," Sanchez explained. "Just pick up the phone when it rings, and say 'Federal Bureau of Investigation.' Tell the old person that I'm James Sanders, an agent, and that they are to do exactly what I tell them to do. Tell them the F.B.I. has a tip that some of their money may be counterfeit and that if it turns out that any of it is we will replace it with good money in return for their cooperation in helping get these counterfeit bills out of circulation. That way I can make this person go withdraw his savings and turn over to me any money they have in the house. I count it and put it in an envelope and give them a receipt for it."

"And then what?" Dimple wanted to know.

Sanchez smiled. "That's it. I take half, you get half."

"All right," Dimple agreed. "Only right now I'm broke and I'll need something to tide me over. I need a suit of clothes and well — " Dimple gave it some thought. He looked at Sanchez and then past him at the pool game going on at the table beyond Sanchez in the dim, cool, cavelike interior of the Black and Tan Club.

"What you need?" said Sanchez impatiently.

"It's been a long time since I had a real nice — " Dimple paused. He looked at Sanchez.

"You mean a woman," Sanchez said. He nodded. "Sure, I understand."

Dimple nodded. Sanchez smiled. "I can let you have two hundred dollars. Two bills, how is that?" Sanchez was suddenly all smiles. "Two bills?"

"That will be fine," Dimple said. Sanchez handed him the money.

"Now go sit in the phone booth."

Dimple folded the money and stuck it carelessly in his shirt pocket. "All right," he said.

He went to the phone booth and sat down. With a wave of his long arm, Evan Sanchez strolled out of the Black and Tan leaving Dimple alone with troubled thoughts, and the usual phone numbers and names scrawled on the pebbled metallic interior of the creaking booth.

In large letters one such scrawl read: "Police." On impulse Dimple dropped in a dime and dialed the police number. "I have something to report," Dimple told the voice that answered.

So doing, Dimple had landed Evan Sanchez in jail. Dimple got his own name in the *Ormund City Times.* Dempsey Mack Morton, hero, protector of the aged, and Dimple stayed in Ormund City instead of moving on south, as he had intended.

And again, as before, the money evaporated. Sanchez sent word from jail that when he got out Dimple Morton's life would be worth change for five cents. The landlady at the rooming house, far from remaining as pleased with Dimple as she had been when Evan Sanchez was first arrested, had by now begun grieving. Sanchez had been good pay. Dimple was three weeks behind and was trying to borrow money from her to buy a new suit so he would look decent enough to apply for a job, he said.

She had turned on him one day as he began his plea for what

seemed the hundredth time, she in her soiled seersucker sundress. The electric fan on the wall behind her barely moved the stifling air in her small bedroom.

"Lend *you* twenty-five dollars!" she screamed. "And you *owe* me thirty dollars?"

The yellow eyes regarded her calmly. "Lend *you* money!" she cried.

She turned her back on him. "I can tell you what you ought to do. You're twenty-one, are you?"

"Yes'm," said Dimple.

"A high school graduate?"

"Yes'm."

"All right — if I was white and a man and twenty-one and owed as much money as you do, Dimple. If I was in your spot and had somebody like Evan Sanchez just waiting to get out of jail, just dreaming of the time when he could get out so he could jam a knife in my cowardly, low down guts . . ."

"Yes'm."

"I'd stay out of nigger clubs. I'd lay off pool and I'd — well, I'd apply downtown for a job on the police force if I was in your shoes."

"Yes'm — but I don't have a nice suit."

"God damn it walk over there in what you're wearing!" And because Mrs. Blackburn was a nervous woman, because she was fat and because Mister Blackburn had left her three years before to go live with a waitress, and because the weather was hot and her feet were burning and aching, the landlady had suddenly burst into tears.

Dimple's yellow eyes had wavered. "All right," he said, but she didn't stop crying. Her shoulders shook. "I said all right!" Dimple shouted.

"Wh-what's wrong with y-you?" she sniffled. "I don't know

if you're h-human or wh-what. Evan S-sanchez tr-trusted you. W-woulda m-made you a f-fortune . . ."

"I'm sorry, Mrs. Blackburn. I apologize," Dimple said. "But I just don't have the guts to rob old folks that way."

"S-somebody e-else will rob 'em," said Mrs. Blackburn, wiping her eyes. "S-so why n-not you, and have the benefit? Oh, what an opportunity you had. And you had to turn Evan in to the police. After all his hard work. Don't you realize all he ever intended to rob was niggers anyhow? *Niggers?*"

"Nome," said Dimple. "I thought it was white people on his list too."

"Well, it's too late now." She sighed. "Niggers," she said. She shook her head and gazed out the window into the green array of shrubs and trees screening and shading and closing in like a jungle against the rooming house.

The walk itself, leading to the sidewalk, was like a tunnel, thronged as it was on either side with bowers of overhanging trees, moss, and shrubbery.

"You better go over there and sign on to the police force," she said. "That way you'll have some protection. You've got yourself on the wrong side for good. Nobody will ever trust you again and somebody — most likely Evan — is going to kill you if you don't."

In a dim way Dimple thought of moving on, but a dull reminder had been lodged at the back of his head like a sore place. He was utterly broke.

"All right," he said finally. He turned and went out, across the porch and through the tunnel to the hot sidewalk and the warm smell of Ormund City. He walked to the police station and produced his birth certificate and his social security number and his driver's license.

Then there was a form which wanted to know if he suffered

from cramps, earaches, sinus trouble, pains in the chest, fallen arches; did he wet the bed, suffer nosebleeds . . .

He turned the form back over to the recruiting sergeant who looked at it briefly and then asked Dimple if he could read the fourth line on the eye-chart next to the calendar.

"E-K-G-F — "

"That's enough," the sergeant interrupted. "Take this chit and report to the uniform shop. That's on Broadway acrost from the newspaper printing building. You'll draw your summer gear and that comes out of your check. The hat's just the same as the cab drivers and what-not wear, only fasten this on it." The sergeant handed Dimple a badge insignia. "And wear this one pinned to your shirt pocket," he said, handing Dimple a badge. "Report for duty at seven-fifteen sharp in the morning. I'll draw your service revolver and cartridge belt this evenin and it will be here in this desk drawer. You'll ride with Carter."

"Carter," said Dimple.

"That's right." The sergeant stood up and stuck out his hand. "Glad to have you on the force. Congratulations."

The men exchanged a limp handshake.

"I was just wondering — "

"Huh?" said the sergeant.

"Do we draw any pay in advance?"

"Naw," the sergeant said. "Any more questions?"

Dimple hadn't any more questions. Feeling rather sheepish and bleak he made his way several blocks across town to the uniform shop. The little Jew, a silent hunchback, took his measurements, took the chit, and as silently as before counted out four short-sleeve shirts, one hat, two hat covers, four pair of dark blue trousers, and one pair of black navy shoes.

"Well, many thanks," Dimple said, hearing the muffled collision of his words against the musty stillness of the drygoods stock with which the shop was crammed.

The Jew seemed not to hear him. He had quietly opened a drawer and taken out a cigar box into which he arranged the chit.

"Many thanks . . ."

But the hunchback gave no sign and Dimple finally took the blousy paper sack under his arm and walked back to the rooming house. About now it would be getting summertime home in Arkansas. He thought of home and of the Memphis jail where friends of his regularly spent their winters and he thought of fishing and hunting and of quiet places along the road where a man could stop and rest and nap and listen to birds twitting and warbling. He thought of streams where a man could bathe and of stones on which a man could stretch himself in the sun to dry off, and his thoughts sprang back and forth between Arkansas and special places along the road.

"What the hang am I doing in Florida anyhow?" Dimple wondered.

At any rate he would have the landlady off his back now. That had been one relief, and he had savored it as he turned back into the tunnel and walked up the porch steps with the yellow sack under his arm.

"Miz Blackburn?"

She had lain snoring and sweating on the parlor sofa. She snorted and woke. "Ha?"

"Uniforms," Dimple had said. He had smiled and rattled the sack.

"Um," said the landlady. "That's good." She had sat up and put her heavy feet on the linoleum rug. "I knew good and well they'd be glad to have you. Evan Sanchez sent word this evenin."

"He did?"

She had nodded, as though aware of Dimple's compounding fear. She had assured Dimple that Evan Sanchez would do him no harm, not now, because joining the force had taken care of Evan Sanchez where Dimple was concerned.

And she had been right, Dimple mused. And as usual, he thought, Carter was late. Dimple shifted his uniform cap. Sweat was running out of his sideburns. He thought of a wild, shady place beside the river, a stretch of bank near a warehouse. It was a comfort just to go there and sit quietly on the bank and watch the water hyacinths drift past in little green rafts and patches, turning and drifting. It brought peace to Dimple's mind, that wild place beside the river.

He was young and he felt as if his muscles were bursting. He wanted to run, but there was no room.

And just then Carter drove up.

6

GUDLIEV

U pon entering you were struck blind. It was that kind of bar. Daylight outside was no preparation for this dim, cave-like interior. It was a little dive on Front Street.

Once your eyes began to adjust, however, you saw the faint orange lights lining the walls of the rectangular room and finally the tables in the midst of the dark invisible floor; the bar and the upholstered bar stools lining it. Then you saw the girls.

Topless waitresses, two of them, moved from table to table removing glasses and taking orders for drinks. As though by some strange signal all the customers but one soon disappeared. One after another the customers went back into the blinding daylight of Ormund City leaving a lone sailor who pretended to speak no English, having long since discovered that his size, his good looks and his comical gestures would get him more of what he wanted — fun — and would sometimes serve to keep him out of trouble as well.

Gudliev had come down the gangway of the Norse freighter straight into the sensuous arms of the waiting city. The lush, welcoming port had shown him everything he wanted to see; had given him almost every sensation he had wanted to feel.

After the riding motions of the sea, after pictures of women in magazines, he wanted the real thing; real women. He had had them.

After pictures of whiskey he wanted the real feeling of slight drunkenness. The U.S.A., tropical Florida, had taken care of this need.

Only one more unfulfilled desire remained. He wanted to drive around in an automobile. The final abiding desire had been singing almost all the morning, like a refrain in his head, while he sat drinking in the topless bar on Ormund City's Front Street, admiring the little breasts of the waitresses. Now and again he pondered in advance the tales he would tell the girls back home in Stavanger about this Sunday in Florida. His stories would be sure to make the girls back home turn gray with jealousy.

Using his strangely comical gestures he ordered another whiskey and a beer to chase it. He thought idle thoughts about the ship. She had brought in a cargo of sheet steel from Japan. Tomorrow she would leave Ormund City bound for Japan with a cargo of U.S. paint contained in steel drums made here in Ormund City, Florida, from Japanese sheet steel. Also riding in the Norse freighter's hold when she departed Florida tomorrow would be several hundred tons of American scrap iron destined to be made into Japanese sheet steel. Paint, steel, scrap iron. Japan, U.S.A.! His brain whirled.

The complexities of the sea; the complexities of international trade; the hiss of high brooding waves; the curl of beer foaming against the human tongue; the heat of Kentucky bourbon hitting one's belly like a sounding fish and breasts, naked as babies, and soft little drawling-voiced switchtail waitresses.

Again he yearned for an automobile to drive. That done, decided he, and he would be satisfied. He could return to the ship
after that: content.

He considered the girls. The taller one, who was somewhat
older, appeared to be more compassionate than the other. A
shrewd notion entered Gudliev's head. He motioned to the taller
waitress and reached for her pencil and pad. She handed them
over obligingly and watched, leaning against his shoulder while
he drew a picture of an automobile. He worked solemnly and
slowly. Then he pointed to his heart and touched the picture
and made motions — his huge hands gripping an imaginary
steering wheel.

"I b'lieve Stavanger here wants a car," the older waitress
said.

Gudliev nodded vigorously. "Ya! Car!" he said. "Car!"

Without another word the tall waitress reached gently down
and took his leather wallet.

The younger one, who was back of the bar, looked up.
Gudliev had made love to both earlier.

"Who'd wanna sell *him* a car? On Sunday?" the younger one
was saying.

"Nah, he wantsa *rent* a car," the older girl was saying.

"Who the hell would be crazy enough to rent him a car?
When he can't hardly even speak?"

The waitresses talked it back and forth, topless and talking.
Their breasts shook. Gudliev drank his beer. He sipped his
bourbon.

"I — me!" he shouted finally. "I drive! License — I have.
Look!"

"So he *does* speak," said the younger one. She made a face.

"And I let him off cheap! Because I thought he didn't he got twice what he should of had for the money. Say, what's it with you anyhow big boy?"

Gudliev shrugged and smiled. He took his wallet gently back and showed the older waitress his driver's license. "International — good everywhere," he said, smiling.

He began to feel full. "Me — from Stavanger," he said now. He said it again. Home was like a sudden tiny nibbling in his heart.

"Look," said the older waitress, taking pity on him. "I gotta car. It ain't much car. But for twenty — *no less* — for twenty I'll lend you my car? Unnerstan me?"

"You got car?" Thoughtfully Gudliev reached a hand out and fondled the nearest breast. "You own a car?"

"Yeah, and don't get your mind off the subject," she said. But she didn't move. "For twenty?" She took the wallet back and got a crisp twenty. "Twenty?"

"All day," Gudliev said, bargaining.

"All day. Just bring it back before sundown and for God sake don't wreck it and kill somebody? You're a careful driver, ain't you?"

"Ya," Gudliev said. Twenty was a terrible price. He well knew it. Money does not come easy, he thought. Father God money was hard to earn. He pondered the offer. "Well," he heard himself saying. "Okay." She folded the new bill over her long fingers and stuck it deep into the secret space between her stretch pants and her skin. It made a little bulge there, with the rest of her money. He let his hand stray over the place. "Okay," Gudliev repeated. Father God, he thought again, but he had what he wanted. She was fetching her car keys. She slipped on a man's white shirt.

"You ready to go?" she asked.

"Ya," Gudliev answered.

"Christ a-mighty," said the other waitress. "You nuts, Christine? How you know he can drive?"

"I got twenty; he can drive," Christine said.

"You'll do any damn thing in the world for money," said the other. "Drunk as he is?"

"He isn't drunk as you are, by God," Christine said huffily.

"Shit," said the younger one. "He wouldn't drive my goddamn car for no twenty goddamn dollars."

"Yeah, but you don't own a car, that's why," Christine said sweetly. She buttoned up the shirt. "You bum rides off me. Come on sailorboy," Christine said. "Now just be sure you bring my car back when you get through with it? When's your ship supposed to leave?"

"Ah — tomorrow," Gudliev said. "I bring car here tonight."

"Fine," Christine said. "Hey, Francie, be right back!" she called to the younger waitress.

"I swear you'd do anything —"

"Well, so would you!"

Viking huge, Gudliev stood up. He steadied himself against a table and followed Christine out the rear door into the torrential, blinding brightness of an alley. She didn't look nearly so young in the daylight, he noted. Her body is young, though, he consoled himself. He had got a bargain there even if the car was costing him dearly. It was, he saw, an old, old Chevrolet. "Farewell twenty dollar," he was thinking.

"You ain't drunk?" Christine said anxiously. Her eyes looked at him from dark frames of eye shadow, from beneath long false eyelashes.

"I'm okay!" Gudliev said brusquely.

She opened the car door for him. He got under the wheel, smiling. She handed him the keys.

"You know how to drive? You really know how?"

"Ja. Okay," said Gudliev.

He got in and put the key in the ignition switch. Kicked the seat back and started the engine.

"Be careful!" she said. Because of the man's shirt she had worn into the alleyway there was no getting a last glimpse of her fine breasts. He waved to her.

"Bye now!" Christine waved.

"*Morn-a!*" said Gudliev. Driving slowly he got the car safely away from the brick building and eased on up the alley. A little tune sang in his head like fiddle music. The car was roasting hot.

Turning into Main Street he began to drive in earnest. The flat streets, the sand, the palm trees. Lazy pelicans sailing over the river. He switched on the radio. Music stampeded out and flooded him, crowding his ears and he knew a delicious pleasure. He drove on and on, slowly and carefully.

Down on Bayside more and more cars whizzed past him, some honking. Gudliev waved. Across the bridge to the island, in and around the hospital parking lot. Confidence began entering him. He felt the car becoming a part of himself. Turning back out of the hospital parking lot he crossed the bridge back into Ormund City, going to the right now, driving straight into the downtown section, past the taller buildings of Ormund City's staid, Sunday-quiet business district. He turned right again, beside a new Motor Lodge and then, at Central, he turned left.

Suddenly the clothes on the sidewalk were brighter. The faces were yellow, brown, black! The Negro section! Gudliev was overcome, delighted. His big hands fondled the steering wheel. The black people yelled. The boys whistled at him. The radio pounded; rushing, roaring American music. A pair of white felt dice were suspended from the mirror beside his head, hanging like square testicles just to the right of his vision. They swayed gently. Felt dice? What next? He began humming. The beer and the whiskey began taking hold in the heat. A heaviness touched behind his eyes. The bar had been cool, the bare breasts had sung to him. Now Gudliev felt himself being baked by the tropics, the beautiful heat . . .

Even the heat was pleasant until a car pulled out sharply and suddenly from a side street. Gudliev spun the wheel. Stomping frantically for the brake he hit the accelerator. Then the fireplug loomed and plunged beneath him before he found the strange, the awkward brake at last, whereupon, before the engine died, water was streaming, spurting, shooting a fine spray in the air and washing into the street gutters beneath him.

Black people gathered, laughing. Gudliev got out of the car. "Beer?" he asked. He got a bill from his pocket. Someone handed him a beer and took the dollar. The police appeared. Gudliev showed them his wallet, solemnly drinking beer and nodding. "*Ja,*" he said. "*Me — Stavanger,*" pretending that he had no words to explain the brake, the accelerator, the fireplug, Christine, the bar, the rushing water, the little naked breasts that had sung sea chanties to him since yesterday.

"We have to take you to the station big boy," the younger policeman said.

"*Ja,*" said Gudliev. He smiled.

He got in the car with them. "*Me — Stavanger,*" he said. He made two of them he was so large. He smiled lazily now and then. The policemen laughed. At the station they got out, already friends. They walked slowly into the little building.

"What's this?" said the desk sergeant. "Ha?"

"Damn if we know. He's off one of the ships. Tore up a car. Busted a fireplug."

"Better call the city engineer, I guess," said the desk sergeant. He dialed a number. "Got his name?"

"Ah — Godlove or Gud — something. G-U-D-L-I-E-V, first name, L-I-D, last name, like a stove lid," said the policeman. Barely twenty-one, he had been two weeks on the force.

"Okay," said the desk sergeant. "Godlove Lid — that your name fella?"

"He don't speak," said the older policeman.

"Me — Stavanger," Gudliev said. He smiled his innocent smile.

"Where's that busted plug at?" said the desk sergeant.

"Over on Central near Woodyard, smack in the middle ah the nigger district."

"Hello? This is Marvin, at Central Station? We got a German or something, anyhow one of the sailors? He run down a fireplug on Central near Woodyard? We'll get the car moved. You fix the plug — okay?" The desk sergeant put his hand over the mouthpiece of the phone. "How bad is it. Much water?"

"All over the damn place."

"It's bad busted," said the desk sergeant. He hung up the phone.

"Me — Stavanger."

"Let's see — these his papers? You have to call somebody. Who I don't know. They got a special kind of do-jigger man to take care of these fellas," said the desk sergeant. "A counsel."

"Can't you call downtown and ask?"

"Okay," said the desk sergeant. "Meantime I guess just leave him here."

"Lock him up?"

"Naw, just make him — ast him to set down. Get him a magazine. Sometimes it can take all evening jist getting the man down here. Specially on Sunday. He picked a hot day for it, didn't he?"

"Sure did," said the younger policeman. "Ninety-five." He motioned Gudliev to be seated. The big Norwegian sat down. They handed him a *Life* magazine. The desk sergeant opened him a Coca-Cola. The two men on patrol left.

The desk sergeant got on the phone again. "I have a sailor here name of Goodlove. Don't speak one word a English a-tall. Name of Lid, like a stove lid. Who is it we're supposed to call? Yeah, I *know* it's trouble. Naw, he's right here drinking a dope and looking at magazine pictures. Wrecked a car, busted a fireplug, happy as hell. Big as a horse. Well he is *sorta* drunk I guess but he's all right. Okay, I'll start trying to get Mister Sappington." He hung up the phone. "I have to get the Norwegian consul. His name is Sappington. This might take a while."

"Ja," said Gudliev. *Vel, vel,* he thought, turning the pages of the magazine.

The black face was bloated beyond human proportions. The patient had suffered a severe cardiac arrest on the elevator coming from surgery.

His thready heartbeat traced itself across an electronic

screen behind him. The nurse watched and waited for him to die and the green lines scribbled and scribbled themselves endlessly across the gray face of the implacable screen.

Because the patient was also an item prominent in the Sunday newspapers and because his death, perhaps even his very maiming of last night, could possibly set off enormous violence, the nurse took more than mere morbid pride in her professional vigil.

She marveled that so frail and obscure an old Negro could cause such furor; and, sitting down, she practiced her exercises. Once every hour, while on duty, she tensed and relaxed her vaginal muscles fifty times in series, as women are instructed after childbirth in order to bring themselves, speaking sexually, back into shape.

Not that the nurse was pregnant, of course, nor even married; but there was a certain supra-passionate surgical resident, and again remembering their considerable moment the night before, she tensed the muscles, gripping and gripping again, rehearsing with all the earnest, mucid professionalism of an actress or an acrobat.

"Make it snappy," she thought. The patient gave a long sigh, and groaned.

7

LEROY

$\mathbb{T}$HINK back to Christmas and come on forward."

Leroy nodded. Lying on the bare mattress with the sun bearing down hard on the roof overhead he wanted to be free of this man, clear of his questions, his clipboard, his ballpoint pen. Leroy wanted to go downstairs and if nobody was using the bathroom he wanted to get a rag and sponge himself a little. He planned first to lay the rag across his eyelids and next to go see if Smith had any spare aspirins.

Downstairs poor old deaf Smith's radio was turned loud as it would go playing the Sunday programs of gospel singing and preaching. Smith was one reason rooms in this house were so cheap. Nobody slept on Sunday morning unless they could wrap a pillow around their ears. Now, hot as it was, even that was impossible.

If he could get away from this white bastard's questions, Leroy was thinking, he could put on some threads and get outside. If he could bum a little silver off Smith and then walk over to Poor Boston's Club and Cafe. By now, if church was out, Hatcher might be there and if Hatcher could be talked into it they might get up a three-way, matching coins with some kid where odd-man always wins.

[67]

"Since Christmas? Can you come forward and tell me just the first names of the people you've had sexual intercourse with? How many girls?"

"Oh, six, I guess," Leroy said. "So my blood come up positive? That's some kinda come up ain't it."

"How many boys — men?"

"Oh — three, maybe."

"First names?"

Leroy gave him first names. "I don't know if I'm remembering them all," he said.

"You're doing fine," said the white man. The first visit he had taken blood from Leroy's arm with a big needle. Maybe a week ago. That time Leroy hadn't said much. Now that the report had come back positive the man was claiming that if Leroy did not cooperate by taking treatment at the venereal disease clinic and by giving the names of everyone he had been with since Christmas, then the police could come and haul Leroy off to jail. So the guy said. Leroy had no reason to disbelieve him.

"Go on . . ."

Leroy continued, giving all the names he could remember. All but one. Leroy held Hatcher's name back. "That's all?" the guy was asking.

"Yeah," Leroy said after a pause. "That's the crop."

"Now let's go back for a quick review. Rosalu. What's her last name?"

"Crenshaw," Leroy said.

"Where does she live?"

"She stay over on Sprigg Street near to Vine. It's a little row of shack houses. You know? So just go this way — to your left when you get to Sprigg and it's like the second or third shack house. They all got a porch down there. I believe maybe one of the porch posts is painted blue if you look close, and Rosalu, she stay there."

"She have a nickname?"

"Hinge Baby."

"*Hinge?* Like a door hinge?"

Leroy nodded.

The honkie wanted a lot more last names and addresses. He wanted them all in fact as it turned out, and Leroy soon was weary with answering questions. He thought of the Gulf not many miles away stretched out on a still day like this like a puddle of used motor oil and the steamy drifting air coming off the water out there and it so hot in this room here that Leroy yearned to be outside. To find a piece of shade somewhere, anywhere, and lie down and wait for nightfall. In the colored part of Ormund City with so many buildings and so much pavement summer made it an oven and you happen to be nigger, you happen to be shut up here and you got like a biscuit that was going to have to stay with it and bake up into the middle of October. It hadn't rained and the neighborhood was hotter by the day. He thought of the Gulf out there, a dragon, breathing steam.

The man had another question.

"My mother, she pulled out and left me, she hauled ass when I was maybe two or three years old. Raised like I was, man? She put food on the floor for me like you feed a dog? Left me all day locked in that room. At night she come home and maybe she got a man with her. When that happen I have to sleep on the floor. Or sometimes the next morning maybe they might take me in the bed with him if he was a nice guy. She hauled ass when I was three. It was two whole days before somebody found out about it. Somebody opened the door and let me out, see? And I never saw her again. She did some kind of a disappearance. One family kept me and another and finally I just went off and lived under the sheds down by the warehouses and the men they would share their lunch with me. Like a cat — that's the way I grew up. So that's the only way I know how to make it, you know? On my own, see?"

"So you can't know if you are eighteen or seventeen."

"That's right," Leroy said. "To me a birthday don't make no difference because I don't have the knowledge of when mine is. So I used to imagine it in my head that a certain day was my birthday. For a long time I used Christmas that way. It made a certain show on kids to say you had *your* birthday then. Today might be my birthday. Because I don't know. I use Smith for my last name because, Smith, playing that radio you hear downstairs, old Smith was always kind to me. If somebody threw me out Smith took me in. If I got hungry he kept me from starving. He gave me shoes. He knew my mother. Smith, he knew who she was. Her name was Foster. Sometimes I go by Foster."

The man nodded.

"My old lady was a grove woman, a black-assted strumpet. You know. She peddled her ass. Who was my daddy has to be anybody's guess. You wouldn't know how to feel like I feel sometimes," Leroy said. "You couldn't have any judgment of what it is like."

"I suppose I can't," the man said. He had a few more questions.

Something stirred the air outside. It was a stench; dark and rotten, and it came pushing through the open window. In such weather, at this time of the year, garbage went down in a fast hurry. Maybe it was rotten fish guts, Leroy thought. It could be anything down below there, down rotting in the alley between the warehouse and this building.

"Francine," Leroy said, answering. "She went by the name Burrus. She stayed downstairs. Stayed with Smith. He was like her uncle, I don't know. Like some kin to her."

"Smith," said the white man. "Where the radio is."

"Right."

"How old is Francine?"

"Maybe fifteen — sixteen. You could ask Smith. Francine has cut out and went up to New Orleans though."

"Would Smith have her address?"

"He might," Leroy said. He shifted on the mattress, turning over on his back, lying flat and looking at the brown marks in the wallpaper where the rain had leaked and made patterns in the paper like clouds, round and fluffy about the edges. Sometimes he saw pictures in the watermarks, shapes that put him in the mind of things. Now he saw nothing. Just the stained edges of the marks made before the house got new shingles a few months back. Thinking: Francine gone up to New Orleans. Thinking how he missed her.

Say if Hatcher *could* be talked into matching silver on the three-way, Leroy was suddenly thinking again, say they could set it up where odd-man wins, then every third or fourth time they could let the kid win and keep him going while Leroy showed heads one time and Hatcher tails. Between them they couldn't lose. When the victim was in deep enough Leroy could offer to match him double or nothing. Sometimes they could even work it with an old man. The trouble was always Hatcher's religion. It didn't allow him to gamble, didn't want him to make it with girls.

Hatcher's religion had him messed up until about all he could think about was work. And he had to be all week looking for work, or if he found it he had to be mixing mortar and carrying bricks until by nightfall he was so goddamn tired in his bones from work and weary in his head from saying "yas-suh" and "nawsuh" to those brickmason charlies, those union-wage somebitches. Well, Hatcher was lucky if he had strength enough left to piss before he fell on the bed and if he *didn't* have work then his mind was so worried it seemed like he believed God was down on his ass.

"Is that all —?" said the white guy.

"I'm trying to think. I mean like say what if I forgot somebody. How am I going to find you if I forgot because like I am maybe sometimes I don't even remember myself who it was or when it was — you know?"

"I'll leave you a card. You can phone me. But the important thing is to give me all the names now so we can start tracing these people down. Otherwise you get an epidemic?"

"A what?"

"Okay. A fist fight between two fellows? You can get that stopped. But what if more and more get into it — pretty soon you've got a war on your hands. So with a few cases of syphilis you have like a fist fight. An epidemic is like you've got a war."

"Viet Nam along beside of some little street corner shuffle — I see what you driving at. Maybe I *can* give you a few more names." Leroy started giving them. The man started writing.

Maybe if this guy got *tired* of writing he would give up and leave, so why not let him have what he came after?

Only leave Hatcher out of it because if Hatcher had it, and he was bound to have it because Leroy had talked and con-

vinced him into going with Louise Hollan. Hatcher was all last
week out of work and looking for it everyday all day long
Monday through Saturday and Leroy had told him, just
yesterday, had told him the way you tell a friend that you just
can't live without, telling Hatcher how if his spirit was that low
that he felt there wasn't nothing on earth could raise him out of
his agony then a taste of chicken might be what was needed,
telling him: "So what I mean if God is down on your ass anyhow and won't give you no hope to find a job, I mean why not
try something different? What I'm talking about, man, it
might *change* your luck." And Hatcher who had gone all this
while and grown all the way up to a man and never touched any
chicken, never the first taste, all this while just living with his wet
dreams or maybe pulling his meat a little bit now and then and
having to tell Leroy about it afterwards how he had started
pulling his meat again and how that was a sin against God too
because somebody back in the Bible had dropped his wad on the
ground and God struck that Jew bastard dead. Hatcher listened to preachers too much and stuck his nose down in the
Bible, reading it all the time for comfort and wouldn't even
touch a good magazine with nice naked pictures in it, nor
comics, never bought a funnybook once in his whole life. So it
was strange how you could have him for your friend and be like
the way you are and him be like the way he is. Like Hatcher has
his mother and his daddy and he's handing them a little scratch
for rent and groceries and he's sleeping nights in the same room
and putting his legs under the same table like he has done
everyday all his life. How could he be *more* different? And he
has put cash in the collection plate every Sunday and some days
walked a mile up Vine — like he did Wednesday — a mile in the
hot boiling sun just to find a morning newspaper somebody

threw away in the trash before they hopped on the bus so Hatcher can read the want ads. Then he has to traipse all the way to the docks, trying to get on over there for something like a bait cutter on one of the red snapper party boats, having to be there before five in the morning to beg for some lousy "yassuh cap'n" all day detail along that line, from the docks then to clear out across town to the other end along the bayside roads where if he got lucky as hell somebody might let him wash windows or mow grass or clip a hedge all day and then maybe hand him two bucks at sundown and tell him to get lost.

"Let me read these names back to you," the syphilis hunter was saying. "Just like to be sure I've got them all. This is a long list, but that's what we want. It's what we have to have." The guy was more like talking to himself. He was flipping back through his pad. "She was infected before Christmas by an ambulance driver. She gave me five names — Knox, Murphy, Foster — that's you — Keenan and Shafer. Do you know of anyone else — I mean who's been with her?"

"No," Leroy said. If the syph man went to Hatcher — well, you could just think what a lucky thing it was Gyp forgot about Hatcher. Maybe Gyp — maybe Louise, she also figured it out that telling off on poor old Hatcher wouldn't help nothing.

Louise, she was something special out of the ordinary. Not like just some ordinary woman. No, and Hatcher saw it too, what there was about her; she had brains and she could be funny and she could make a man laugh and make him feel something extra like what he was and what he did was pretty damn swell, and something had been bound to happen between her and Hatcher. If a man looked back on it he could see how it was bound to happen between Hatcher and Gyp, but then like they say hindsight is all twenty-twenty perfect.

The syph man had crossed his legs and lit another cigarette without offering the package to Leroy. Leroy reached under the pillow and took out one of his own weeds. It was a king size. He got his book of matches from the place where he kept them between the floor and the mattress. Just before lighting the cigarette he thought about tearing it in half, but he decided it wouldn't look good if the white guy saw him half it. The air stirred again and the stench from the alley came through the window and lingered, exactly like a fart, except the alley stink was worse. It had to be rotting fish Leroy decided, and here it was only Sunday and there it was only yesterday Hatcher finally gave in and was ready to try something — anything.

So because he had money and Leroy was broke Hatcher bought the beers at Poor Boston's, a whole sixpack. Leroy carried the package. They walked over to Sycamore and found Gyp just leaving her sister's house and here was Hatcher who had lived his whole life three doors away from the house Gyp Hollan stayed at and plainly he had never one time let himself look at her or think about it. She had on blue shorts the color of a spark of electricity and a red blouse with the shirt tails tied together in front in a knot just above her belly button so you could see how smooth she was between the shorts and the blouse, where her middle was left open and naked.

Gyp was saying she had to get her hair pressed and change her clothes before Leroy made her feel the sack, how cold it was, and he winked at her and sort of nodded his head at Hatcher so she got the idea and then she's saying "Well baby late as it is to get dark now I got the time but who has the place without taking too much time to get somewhere — you know?" And quick as anything Leroy said, "The warehouse," because it was never open Saturdays and if you slipped through the alley it was a short climb to the roof.

Hatcher just stands there with his mouth open and that sad look he always has when he's out of work and Louise says okay just let her get a blanket from her sister. She goes in the house and comes back with the blanket and Hatcher still looks at her that same sad way so you know he has got to be trembling like hell inside and Gyp, she's saying how she can already *taste* the beer but godamnit hurry now as she has made her plans to jump all night, so let's get all our business tended before sundown? So they all three set off walking and Hatcher takes out his handkerchief and coughs . . .

The white man was wiping his face. He mopped his neck. Then, closing his writing pad, he opened his briefcase and put the pad back in it, snapping the briefcase closed and fastening the little straps, and standing up. He's still talking.

"Your treatment will begin Monday. Report to the clinic about 9:30 and hand this to the nurse at the desk." He smiled. "You'll probably see Louise Hollan there too."

The syph hunter wanted to shake hands. Wearily Leroy stood up. "Thanks for your cooperation," the man was saying. Leroy put out his hand. They shook on it. They agreed that Leroy would be at the clinic at 9:30 Monday. "And Mister Smith is next. Downstairs, you said?"

"Right under me," Leroy said. He stood up. "Right under where we're standing. Just go to the radio. Just walk in because Smith, he can't hear you knock. Smith won't mind."

"Thanks," said the man. "By the way my name and my phone number and address — it's all on that card. So if you should remember anything, as you say, just call me." And he went out the door.

"Hotamighty damn," Leroy whispered to himself and it was like you could smell the salt steam where the city was pushed and crammed, crowded down beside the Gulf and the sun had swung up by now and would be over the ocean like a ball of blood just hanging there a bloody eye-socket above the brassy cheek of the sky. He took his rag from the paint-blistered windowsill and went downstairs. The hall was a little cooler. Smith's radio was no longer blaring. Leroy closed the door to the bathroom and pushed the barrel bolt latch. He stripped, putting his shirt and pants on the white painted chair. He felt the heat again in the closeness of the room and the soft touch of it on his lean-muscled slender body. He used the toilet and then stood before the lavatory, wetting the rag and sponging himself, rubbing the rag across his face, leaning down now and again to take a drink from the water spigot, taking his time. You let yourself wake up slowly and the cool cloth is the best, grazing over your skin. Wear the world like a loose garment.

With the sponge bath over he was hungry but it was never any good to eat early in the day. If he did his stomach was no good. In such hot weather a man could ruin his best shoes, the one real good pair he had saved up to buy — hot damn — (because you can't walk in and steal expensive ones. The good ones come in a box and they got a man watching you) — but leave thirty bucks worth of shoes in your closet a week in this hot weather around *here* and you got mildew. Your threads rot and ruin the same way, *they* feel damp too and they go sour even before you put them on. So around this place everything rots and why they ever decided to make a city here in this location of the world when there has to be some place better if only a man could get out of this one someway and find out where he wants to go and be the rest of his life.

Like he told Hatcher and kept telling him, "Man, there has got to be something better than this," and Hatcher, with that same look on his face saying 'Well there *is* because that's why they have heaven because I know that whatever you want and whatever you need it has got to be up there. And they's why I am trying so hard. So there is some place better."

"But I mean down here on this earth."

"All right — well, you got to try in that direction too, don't you know. But you don't even try, I mean like have you *ever* been to church?"

"You know I went a couple of times with Smith and once with you and your folks that time when we sat next to Linda. I got to know her and that was okay."

"But by yourself without nobody arguing at you to do it. I mean did you ever once try to make up your mind and try to *want* to give your heart to Jesus?"

Hatcher could run on that way for hours. And just try to tell him that well of course *he* grew up in a house and they found *you* locked in a room like some cat or something when you were maybe two or maybe three years old and whoever dropped you, whatever it was *you* had for a mother if you could call it a mother — more like some nigger whore — was leaving food on the floor if you could call it food and raising you locked up in a room like a hog to eat off the floor? And where they took you to live the first time after they found you almost starved to death — you ate toothpaste and soap and everything else? But just try to tell Hatcher and explain to him a little bit what the difference is when you get whipped and slapped and they hand you one orange that that's Christmas, no man knows your birthday, and you run away and sleep in the alley or any other place you can find, so ask it this way, if there was some place else on earth better where a man could just b-r-e-a-t-h-e?

Leroy went back upstairs to his room and changed into his

good clothes as fast as he could, still hoping maybe he could talk Hatcher into matching silver on a three-way. Then run it up to something decent and they could both go have a shoe shine, could sit up there on that throne like two kings and let that nigger admire their shoes because you couldn't hardly tell them from real fifty dollar ones. And Hatcher would have to be told he had *it*, that he had caught *it* and his blood was lousy, that if he would just turn himself in up to the clinic then they would treat him. Telling him might be something to keep his mind from worrying while he was out of work. Say if he had some place regular like the clinic to go and maybe while he was there he could ask them if they needed help? Maybe they might let him sweep the place out and wash the toilet bowls and dump the trash. Having syph might open up a whole new life for Hatcher, you never could tell.

8

CUTLER

A Middle Tennessean, slightly built man, with sloping shoulders and narrow hips, Rann Cutler's face was long and his nose was large. When he was younger he had hoped that his nose would get broken and thereby improve his looks. With maturity he had ceased to worry about looks, for as is true with many men, age improved Cutler's appearance. He had light blue eyes. Behind them lurked the belief — by now a conviction — that all the luck he would ever have was bound and fated to be bad. Rann Cutler was a Southern aristocrat, and his life so far had been a definition, one at least, of what it is to be Southern and well-born.

An exile, he lived in Florida. The Marine Corps had offered Cutler during the years he was serving his enlistments, exile of another sort. Sometimes he pondered his birth, his life — the quicksands, that jungle trivia and happenstance, the bygone past. His life. He was thirty-five years old; thirty-five more and you get your seventy. Back you go then to wherever you came from: I was not; I am; I will not be. Ideas often troubled his dreams, disturbing his slumber.

During the interim — life and being — what was man to do with himself?

Of late Cutler had been working for a Negro. As for the sort and kind of bad luck this surely would bring — well, there was never any need trying to psyche out the always horrible future (considering the past could be hard enough), but the nigger would somehow turn out to be bad news. Cutler was sure.

"That's all I need," Cutler told himself, coming wide awake. "Ten years in the pokey."

He got up off his hard mattress and stretched. "Ten years," he said aloud. "Then I'm forty-five."

"You finally woke up?" It was the girl. Like most she couldn't take Cutler's hard mattress, so like most others she had slept on the fold-down studio couch in the front room of Cutler's Bayside studio apartment. She had folded the couch back, he saw. She had replaced the sofa cushions. She was already dressed. An empty coffee cup on the low table spoke for itself. This girl was an improvement over the most of them, Cutler thought. She got up in the morning anyhow.

"I don't see how you stand your mattress, it's like concrete." She was serious.

Cutler smiled. He never felt like talking in the morning. He went to the efficiency kitchen, poured himself a cup of coffee, and walked into the front room with it. The glare of sunlight beyond the wide picture window of his apartment told him this day was another in a long series of scorchers. Sunday. He sighed.

"You have to be a hard up son of a bitch to stay here in the summer," he said. He took a sip of black, bitter coffee.

[*81*]

"It didn't rain this morning," she said. "No rain again."

Because it so often rained early in the morning at this season everyone in Ormund City was talking about rain, when in truth such brief tropical rain didn't help break a heat wave like the present one. Nevertheless everyone talked about how much it would help. They prayed for the morning rain, hoping each morning it would storm in from the Gulf.

"If it would rain," she said.

She was pretty and coltish. A very nice girl, really, Cutler thought. She had lovely, almost Indian features. Her hair was heavy and dark. She wore it long. She had fine eyes and a clean, pretty mouth. She was athletic and she had the right kind of nose. She was really a nicely proportioned girl and she was calmly bred. Sound breeding, Cutler thought.

Only one thing was wrong with her — she spelled t-r-o-u-b-l-e.

A grocery millionaire, Alabam Webster, was letching after her — not so surprisingly. This would have been all right too were it not for the nature of Cutler's own employment. Three weeks ago last night the girl had first come home with him. She had been a virgin. Quite a surprise. Again, everything would have been all right but for the *fact*. Inwardly Cutler felt himself wincing. The girl had meanwhile taken her empty cup and saucer from the low table. She went to the kitchenette. She moved beautifully, beautifully, he thought.

Cutler tried to force the fact, the problem out of his mind. He chain-lit a second cigarette using the butt of the first one. In his mind's eye he saw the grocer again, as though for the thousandth time, poor old Alabam Webster — clodhopper written all over the old bastard's drastic face, money running out of his lowdown ears. Webster was also a Tennessean — a West Tennessean. The western variety was a different breed. They trusted strangers. The maxim had crept in upon Cutler, like a cloud, very slowly:

"East Tennesseans trust nobody; Middle Tennesseans trust very damn few; West Tennesseans trust everybody, but especially, other Tennesseans."

That poor old Alabam had happened to be a West Tennessean had been the icing on the cake, for Cutler's purposes. Cutler no sooner contrived to make the grocer's acquaintance than Alabam was touched — the hapless bastard loved his home country, low born though he was. Did the lowborn have more such love in their Southern bones? Cutler wondered sometimes.

The girl came back. "Something's on your mind," she said. "Want me to go home?"

"No," Cutler said, automatically courteous. "Please stay. Pretty Girl you know what happiness it is just to look at you? Just having you here? If you try to leave I'll break your neck."

A slow smile came to her face. "What makes you tick, I wonder?" she said. "Do you know you never tell me anything?"

"Never explain," Cutler said. "Never make excuses."

"I love you," she said.

He nodded. He put out his cigarette in the ashtray she had given him — for his thirty-fifth birthday. He put his coffee cup beside the ashtray and sat back in the dark green, overstuffed chair. "I believe you, Pretty Girl," he said. And then: "Come here."

She came. She knelt and rested her head in his lap. She sat for a long time at his feet with her hands clasped over his knees, holding him gently, loving him. He caught at the cool, heavy folds of her fragrant hair.

"Tell me something," she said.

[*83*]

"What?" he said.

"About you. When you were a child. Do you mind? Rann — ?"

He was silent.

Then: "Yes, Pretty Girl?"

"Is it too much trouble —?"

"Of course not," he said. He didn't want to tell her things, of course. Anything he told could only bring them closer together. Because he didn't like to hurt people, and because he had been this route so many, many times in the past, something deep and spinal in him sounded a warning. If he fell in love with her, what then? He had nothing to offer but himself, and that wasn't enough. It had never been enough. In this case, besides — especially now — there was no possibility that anything ever could work out between them. Telling her things, talking to her could only cause him pain later on.

"Please?" she said. *Please*, in that soft, low voice he had come to know well. *Please*, a word she whispered when he made love to her. And it summed her up — beauty, the innocence, the youth — the vulnerable, beautiful self on its knees to him, begging him to accept the gift of her, pleading with him to love her. Love me. Love me . . .

"Of course," he said. (Giving in made him a little blind.) And he thought: Christ — such a girl. "I was born in Nashville. Middle Tennessee," he began.

Then, as though for an instant, for one of the few times in his careful life, he had slipped his tongue. Cutler heard himself telling her things.

Horses, for example, all about horses. Your hunter, he was telling, the hunter has to be a mix. He needs some Arabian in him but has to have the muscles of the draft horse, strength to

[84]

loft him over the jumps. And although your Thoroughbred doesn't make a hunter, still your hunter needs a dash of Thoroughbred in him for speed. The draft horse blood gives him something besides muscles. It gives him what the Arabian lacks. Cutler paused.

She wanted to know *what*. She opened his hand and kissed him in the palm.

"Calm bravery," he said.

"If you grew up with horses then you grew up with money," she said.

"Yes." The old bitterness came back. "The Cutlers had land and the Cutlers had money and by 1939 they had spent all of it. The house I grew up in had seventeen rooms. We had servants on the place — darkies." Cutler smiled at the bitter memory. "Even though my father had spent it all by 1939 it took him three more years to realize it. I think he didn't realize it until my grandmother died. Then it finally dawned on him."

"What is it like — to have had it that way and then to lose it?" she asked.

"It's like getting kicked out of prep school," Cutler said. "It bothers the living hell out of you. It follows you and you never quite get over it. Rather than to have had it and lost it I think it's probably better never to have had it," he said.

"I can't see how you can say that," she said. "Of course I've never really lost it though." She pressed his hand to her cheek.

"You know everything it can buy," Cutler said. "You know all the people who have theirs still intact. In your dreams you still have it. You dress like them and talk like them and think like them but God damn it you aren't one of them. Not any more. So what are you? I don't know," he said restlessly.

"You make it sound so awful."

"Take my word for it, it is."

She wanted to know what Middle Tennessee was like and he began telling her. He described the most beautiful country in the world. Clear, shaded creeks flowing over ledges of limestone; split rail chestnut fences; emerald meadows; soaring, treecovered hills. Would he ever take her there? she asked.

"I couldn't bear it," he said.

"Then it's that bad." She kissed his hand again.

"Yes," he said, perhaps only now for the first time realizing himself how bad it was. Not that he hadn't known before now what a mess his life was, but knowing a thing can't hurt; whereas realizing always can — does hurt, he thought. *Always.*

"Your sisters, for example," he said. "I had five sisters. Christ — it ruined them. Because when the worst happens to a girl she panics. She marries some bastard because she wants to get it all back. Because she can't marry for love — not the first go-round anyway — she marries money. Or gets herself knocked up —"

"You speak as if . . . they were dead."

"No — they're alive. All of them — divorced, remarried, knocked up and what not — alcoholics unanimous." He smiled.

"So what did you do, Rann?"

"Joined the Marine Corps."

"I love you," she said. "After the Marines, what then?"

"Came here. Played bridge and poker and gin. Taught a class of Ormund City society cunts how to shoot pistols. Shot skeet, played golf, fished the tarpon. First my luck, then the money ran out — everything — because nobody ever taught me how to be lucky, or how to live without spending. I could save as long as I was in the Corps, but once out —" Cutler sighed. "I'm boring your sweet, beautiful little . . ."

"I'm *not* bored," she said softly.

"Get out of the Corps? Immediately you're a Southern aristocrat again — right back where you were when you enlisted at eighteen. Broke as hell."

"Then what did you do?"

"Went to work for a nigger," he said.

The nigger had been looking for some time for a certain type. He had wanted a white man with peculiar qualifications and he had hit upon Cutler not quite by accident. The approach, indeed, had been very direct.

A polite phone call was the first step. The nigger had inquired and through the bartender at the yacht club whose brother drove a cab . . . did Mister Cutler perhaps know the bartender, Smith?

Yes, Cutler knew him.

Well through Smith it was understood that Mister Cutler knew a great many people in Ormund City by virtue of gin rummy and bridge, which was not to say that Purchase Walker in any sense felt that Mister Cutler gambled professionally. Yet on the other hand other connections in the business community had indicated to Purchase Walker that Mister Cutler was occasionally short of funds. Purchase Walker hoped Mister Cutler wouldn't take it unkindly?

"In other words you've already checked up on me," Cutler had said.

"Yes, and from everything we have found you are the man I am seeking," the nigger had said. "I believe you can get what I need and I am prepared to make it well worth your while. You understand of course that I'm a Negro."

Cutler admitted that he had heard the name Purchase Walker. In what connection he didn't recall at the moment.

"If we could arrange a meeting," the nigger had said.

Rann Cutler had agreed. It was a late afternoon near the end of May, one of the last few livable days when evening, thanks to a raft of almost translucent clouds rolling across the Florida sky like pink feathers festooned with streaks of slate dust, gave a sense of cooling freedom to the air. The Negro had sent his limousine, a brand new vinyl-top Cadillac Sedan de Ville with a wryly grinning little driver perched monkey-like under the dark wheel. It had come to Cutler as the sedan carried him smoothly away into the Central District, it dawned on him as he sat in the center of the back seat measuring the distance between himself and the driver of this nine-passenger ten-thousand-dollar automobile, that Purchase Walker was the black vice lord of Ormund City.

The meeting was brief, though not perfunctory. Purchase Walker wanted a background file on the Webster Kutrate supermarkets. He wanted every smidgin of information Cutler could get. The volume of business, the mark-ups, the worth of the two huge stores, future plans for expansion. Everything.

"The business is owned by a Mister Alabam Webster. I believe you know him."

"Yes," Cutler had said. "I have met him."

The Negro's business office, tucked in behind one of the larger Black and Tan Clubs, was luxuriously appointed. The crumbling brick walls of the alley outside gave no indication of the polished and upholstered interior. No more than the club itself with its topless dancers, the grimy little band, the B-girls and the prostitutes; it was difficult in one sense to believe that behind two such unlikely facades there could dwell offices such as these, but taken another way, that is, taking into account that the entire fleshpot pyramid of the city from dope to gambling to prostitution and even the cab companies, was owned and controlled by Purchase Walker, then offices such as these and a suite such as this became inevitable once the doors opened and one was ushered into the presence of the man who was the boss of it all.

The Negro chose to live surrounded by French antiques. He chose to wear slash pocket suits, alligator shoes, cuffless trousers, beautiful shirts, and ties that must easily cost him fifty dollars apiece.

He had been very open about it. He had his bookkeepers and accountants. That room was cheerfully blue, from tile floors to bright walls. The accounting personnel worked heads down. It was like a scene in a bank. Another division contained the cab dispatchers' communication center. Girls worked the switchboard; men operated the two-way radio sets.

The money was collected, accounted for, banked. The winners were paid promptly in the case of the baseball cards, the bolita, and the numbers. Books were kept on income from prostitution.

"It's like collecting rent. We license them, supervise them, protect them and take a percentage. They pay their income taxes and so do we. Otherwise you have the Federal Government."

"And nobody wants the Federal Government," Cutler had offered.

"Yes," Purchase Walker had said. "Being as you worked for it — in the Marine Corps — you understand that nobody wants trouble with the Federal Government. So naturally we avoid it ourselves. We have the sheriff and the police on our payroll. Now and then the Federal Government will get one of them for tax fraud, but we avoid it." The Negro had shrugged.

It had been back to the Negro's office then. "What I'm

[*89*]

asking, if you decide to take the job, is nothing dishonest or illegal," the Negro had said. "I can pay five hundred a week and expenses."

"Why do you want the information on Webster's Kutrate?" Cutler had asked.

The Negro seemed to consider the question. Perhaps he was weighing just how much he should tell. Perhaps he was wondering how far he should trust Rann Cutler not to betray him.

A silence seemed to slide between them in the scented recesses of the room. A French clock on the fireplace mantel brought an incessant quality to the pause with its expensive ticking, as though to tell Cutler that here in every object was something he would never afford, never own, such that when the Negro finally spoke it was as though he had not spoken before at all. What the Negro said might have been the first words to pass between them.

"You may as well know," the Negro said. He had offered Cutler a cigar which Cutler accepted. They had sat smoking.

"Webster came here a few years back. He had worked for the chain stores and had decided to go independent. You'll discover all this. Well, he makes nothing but money. From one little operation here in Central he grows until he has what you see now. The two biggest supermarkets in the state of Florida.

"Villa on the island, membership in the clubs . . ." The Negro paused again.

"And don't get me wrong. I don't begrudge him. Because this cracker made it. I'm glad to see him make it. The trouble came in when he decided he wanted a cab company. So he applied for the franchise and he got it. Nothing I could do. No influence I could bring in Tallahassee, nothing I could do in this town. They had a hearing and he got his license. Says he intends to run a clean cab operation."

"Excuse me if I still don't get it," Cutler had said.

Preoccupied, holding the cigar in his long, articulate fingers, the Negro seemed to be staring at nothing. Suddenly then, he looked at Cutler.

"The cab companies happen to be the importance," the Negro said, speaking that strange lingo. "The importance," and not so strangely, the manner of his speech had set the two men as much apart as the difference in skin and hair, bone and facial structures.

"Come again?" Cutler had said.

"Three things every cat has the need of, Mr. Cutler. Women, gambling, and a way to get there? Throw in grass and lap, man must have those too."

When the Negro saw the puzzlement in Cutler's face he laughed softly. "Grass, lap?" Cutler said.

"Marijuana and whiskey. Lap is whiskey. What I want you to see is that Webster, who calls himself Cousin Alabam and has made himself very popular with the colored people of Ormund City, all the way from Durban Heights to the Wood-yard to the Bottom, Mr. Webster is horning in on an important part of my business. His cab operation is going to hurt me. It's already hurting me. He's hired away some of my best dispatchers. He's got some of my best white drivers on his pay-roll. Next thing you know he's going to have some of my colored guys lured away. They will start to running women on their own. When a man is after shot does it matter to him who he buys it from?"

"Shot?"

"Pussy."

Cutler nodded.

"So whatever Mister Webster says about running a *clean* cab company is nonsense, Mr. Cutler. I need him out of that business. He just bought over one hundred air-conditioned cabs. So I had to buy over two hundred air-conditioned cabs or lose my business down to a dangerous level."

"I see," Cutler had said. "So you want information enough on Webster's grocery operation to squeeze him out of the cab business."

"Now you see what I want," the Negro had said. "If you need to let him win at cards to make friends with him. If you have to give him presents. If he needs the idea in his mind that you are rich? See? For from what Smith tells us, from his observations at the yacht club, Mr. Alabam Webster is not as long on friends as he is on money. A man like you could become his friend. You have the class to turn him on, to get next to him."

It was flattery of a backhanded sort, as Cutler had realized. The Negro credited him with class and almost in the same breath called him a judas goat willing to lead another man to the slaughter by using that "class" in order to abuse and ulti- mately to betray a friendship built entirely upon false pre- tenses.

"It is not illegal," the Negro had said again, as though sensing Cutler's qualms struggling to cross the silent distance of his hesitation.

"Five hundred a week and expenses," Cutler had said. After all the Negro was right. On all counts. Cutler had been hurting for money.

"That's my offer," the Negro had said.

"It's very fair and I accept," Cutler had said. "I'm just the son of a bitch you've been looking for . . ."

The only question had been how long the process should take. They had finally agreed that Cutler should have the information in the Negro's hands no later than June 1. It was now June 11. There was also to be a bonus for Cutler upon receipt of the report. The bonus meant fifteen hundred dollars on delivery, and once again, Cutler needed the money. He needed it now. He had therefore promised to deliver the report today — June 11, Sunday.

Today.

9

LEROY

CLOSING the door after him, Leroy went downstairs to the street. Smith had located another gospel program because the singing, like hollering straight out of the goddamn jungle, could be heard even down in the alley. Leroy held his breath to pass the garbage. Then he stopped because he saw a movement. It was a mutt of some kind, he saw, and it was sniffing and picking through the trash. That's how he had to make his living too, this little mutt. He was a little black mutt like a rat terrier. Maybe he had been kicked on his can more times than sand in the ocean because there was mange on him and he had a black scar on his side the size of a half-dollar.

"Hey little man."

The dog wagged his tail.

"How come I never seen you here before?"

He could be a right nice dog if he had somebody to take care of him a little bit. Give him a bath, cure his mange. Get him a little collar. Give him a name. Maybe old Smith would want a dog?

"I tell you what little man if I see you here sometime when I ain't in no great big hurry maybe I'll take you upstairs and introduce you to Smith. Yeah!" The mutt wagged his tail again. He made like he wanted to follow Leroy. "Uh-*uh!* You don't want to go with me, baby! I'm traveling too fast for you!"

The mutt's ears went down. He turned back to his hunting.

Leroy continued on his way. He wondered if Hatcher would be at Poor Boston's. And what would become of Hatcher and Gyp Hollan?

Because Hatcher had to take everything he knew second-hand, from some preacher or from the Bible, it was pretty hard on him yesterday when they climbed the iron ladder up to the roof of the warehouse. Louise Hollan went first wearing tight electrical-colored pants. Then came old Hatcher right behind her with the blanket and Leroy behind Hatcher with the bag containing the beer, and Gyp saying the beer would not be getting no cooler if somebody didn't hurry up!

When they all three got up there and Gyp spread the blanket in the regular place near the housing where the silent exhaust fans were mounted, where shade could always be found. It was very quiet up there and very private. She came out of her clothes and folded her garments neatly on a corner of the blanket. Then she took the tissue paper out of her purse and put it where she could reach it. All this while Hatcher's face seems to be saying, "But this will only get us into trouble." Leroy looks at him.

"Open me a beer," says Louise Hollan. Leroy opens her one. He opens one for himself. Hatcher says no that we will not have a beer and Louise Hollan says well nice because it will mean one more for her. Leroy has his pants folded and his shirt off before he notices how Hatcher is just standing there. Gyp says didn't somebody mention this was a three-way and says maybe some people need help or maybe they just like to watch which is all right by her but she heard *somebody* say it was a three-way and here she was and baby, let her make it plain that when it got dark she had to cut out because if she don't jump on Saturday why the rest of the week forget it!

It comes to Leroy that he must do something. He reaches and unbuttons Hatcher's shirt for him three or four buttons. Hatcher's hands move, then, as though they are not a part of himself. A moment later he stands naked and pure as the day he was born, he seems. When he still doesn't move Leroy and Louise Hollan take his arms and lead him to the blanket. They get him stretched out on his back and Louise is saying, "Now baby all I want you to do is shut your eyes. Relax and dream." She kisses Hatcher's nipple and he gives a little sigh. Leroy turns away. Because what takes place on the blanket is different, not what Leroy expected, he slips into his clothes and stands just at the edge of the warehouse roof where he can look down into the street and see Saturday. He can look down from on high at people in the street with nothing but Saturday on their mind, with no idea what is happening under the sky above them.

Presently Gyp calls Leroy. He goes to the shade where she is standing. "Is he crazy?" she whispers.

"Well," says Leroy, "this here was Hatcher's first taste."

"Don't put me on, man!" But she believes him. Her lip quivers. Then without warning a beautiful smile runs into her face. She's saying, "Well!" And "Well!"

She gets two dollars from her purse.

"Go down to Boston's and buy another six-pack. You don't mind, do you?"

Leroy shakes his head. He takes the money. He runs the whole way. When he gets back the roof is quiet.

Leroy turns his face toward the gulf. Gyp takes the beer and returns to Hatcher.

Daylight slides into evening. Lights glow against the sky. Looking beyond the stretch of the lights gives the world magic. Everything so awful by daylight disappears with nightfall. Man's blood tells him he could run and run and run on and on and never be tired of running.

Hatcher has started talking, saying words he has never before spoken. His voice rises and falls away in the darkness. Hatcher calls her "Louise" instead of "Gyp." He talks about his plans.

Well, Jesus B. Christ, Leroy thinks. He walks to the ladder. They pay him no mind. Leroy feels very lonely and he wants to feel bitter. He wants to let Hatcher and Gyp know but he can't think of anything to say. Hatcher and Gyp don't know another person is alive in the world. There in the dark Hatcher is so happy he could crawl up inside that woman and drown himself and never come out again he would be so pleased right this minute to die. Not worried no more about heaven, about jobs, or God being down on his ass. So because three's making a crowd Leroy goes down the ladder and walks to Poor Boston's with Francine on his mind like a live pigeon that won't fly off and leave him be, and Boston lets Leroy have a cup of coffee on credit. After that Leroy feels worse so he walks back home and lies down on his mattress. He tries to think what words it was he said to his own girl once and how she talked but he can't even do that because Smith has the radio playing downstairs and Leroy could go ask him and Smith would feed him but there is not enough food in the world to satisfy what Leroy wants and desires.

"I love you," said Leroy aloud.

He pushed open the door to Poor Boston's Club and Cafe. Sure enough, there was no sign of Hatcher. Boston, a puffy-eyed old man, said he hadn't seen Hatcher.

The place wasn't too busy. There was a game of dominoes going at the table. The light over one of the pool tables was on and a game going there between a spry little man named Bolls and a tall kid in a red shirt. Leroy had never laid eyes on the tall kid before. And Bolls, acting like he wasn't very sure of his game, was busily setting up the kid to hustle him. "I don't know," Huey Bolls was saying. "It seem like my vision or something is wrong this evening." One of the domino players winked at the others. "Shoot you a dollar," said the tall kid. He was racking them up.

"Naw, Hatcher ain't been here today, Leroy," Poor Boston was saying.

"What about Gyp?"

"Let me see —" Poor Boston raised a hand and covered his puffy eyes. "Well as best I can remember I didn't see no sign of Gyp last night. No, not a glimpse. And you know that's something strange." He put down his hand and looked at Leroy. "And I damn sho ain't seen her today. But the fact she never came down this way last night — that's something I can't figure. I mean she be so regular on Saturday. I don't know. Nothing don't feel right today. It's too damn hot. Nothin doing — nobody stirrin and I been all day trying to figure why I feel this way. I mean maybe nobody else feels it. But they not stirrin much. But they not complainin you know what I mean. Do you feel something? And Watridge stompin that old man."

"I don't know," Leroy said. "Maybe that's how I felt all my life."

Poor Boston let a sleepy grin appear on his face. Then just as quickly as it had appeared it slid away. "I know *that* feeling boy, but what *I'm* saying — you want some coffee?"

"I'm low on scratch — I —"

"You ate anything today? Look, sit down." Poor Boston turned to the hot plate and poured a cup of coffee. Leroy sat down at the counter. Poor Boston pushed the sugar jar to him and got the can of Carnation milk from the refrigerator. Leroy loaded the coffee with sugar and poured in plenty of milk.

"These here didn't sell last night. This here one is egg salad and that one's a ham." He pushed the two triangular packs across the counter beside Leroy's coffee cup.

Poor Boston got sandwiches from the Mother Baker's Sandwiches driver — whatever the driver happened to pick up as stale, to be replaced on the counters of the drugstore soda fountains, the concession stands, and in beer joints all over the city — whatever was stale and ready to go bad the driver brought to Poor Boston who got the sandwiches cheap that way. The same thing went for the stale snack crackers wrapped in cellophane. Poor Boston ran the place with secondhand food. Fridays he drove out to the dump and was waiting when the truck from the potato chip bakery appeared with all the stale chips and back Boston came to the cafe with a carload of chips that he had got absolutely free. As Hatcher often remarked, "Ain't nothing poor about old Boston Humes. I wonder sometimes who is he trying to fool anyhow?"

"Go on," Poor Boston said. "Eat your lunch."

[*99*]

"Yeah, but I tole you, I'm almost broke."

"All right, can't I give you a couple of sandwiches, man? Don't take it so hard when anybody tries to give you something."

Leroy opened the sandwiches and began to eat. The first one was an egg salad. The other was ham and opening a sandwich that way, opening and eating it and all the while knowing that here was a sandwich that nobody else had wanted to buy, something that several white honkies across town had maybe looked at or even touched, to take it another way maybe some beautiful chick, some lovely secretary picked the sandwich up and was just about to pay for it when she changed her mind — it gave a man ideas he could dream about such as whereall this here very food he was eating had been. A man could be happy about it or blue over it. He could feel good about secondhand food or it could put him down and mash his spirit, all according to what dreams appeared in his head.

"How are they — okay?"

"Yeah, okay," Leroy said. "I was ready to eat."

"I been all down the road you're walking now. I know hunger. I know thirst. I know what it is to be cold — because I used to live up in Atlanta, see — and that place can freeze your balls, man."

"Yeah," said Leroy. "I wouldn't know because I have never left this town. So this one place is all I know. But I get the itch now and then I want to travel. I want to see New Orleans."

"And now this town has been teaching me about heat," Poor Boston was saying. "You know what the power company would charge a man if he ran just one little air conditioner?"

"How much?"

"Fifty a month," said Poor Boston, nodding. "You can't run no electric fan down in this place for less than ten a month and then it's got to be so small . . . hell a fan that would exhaust this place pretty good and pull in breeze from the pavement, even if I could afford to buy a fan what I have to say, 'Man, I could not afford to run it!' "

Leroy nodded, putting the last bit of ham sandwich into his mouth. He took a sip of hot coffee.

"But I know something don't feel right."

"Maybe you need aspirin for your nerves," Leroy said. "Maybe you getting nervous lately."

Poor Boston again covered his eyes with his hand. "I don't know — I just wonder if my peoples back in Atlanta is okay. It's like you feel before that knock raps at the door, that somebody, that something is about to knock and that something is out there waiting, wanting to see you. I have this business where sometimes I can feel it ahead of time when something ain't right."

"It needs to rain, that's all," Leroy said. "Cool this whole place down so somebody can get peace and rest. I got waked up out of my sleep this morning. Some white man knocked on my door and woke me in the middle of my dreams."

"What he want?"

"You don't know whether the bastard wants to sell you insurance or ask you to hustle him some chicken."

"What did he say?"

"He said he had questions for me."

"And what did you have to tell him then?"

"When he woke me up this morning out of my dreams? I told him, I said, 'Man, if you got to do business with Leroy you got to learn that Sunday ain't no moment to come waking him up out of bed.' I tole him, I says, 'Come back tomorrer during business hours.' "

"You knew he had to be a phony coming at you wid that phony approach that way."

"Sure I knew it."

"Was he a detective cop? They got a couple of guys snooping around the neighborhood. I believe somebody said they got on a campaign about the bad blood — the syph and the clap, the disease. Where you have to go down to the clinic and take the treatment — take a treatment every so often and they draw your blood and all," Poor Boston said.

"Well, I tole what I knew and then I said cut out of here, fella, and let Leroy alone unless you got some silver you want to give me. Because Leroy can always use a little scratch."

"He was wanting something free. Every man in the world wants something free. Mankind is all looking for gifts," Poor Boston said. "So then what did he do?"

"Oh, stood around. Tried to talk. When he saw he wasn't getting nowhere he left out and that's the last I seen of him. First I thought maybe he thought it was a whorehouse and walked into my room by mistake. I never know what a white mother's got on his mind."

"You don't trust him."

"Don't believe nothing he says because he don't half the time know what he *is* saying."

"Yeah," Poor Boston said. "I know how you feel and I keep telling myself how the world is changing when you can meet up with a man like you, Leroy, and know that in all this green and black world it ain't one white face you trusts. I'm satisfied you don't know anybody trustworthy belonging to the white race —

but you take now it wasn't always like that. I mean it is not like that everywhere all over this country. Not yet."

"Say it ain't."

"I mean it was a time some years back before you was born in the world when I couldn't find many colored men or women either that didn't have at least one white friend, one member of the white race, they could trust. Some member of that race they could go to in a time of need and receive help and be comforted. You take in some small places it is still that way — but look at this God damned town. Look how many kids you know like yourself that have come up and been raised in this neighborhood now and they don't know *any* white person unless he's some kind of cop or officer or like what you had walk in your room this morning. So I mean what is getting scarce around here is any human feeling between the white and the colored. So something is wrong. Try to make one thing right, demand and go after our freedom, and something else goes wrong."

Leroy smiled. Old Boston could get so wound up and so serious until he didn't make sense either, but if somebody would just listen to him at least it might end up that for listening a fellow could get a little something on his stomach and with any luck at all Boston might forget it and not put Leroy on the credit list for what he ate. So Leroy pretended to listen.

"It's like Hatcher is always saying," Leroy spoke up. "Everybody goes about talking about jobs and freedom but nobody does nothing about it."

"Hatcher's a smart man all right. I believe Hatcher is a deep thinker," said Poor Boston. "I would have to say you are lucky to have Hatcher for such a close friend and Hatcher's fond of you. Yet one thing about you two continues to bother and worry me."

"What's that?" Leroy asked.

"A question occurs in my mind. I wonder will you become like Hatcher or will Hatcher become like you? Because both of you are not alike to the other one in any way. So one is going to have to fall under the influence of the other. So whose way of life is strongest. Which man is going to be changed?"

"Hatcher's coming my way," Leroy said.

10

CYNTHIA

THE instant she sensed that a man wanted something Cynthia resisted. It had been at long last Cutler's maddening, infinite patience that finally had captured her. How strange it was — knowing he loved her. Yet all the while something kept him from admitting what he surely felt. Purposely perhaps, he kept her wondering. She watched him.

Cutler had fallen silent. He was suddenly withdrawn again, pulled back again toward the mysterious inner self she had never before really penetrated. Getting up she leaned quickly forward and kissed him. "It's almost time we left," she said.

Cutler roused a little. "Yes," he said absently. "Call a cab. Pick up your car. Go on ahead of me. We mustn't be seen arriving together."

Why was he so silly? She wondered. Why was he so careful of Webster's feelings? Poor old foolish old Alabam Webster. Rich old outlandish old Alabam . . . who was actually a very sweet man, very kind, very generous, very loving and extremely shrewd. It was unfair of her to dislike him so. But-I-do, she thought.

"What's the difference?" she said. "Isn't he bound to find

out soon? Has it got to be everywhere in separate cars? Mating in dark corners — like spiders for God's sake? Rann — are you ashamed of me?"

"It isn't that," Cutler said.

"Then what is it?" she said. His silence met her head on again. "I'm not Alabam Webster's girl. I'm your girl!"

"If you don't leave now you'll miss the noon meal," Cutler said. "Why make him suspicious? Why hurt his feelings?"

He wore white boxer shorts, his usual sleeping attire. His evenly tanned body was lean and finely muscled. Everything about him attracted her. His calm voice, the slow, diffident drawling manner of speech — as if nothing in the world really mattered, really bothered him; and his eyes, his eyes especially, that blue, fearless quality of his gaze; the perfect blend of kindliness and cruelty. One such glance and something inside her seemed to melt. He's going to marry me, she thought despairingly. And then: I'm going to make him happy.

"It's important to me, that's all," he was saying, so utterly calm, so supremely relaxed. So sure within himself. Hard as glass, she was thinking. "Alabam just mustn't know about us for now. He must not even suspect. And Cynthia, Pretty Girl, if you love me —"

"Love you!"

"I'm sorry," he said quickly, quietly. "Don't misunderstand. I don't mean anything cheap. I don't intend anything cheap. That sounded cheap of me."

"You need something from him," she said. "Don't you?"

"I'd rather not go into it just now if you don't mind," Cutler said dryly.

"It has something to do with that nigger, hasn't it? Or were you lying? Do you really work for a Negro?"

"I don't lie," Cutler said in an even voice. "I need a shave and a shower. Why not get your car and get out there before Alabam gets impatient or uneasy? I'll be along in a minute or so. This is something we can work out later between us — isn't it?"

"No," she said. "Tell me what this is all about. Tell me now. What is this work, the only work you know how to do? What are you doing? Who are you working for? Tell me? Please — ?"

"I can't," he said.

"But you do need something from Alabam. That's why you made friends with him in the first place, isn't it? You're after him. Hunting him."

Cutler smiled. "Maybe," he said.

"I ought to warn him."

"You won't," he said. "You wouldn't."

The fear no sooner crossed her mind than she told it. "You're using me." And then: "Are you?"

"No, God damn it. The point is I'm really not. I certainly won't," he said in the same bored drawl. "I really wouldn't."

". . . because if you are I don't know what I'll do," she was saying. "If you are!" She felt silly.

"Come back here," he said.

She stood at the window, refusing him. Beyond the glass Ormund City was slowly roasting. Standing here the cool, constant slide of refrigerated air kept her comfortable; but what of others there beyond the glass? What about the really poor? How did they stand it? She could see the river. Gulls were wheeling in the sultry air above its flat waters. There was also a view of the Bayside Bridge, where it swung upward in a graceful curve crossing to the island, and beyond the bridge she glimpsed the tropical white gleam of Ormund City General, the hospital, tower-like above the reach of the dark, distant trees. The island. To the left of the island, west and beyond the dark width of the river stood the tall buildings — downtown Ormund City. Here where she stood, in what was called "Bayside," everything was clean. Everything beautiful; every room was cool.

"I'm not going today," Cynthia heard herself saying. "I don't feel like going."

Cutler had showered, shaved, slipped into his casual clothes and walked out of the apartment. Now just as suddenly she saw he was back — with a thick Sunday newspaper — but ignoring her still. He sat reading the paper in the same dark green chair and smoking, paying no more attention than if she had been a cat.

"I'm not going," she said.

Cutler whistled. "God — godamighty," he said. "The bastards — poor stupid bastards."

"What?" She answered in spite of herself, thinking: Damn you! Damn you!

"Oh? An old nigger gets arrested down at the Woodyard. The cops handcuff him. Then the proprietor —·a white man, Felton Watridge — kicks the helpless bastard in the mouth. In front of God and everybody. The nigger has to be put in the hospital. The poor nigger says the cops stood by and let it happen. Watridge says something else. The cops say the nigger resisted arrest. Witnesses say the poor old son of a bitch was drunk all right and rowdy, but that he was down, helpless and handcuffed, when this plus two-hundred pounder, Watridge, lets him have it in the guts, the mouth, the side of the head. Christ — the stupidity."

"I said I'm not going. And I'm not." She folded her arms.

Either he didn't hear or he wasn't listening? Or what was closer to the truth? He didn't care? Cutler wouldn't let himself care. Cutler wouldn't let himself make her go to the club even though her going, obviously, was so important to him. Almost a case of his survival, she thought.

Just as independence was with Father, Cynthia thought. Independence had been Father's source of selfworthiness, and what he was not and could never expect to be nor become in the business world, in downtown and dockside offices, (which he quite naturally envisioned as part of the world's sham) Father became at home. At home he was important, Father was *somebody*. His timidity disappeared. People respected and feared him — at home.

Father died so suddenly.

He died at the office, a ". . . shipping company employee, for thirty-five years associated with Bonello & Sons, Inc., of Ormund City and New Orleans."

Father's wife who had not set eyes on him in ten years at least, had suddenly appeared. It was as though the ground suddenly opened up. There stood Mother, his wife: or now better said, Father's widow.

As Mother said, the man's independence had been like a strange unhappy mania. To her mind independence was like an infectious disease. She wasn't, said she, about to be prostituted to it.

Mother had left him therefore, years back, for points north, for Philadelphia where she had come from in the first place. For New York, where she had always wanted to live anyhow. Cynthia had been free to choose the parent she preferred. Occasionally, through the years, Mother had sent money. She had enough of it, Mother had. (Her money had always rankled Father. Her God damned money which she was always flinging around, said he. Why hadn't she married some Eastern money-bags then instead of picking on a simple Florida cracker like himself, Ormund City born and bred?)

Mother's family once upon a time had wintered in Ormund City. They were Quakers and hadn't quite known what to do about a daughter's sudden penchant for such an ordinary Floridian, for Father, so they let Mother marry him — *damn them* — Mother always afterwards said. Damn them—it had cured *her* of Quakerism.

Father hadn't wanted their money, hadn't accepted their earnest offers, hadn't been gently persuaded nothing was lost did he accept a loan at least and go into business for himself, or better still, move to Philadelphia and try his hand at banking — in their bank?

What finally smashed the marriage was a Christmas gift. Ten (count 'em) crisp one thousand dollar bills. Philadelphia money, earnestly and lovingly given.

(Father *had*, finally, realized the true spirit of the gift, or pretty much so, before he died.)

The bills had been from "Santa Claus to our own dear George," in a neat brown Philadelphia envelope. The money was implicitly a downpayment on a somewhat larger, somewhat newer, somewhat more fashionable house — a place on the island as opposed to the family's smaller, quieter little place in Bayside — backstreet Bayside, to be sure.

Had they been hundred dollar bills "Santa's" gift might not have come to and caused so much storm and grief; but hundred dollar bills they positively and obviously were not.

Father had waited calmly till after the Christmas meal. No

need (in his estimation) to spoil appetites. It had been the traditional late-morning Christmas breakfast, a combination morning and noon feast.

Everyone, including Cynthia, was lazily full and somehow wondering in various ways how the rest of every year's consistently most awkward day — Christmas — was to be spent and endured.

Give Father credit for having a few drinks. The Quakers even broke their rule and sipped a couple of "Pink Ladies" before the meal. Cynthia herself had been allowed a tiny taste.

Now Father produced the envelope from beneath his plate. He took out the beautiful bills. He spread them fan-shaped like a hand of playing cards. Every gaze at the table came quietly to rest upon the money. Perhaps they anticipated a speech, a few words of thanks, some simple and sobering wisdom upon the Day of Days?

Father pushed aside the egg platter. Father reached for the silver candelabrum. Its three Christmas green candles were a bit guttered now but still bravely green, wicks sternly black, flames firmly erectile and yellow.

Father stood up slowly, and one by one, he began burning the bills. One by one he dropped them (bereft of all green worth and power) black ashes in his plate. Halfway through the burning he began smiling. As the last bill burned down towards his tanned, trembling fingers Father began laughing.

As for the others at the table, not one it seemed had stirred, spoken, raised a hand, coughed, swallowed, blinked.

Mother (far from admiring Father's courage) had quietly decided this was the bloody end.

"I suppose," Mother had said after his funeral, weeping a little. "I suppose you would have to say for him, for your father, that he was, is — no was — God! — the only son of a bitch that ever lived who actually burned so much money. Darling, wouldn't you agree?"

For the first time in more than ten years Mother and Cynthia suddenly embraced, weeping and laughing; laughing and weeping. Mother couldn't stay in Ormund City, of course, but she had set Cynthia's life into a pattern of order before going back to New York.

Father's tiny estate was converted to cash and invested in municipal bonds. Cynthia found a suitable apartment. Mother calculated a budget. Since the funeral there had been a check from Mother every month.

"I *won't* go to the Club today," Cynthia said.

Cutler lowered the paper an instant, looking at her. "Well then, God damn it, *don't* go," he said pleasantly.

When it was almost time to leave he stretched her out flat, face down on the little cotton rug. She lay with her cheek resting against the folds of her dark hair. Like a man with all the time in the world he began to rub her shoulders, kneeling astride, in the attitude of proper artificial respiration, resting, pausing lightly now and then, one knee between her legs, and a slight, very slight, and an occasional, very occasional, pressure against her buttocks. All the while Cutler's strong hands patiently kneaded her long back muscles, one by one, from neck to pelvis along the comforting, curving sections of her spine.

Soon adrift in strange daydream contentment Cynthia was conscious nonetheless that Cutler could do anything with her — anything at all. Anything he pleased.

Because he never offers to force me, she thought. Independent as sunlight. Take him or leave him. Nobody else could, can, ever will, she told herself.

Every secret place, now, and forever, was his — his alone.

It was like bleeding, like dying, like bleeding slowly, deliciously to death.

Let the world burn, she thought. She didn't care.

Afterwards, while she dressed, he told her about the Negro, Purchase Walker; about Cousin Alabam's cab company, about the Negro's need for information about the Webster Kutrate Stores.

She listened. "So that explains the typewriter *and* the adding machine," she said, looking at the strange instrument on Cutler's dining table. "And here I was thinking you were secretly writing a book. Poor dumb little me," she said.

"Tonight I have to take the whole thing to him," Cutler said.

"So you're in the betrayal business," she replied.

"The nigger said he might find another assignment for me if I complete this one, if this one turns out satisfactorily," he said.

"So after tonight we can tell Alabam about us," she said. "But I have to be nice to him today?"

"It would help if you could hold your potatoes another twenty-four hours," Cutler said. "I have a couple of questions for poor old Alabam and I do need the fifteen hundred."

"Are you going to marry me?" she asked.

"Probably not. What you need is some nice young man in the insurance business."

"You don't mean that, Rann."

"Cousin Alabam might be another bet. He's got something to offer you."

"I know you don't mean it," she said. "I thought yesterday

[*113*]

that once I marry, that once I'm pregnant — then I'll never be free again. I can never walk out a door and decide for myself what I can do, where I can go. Now I'm free. If I could walk out that door now and never see you again. If I could tell myself I don't love you and believe it."

"I'm bad news," he said. "But you've realized one thing anyhow. Once you do marry, once you are pregnant, then you join the big kids. I don't think you're ready."

"When are *you* going to join the big kids, Rann?"

"Me?" He smiled. "Maybe I really have. Or maybe I never will."

"The same loss of freedom doesn't necessarily hold for a man, does it?" she said. "Because nothing physical has to happen inside him. He can mate and walk away from it and mate again and still walk away from it. He's not caught, not forced down so he can never again make independent decisions."

"If I married you I'd ruin you," he said. "But maybe I'll ruin you anyhow. If a ceremony will make any difference let's have the ceremony. Will you marry me, Cyn?"

"I suppose," she said. "It isn't going to work out. I'm too young. You're too old. I want babies and you —"

"I want babies. The older a guy gets the more he wants them."

"Then I guess you better marry me," she said.

At least that's done, she thought.

11

PURCHASE

THE church fans — like the wings of so many, of many-many butterflies. The fans were stirring all about Purchase Walker like an uneasiness in the unforgiving heat.

Comes the time, the signal from the little priest, Father Ned, for kneeling. Purchase kneels beside Ton-Ton. She is fanning him with one of the ceaseless cardboard fans. He feels the press of her teat against his elbow; he, Purchase, ponders the deep faith that is the whole of the reason he, Purchase, natural son of Big Cuba, brings her, his Ton-Ton, brings her here these Sundays and many Sundays past for some months now. And now are come the brutal months when it would be easier on (and much nicer for) everyone to remain home in the comfort and the coolness but instead here we sit like so many eggs in the chicken incubator, he thinks.

When she kneels Ton-Ton holds her sweet body very slender and very erect, earnestly following the responses, reading and always earnestly reading the prayerbook and having him, Purchase, bring her here Sunday after endless Sunday right down and into the brutal days, strangewonderful, strangebeautiful girl she is, is Ton-Ton, with her wits and brains and ways of courage, a boss woman to be proud of — yes. Into the brutal days — and Purchase, he allows and wills that the range of his thoughts wander like an eye all seeing above the flat calm of the near-distant Gulf, between the blinding flash of the feathery sun and the pluming green reluctance of the waters below, down and down then and along the tideflats and amidst the little islands of sand and vegetation to the mouth and the wedding place of the River Meade where the water hyacinths green over black, sunflash and tidesuck and life crawling out of death and slime, the water hyacinths and crabscuttle and tarponsurge. Tarponlunge.

The tidelife uneasiness of the church fans; the ocean flow gulfwarm of the priest's words Father Ned and they believe, and they believe, and they believe kneeling and kneeling in the undersea breath and singing-standing, down the long chantries through and in through in the seachambers of the bloody heart and the pulsetide where it is all inside forever — not quite — working pulsing in darkness. *All blood is black until spilled,* said Tom, my father, said Big Cuba and my midwife mother: *So I have heard it said. Big enough to bleed big enough to butcher, my people say,* said she, *Cut out your heart and devour it like a watermelon. Spit the seeds and the pulp into the sand. That's the branding burn of hot-iron love you can't beat,* she says and he laughs; and plays it on the guitar and his flesh and her flesh, *and I will cut-cutout your heart and devour it like a watermelon; spit the seeds and spit the pulp into the sand, the gritty sand and search the island seas for the turtle, oh the turtlegreen, until blindness have my salt eyes found, till blindness have my salt eyes found from staring all the salt sea round; go and seek the turtle, steal her round-round eggs.* His flesh and her flesh; him laughing, Big Cuba chording it on the Spanish guitar.

Ton-Ton — my flesh and her flesh. Purchase-me-Walker.

Children of the world in swarms like the billion swarming sea shrimp and God flying alone and above like the torn pelican soaring in wisdom aloft and the sea-swarm below, of all God's creatures; *the blood of our lord jesus watermelon preserve thy body and soul unto everlasting life and*

the body of our lord jesus seedpulp feed on him in thy heart with thanksgiving and be grateful: christ died for thee

so to eat his flesh and drink his precious blood and preserve thy body and soul unto everlasting spitsand. Amen and amen and amen; all men, all mankind.

Comes then the final blessing and the end of the service. To Purchase Walker's relief, all stand up to leave.

"Well?" says Father Ned at the front door. He takes Purchase by the hand.

"Swell," says Purchase. "Swell as usual."

"You got my message, did you?" The little priest grinned. "So the message reached you? It didn't reach you? I thought I caught your eye — "

"I beg your pardon?" Purchase said. "*What?*"

"Maybe you and Miss Ton-Ton wouldn't be in too much of a hurry, I mean."

"Yes, Father Ned?" Ton-Ton says. "You need us?"

"If you would wait in my office I do have something." The priest waved his hands. A vague motion, like hands waving through a swarm of gnats, thought Purchase. "Something to say to you," the priest said. "Problems — "

Purchase felt Ton-Ton squeeze his bicep. He looked at her and back at the priest. "All right."

"Just wait in my office? Some young people are in there. You know Hatcher? He's seeing me about arranging his marriage to a young girl. That fine young lady he brought with him this morning."

The priest was shaking hands with the people. Looking across the churchyard Purchase could see his waiting limousine. Maco would be wondering what was the holdup.

"What the hell can he want with me?" Purchase said, going back inside the warm building with Ton-Ton.

"Be patient, lover," said Ton-Ton. "You don't have to come this way but one day each week. You can give Father a little time."

"He's a nut," Purchase said. "He's got brains though. I give him that."

They walked back through the shoddy Sunday School rooms. Above the mirror in the children's room was a sign: "Am I neat?"

Opening the door to the priest's study, Purchase saw the girl. A quick search of his memory told him. She had danced in the go-go line at one of the Black and Tan Clubs. Then she had dropped out of sight. Ton-Ton was smiling at the girl and saying hello to Hatcher.

Father Ned arrived. "A premarital conference is a good idea. It makes you ask yourselves questions that should be answered before people join in holy matrimony."

Hatcher nodded. The girl was looking down. She had folded her hands in her lap. The office was stuffy. Purchase sighed.

"We want to be married as soon as it can be arranged," Hatcher said.

"All right. Day or two won't make any difference will it? You'll want your blood tests."

"I was thinking maybe it wouldn't be no bad idea to wait a few weeks," the girl said uneasily.

"I like a *series* of premarital conferences where the engaged couple have time for it," Father Ned was saying.

"I don't want to wait that long," Hatcher said. "We've made up our minds. So why wait?"

"Impatience is the virtue of youth and the vice of age," said the priest. "Can you meet me in this office tomorrow afternoon? Or if you like you can come to my house."

"We'll come to the house," Hatcher said. "Isn't that easier for you?"

"Yes," said the priest. "Be there then at say two in the afternoon."

Hatcher nodded. He stood up.

"You know Miss Ton-Ton and Mister Walker. This is Hatcher and Miss Hollan."

"Good luck," Purchase Walker said. He took Hatcher's hand and looked at the girl. She looked away, as though frightened. Ton-Ton smiled at them, and they left. The priest closed the door.

"Please sit down." He waved at chairs and a sofa, old over-stuffed furniture with suspicious stains and odd watermarks on it. Sitting down, Purchase smelled mildew.

"An occurrence last night which I tried to work into my sermon," the priest began. He interrupted himself. "My teeth have been giving me trouble," he said. "It may be that I don't speak as clearly as I once did. Yes, that may be. Well, in any event you should be aware of a scuffle, an uproar in the neighborhood last night? Felton Watridge — do you know Watridge?"

"Yes. He bought a store from me," Purchase said.

"That's the one," the priest said. "He kicked a man. I believe it is in the papers. People tell me it is. I don't see the papers."

"It is," said Ton-Ton.

"Ah — then you know what I'm talking about. My point is this. The Woodyard is a powderkeg. Why?"

"Just such as this," Purchase said.

"And what does it mean?"

"It means more trouble than anybody can handle or control if it ever once gets started. Because once started it will be out of hand."

The priest rubbed the side of his face. "Yes, my point exactly. Now Watridge seeks your forgiveness. He asks you to have mercy on him because he knows, just as we know, that what he did last night could have caused a riot. It could have started something we would all regret. Something that would profit nobody. The nature of violence is that there is no profit in it. Everybody loses."

"He wants my forgiveness?"

"Mister Walker, do you intend to kill him or have him beaten or to run him out of town? I don't like having to ask such a question but Watridge told me some things and I believe him."

Purchase smiled. "Father Ned, some parts of the world are jungle."

"Does Watridge have a choice?"

"He *had* a choice. All he had to do was stay clean. Now he's made himself into a public nuisance. If he stays here, if he remains in business, then he's a daily irritation. He's like a speck of sand in my eye. You get something in your eye, Father, and if you have good sense you remove it. Or you have it removed."

"He wants you to know he's sorry."

"If you should see him again tell him I'm sorry too. Yes, and tell him I knew *he* was sorry to begin with — a sorry man with a sorry record."

"Depending on what your reaction is — I mean to the people in this section of town — toward Watridge, depending on that we could have peace or we could have trouble. Watridge could be allowed to stay in business or he could be allowed to leave town peacefully. It's in your hands. In what you do when you leave here, Mister Walker!"

"You have an exaggerated notion of my power. I'm just a businessman."

"Mister Walker — in his behalf, in behalf of Watridge, I'm asking you to have mercy. Let the man depart in peace."

Purchase nodded. "If he *didn't* get out of Ormund City all in one piece what then?"

The priest stared at the floor. "The police would retaliate. The people would react against the police. I tell you, Mister Walker, in terms of nuclear energy. We're approaching a critical mass. Yours is the trigger finger!"

"You got this all enlarged in your mind."

"Will you protect Watridge, Mister Walker? How *many* times in the past have we talked about what has to be done if we are going to get through these next years without blood in the gutters?"

Purchase smiled. "Now why would *I* want a riot? Even if I could, as you say, start one?"

"Of course you wouldn't want a riot," the priest said. "Can you assure the safety of Felton Watridge?"

"I can't assure anybody's safety, Father. But leave it this way. I'll think about what you said."

"Fine. That's enough. Because when you've had time to think I know there's only one conclusion you can draw. In this instance you have the power to steer us either away from trouble or straight for it. Now I've taken too much of your time. But I promised poor Watridge. He's a broken man."

"So is the cat he put in the hospital a broken man," Purchase said.

"Let's go," said Ton-Ton. "Father — can we give you a lift anywhere?"

"I have my car, thanks," the priest replied. "I must go to the hospital. This weather makes it especially bad for them up there." He smiled. "When I think of Hatcher getting married. She's a pretty girl."

"Yes," Ton-Ton agreed. "She is."

"Hatcher has the reputation all over Central for a good kid. He plays games with the small children in the park. The little children all know him and call him by name. The Woodyard kids love and admire him. I think Hatcher is rather unusual and he's striving upward. If he could get a steady job he'd make somebody a good man."

"That's true," Purchase said. He and Ton-Ton stood up. "I've watched Hatcher. He has a lot of family pride back of him."

Purchase didn't say what else was in his mind about Hatcher. That the trouble with him was he's a Christian without ever realizing how he's taken the white man's religion and being black therefore reaps all the disadvantages while getting none of the benefits. So therefore he is in the struggle fishlike already netted but nonetheless trying to fight his way up, aiming to be what never he can be, thinks Purchase, aiming to be white without it once ever dawning on him that he can't be white even if he made it the legitimate way. Even if somehow he broke out and even rose very high and bought him a house, a fine pad over towards Bayside. Still he wouldn't be anything more or less than a poor black fish playing the game, netted beforehand by the white man's rules — so you feel sorry for Hatcher. Because otherwise, if his kind, if the Hatchers would *accept* the Woodyard, begin and drive a taxi and then work up, learn how to keep books on the numbers, use brains in other words and get their mind off the white man's everloving Bible, Hatcher was the kind Purchase might run for some minor office in the Ormund City government. Hatcher's trouble was nobody could talk *sense* to him.

So now he marries. He handcuffs himself.

"I enjoyed your sermon," said Ton-Ton, taking leave of the priest.

Purchase opens the door for Ton-Ton. Out they go then through the Sunday School side entrance, outdoors. Into bright downbearing sunshine. Purchase slips on his dark glasses.

Maco opens the door of the limousine. Ton-Ton slides across the seat, making room for Purchase who climbs in beside her.

"Now for *my* Sunday," Purchase says.

Maco laughs. Sitting in the front seat driving the Continental, Maco laughs again. "Got a cold melon for you this time — cold!" Maco laughs again.

"I don't know about that preacher," Purchase says.

"We having a melon party?" says Ton-Ton.

"It's my Sunday now," says Purchase, nodding. He smooths a big hand over her leg. "Father Ned has got some real far out notions and ideas."

"How do you mean?" Ton-Ton says.

"That riot talk. He thinks I have the power to start one or stop one? He thinks Watridge has given us some kind of opportunity or excuse? I keep asking myself what would I want with a riot? Or put it this way." Purchase paused. He closed his eyes. "If I could have a riot on command, what else besides Cutler's find-out papers would I *need?*"

"I'm thinking the same thing," Ton-Ton says beside him.

"Assume Father Ned is right. Say I have somebody to lean on Watridge pretty good. Then the police would retaliate? Lean on Watridge just a certain way. Let it be very much apparent that we leaned on him because of what he did and because he's white. A show of revenge and defiance, in other words? Make the Ormund fuzz nervous and angry. Take advantage of this weather?"

"So instead of waiting on a riot you create one," says Ton-Ton. "Does it make you feel a little bit like God?"

"The way Cutler talks about his find-out report I wouldn't need anything more: Just the report and a little trouble in the streets and I could apply the squeeze — to Mister Cousin Alabam!"

"It might all be a crazy idea. I don't know."

"I want to talk to Miss Sula, which reminds me. Maco? Let's swing by on the way home and pick up my mother. I want her in on this melon today. I promised her last Wednesday," says Purchase.

"Gotcha," says Maco. Laughing, he makes a smooth left turn and then another one. Purchase kisses Ton-Ton. She bites. He kisses her again. He slaps her a hard spank on the rump.

Maco honks the horn.

"Set up here and behave yourself. You want Mother to see you acting this way? Will you behave, please, Miss Lady-gal?"

Ton-Ton refuses to get angry. She merely makes a few adjustments, sitting up straight and patting her hair. "You big bastard," she says pleasantly. Maco climbs out and opens the front passenger door for Miss Sula. "Watermelon —" says Miss Sula. Not so spry as she once was, she is no longer the little midwife of years and years gone by, but her eyes still hold their hooded sparkle. Maco gets back in the car.

"Purchase don't forget you, Mrs. Walker," Maco says.

"Purchase don't forget his *name*," says Miss Sula. "Do you son?"

"I got a problem on my mind," Purchase says. He proceeds to explain his idea to Miss Sula. She nods.

"I knew Watridge put a man in the hospital last night," she says. "But it never came to me what *you're* talking about. It never came to me that we could begin the *formulation* of the kind of trouble *we* need. If we do decide to knock Mister Watridge around and let him be the bloody chicken, let him bleed on some uniforms and take the message to headquarters — yes!" She continues nodding.

"I wonder how bad Watridge really hurt that fellow?" Purchase says.

"Over to the hospital," Miss Sula says. "Over there they sayin he's pretty bad. Watridge denies it in the newspapers but you can't argue with what's laying over in that hospital."

"Peoples have a long enough memory. Colored folks piece it all together anyhow no matter how the paper prints it," says Miss Sula. "I always said Felton Watridge was stupid. Take the price we got out of him for that store. Selling it was maybe the smartest move *you* ever made." She turns around to smile at Purchase. "It may cost Watridge a very high price and pay you a very nice profit. What *you* say about it, Ton-Ton, honey?"

Ton-Ton takes a deep rapid breath. Opening her mouth she slowly licks her lips. "Yes," she says.

"Purchase, son, how you feel?"

Purchase pauses. He feels his heart pounding. "Yes," he says. He nods. "How's it sound to you, Maco?"

"I'm also *yes*," says Maco. "It sounds gorgeous to me. You got the power to cause anything you want to cause. You *know* it, Purchase!"

"So we lay it on Watridge," Purchase said. "Who does it and when?"

Miss Sula frowned. "Maco does it?"

"We need a first rate mechanic," Purchase says, shaking his head. "We got to have an artist — maybe two artists. I don't want Maco involved. I don't want any of us involved. I want it done the automatic way, from a distance. I will make the call myself."

"You don't want him killed either," Ton-Ton says. "We don't need a heavy mechanic."

"Hey-hey! Ho-ho! Felton Watridge got to go!" Maco chants.

"Cool it!" says Purchase, planning what he must do.

Maco laughs again, a low chuckle. Maco clucks — a chicken sound. Then he makes a neat left into the alley and hits the signal button. The automatic garage door behind the 312 Club slides up and then rattles down behind the limousine. Purchase hurries out of the car and into the hallway. He wipes his feet on the bright red carpet as though to wipe off the uneasy feeling of church. "Bring the melon," he shouts over his shoulder.

In the kitchen he picks up a phone and dials a number. "This is *me*," he says in response to a muffled "Hello?"

"Listen to me good and close," Purchase says. "Ten minutes from now I want something to happen. The name is Felton Watridge. The place is the Woodyard. The location is the

Papa John's. Mister Watridge calls the police to come get him because somebody makes him call the police and when the police get there they find Mister Watridge a bloody mess. They don't find him dead. They don't find him knocked out — they just find him in a condition where he wishes he was dead or knocked out — they find him needing a doctor and a hospital? And they find him in a real angry frame of mind because he has been cussed and he has been told that the same thing will happen to the police who let a certain nigger get stomped? Have you got all this down on your brain?"

"When you want this here?" says the muffled voice.

"Ten minutes from the instant I hang up this motherly phone. Not nine minutes, not nineteen minutes? Got it straight? Or you want to go *back* to prison?"

"If he ain't dead we can't let him see us so he can identify us. So maybe we have to wear a lady's silk stocking on our face if that's okay with you?"

"Okay by me."

"But ten minutes, that don't leave much time to think about it."

"That's right, sport. I want you to call *me* in fifteen minutes and tell me it's all taken care of?"

"All right. Lemme get it straight. We catch him first and make him phone the cops to come after him. Next we work him up to where he needs the hospital real bad but so he can still talk and tell the cops some of them might be next if we catch out the ones from last night that handcuffed the guy and let Watridge stomp shit out of him?"

"You got it. Get going!" Purchase hangs up and turns away from the kitchen phone. He fetches a knife from a counter drawer. Ton-Ton and Miss Sula have come in followed by

Maco carrying a big green melon in his short, sturdy arms. Placing the melon carefully on the table, Maco stands aside. The cold frost on the melon is visible to all. "Cold! Amen!" Maco whispers.

"You made the call?" Miss Sula asks.

Purchase nods. "Gin," he says.

Ton-Ton brings two bottles — "Beefeaters." She opens them. Working carefully Purchase cuts the plugs out of the waiting melon. Laying the knife aside he takes both bottles at once and suddenly upends them, one each to a plug. Slowly, like a live thing the melon begins to guzzle and absorb the gin.

"*Now* the devil has horns," says Miss Sula. She smiles. "And since the call has been made we can all relax and see how it works. We can relax!"

Maco brings the long plastic straws. Purchase carefully cuts tiny plugs.

"I taste him already. I already taste his sweetness," Miss Sula says in a slow, musical voice. "His bitterness has faded."

Ton-Ton kisses Purchase Walker's neck. "Let's start," she says.

"I want him full. Want him satisfied before we have him," Purchase says. And suddenly he is caught — caught and held in the enjoyment, in the sweet agony of waiting for the first straw to be slipped and slowly slipped deep into place. Deep, deep within the dying melon's vital sweetness.

12

THE POLICEMAN

Papa John's in the Woodyard," said the police radio. There was a pause. "Carter, run over there and see about Mister Watridge. He says a coupla niggers beat hell outta him. He needs help. Get over there and help him and see what it's all about and then report back to me?"

"On the way," Carter replied in a monotone. Carter and Dimple Morton were the same age. Carter drove the patrol car; Dimple rode shotgun.

Carter was married. He spent a lot of time talking about how his wife shampooed his hair and made such good coffee. Carter had been a football player in high school and he carried his athletics on now in the form of bowling. He also talked about bowling a lot.

He would describe an evening from beginning to end. He knew a lot about bowling balls and shoes and ball bags and the best kind of socks to wear. Carter was a goldmine of information on a number of subjects, but of all subjects he was most fond of talking about his wife who had been second maid in the Miss Ormund City beauty pageant.

[129]

Carter was a policeman because his father was a policeman and two of his uncles were deputies. It ran in the family.

Dimple rarely got in a word edgewise with Carter.

"I tell you," Carter was saying. "I gazed at those perfect tits of hers last night. I mean until you have seen perfect tits you don't have any way to judge other categories such as you see in the street. You know those small sweet grapefruit, Dimple? I don't mean the big ugly ones with the thick rind and I'm not talking about pink grapefruit. Some people think that pink grapefruit is sweet but the best is the thin rind small grapefruit like they grow just north of here, you know what I mean?"

"Yeah," Dimple said.

"Well, that's the size of my wife's tits. That would describe them almost exactly. I'm telling you one look at hers and you wouldn't be able to look at anything else for a God damned month. Anything else would make you sick. I take her out bowling and the other fellas practically fall out of their pants she's so perfect looking. She never looks their way. I don't mean she's snooty, understand. But she never *looks* at them like she would want to have anyone else in the sack but me. God damn they practically just about fall outta their *pants*," Carter continued.

Dimple sighed.

If Carter was the least concerned about Mister Watridge's complaint he didn't show it. He drove with one hand on the steering wheel. That left his other hand free to describe his wife and to help him tell how last night they went in the bathroom and locked the door and Nan of the perfect tits was naked but Carter had a towel about his waist and Carter's mother-in-law knocked on the door and wanted to know what they were doing in there because she didn't think it was right, Carter's mother-in-law didn't, for them to be locked up in the bathroom together. His mother-in-law was a thorn, the cloud on the otherwise clear horizon of Carter's existence, and poor Carter had the misfortune to live in his mother-in-law's house. "So Nan has to slip on her robe and open the God damn door and plead with her old lady that she's only shampooing my hair and the old lady says 'Well just don't lock the door.' Sometimes I get the idea she's about halfway nuts. I mean if we're married what's the diff whether we lock the door?"

"Yeah," Dimple said, thinking of Evan Sanchez. Now that Sanchez was out of jail he was dunning Dimple for the return of the two hundred dollars. Sanchez spent his days lying around the rooming house smoking one cigarette after another. Evenings he operated an answering service for call girls and between times he talked about the two bills Dimple owed him. He also complained about having gone to jail.

"How does it feel to be Judas?" he would ask, always in front of the landlady, perhaps because he knew Dimple wouldn't crawl his frame with the landlady present.

Dimple had finally formulated a reply. "How does it feel to be Jesus Christ?" Dimple had shot back, just this morning and Evan's face had darkened. The remark had hit home, Dimple reflected, and so thinking he was halfway sorry he had softened his blow by adding: "But I tell you, Sanchez. Just as soon as I pay for a decent suit of clothes so I'll be fit to be seen in church I'm gonna start paying you back."

"Ah, yeah," Sanchez had said bitterly. "Sure!"

Carter was drumming his thick fingers on the steering wheel and whistling. "Say, Carter," Dimple said. "I got a pretty terrible problem. I hate to bring it up."

"Listen, on the force there is not one thing that cannot be discussed between brothers," Carter said. He was instantly sympathetic. He stopped drumming the steering wheel.

"Well," Dimple said. He paused. "It's my sister back home in Arkansas. She's got to have an operation. She's broke and I'm short of cash —"

"How much does she need?"

Dimple shook his head mournfully. "About three hundred dollars. Got a letter from her this morning. She needs it right away, my sis!"

Carter nodded. He brought the patrol car to a stop in front of a rundown building in a sandy street shaded by mossy oaks. The street put Dimple in mind of the tunnel connecting the rooming house and the sidewalk.

"Tell you what, Dimple," Carter was saying. "Maybe I don't have that amount, but between myself and my dad and other guys on the force we'll raise it. I mean I don't want you to worry about it because that's what it means to be a brother on this force, working in this department. We know how to put our shoulders together and chip in to help another guy wearing the Ormund City badge. You'll get your money in a couple of days or maybe sooner. And you can pay it back bit by bit, week to week."

"Thanks," Dimple said, now sorry that he had not asked for five hundred. "Sis sure is sick," he sighed.

"I know it must be just about worrying you right out of your pants," Carter said. "But you came to the right fella. I'll raise the dough. Now let's see what's buggin Watridge."

Dimple followed Carter into the building. "By God, you taken your time!" said a thick voice.

As Dimple's vision adjusted to the dim interior he saw a

bruised and bloodied face. The huge man, Watridge, was seated on a chair with his arms propped against a table.

"What happened?" Carter said.

"Two of 'em. They come in didn't say a word. Had ladies' stockings on their face, didn't say a word, stockings pulled down over their heads. One held me and the other whipped on me until he was tired and then the other held me and the first one whipped on me. I hollered for help. Nobody come. They twisted my arms just about out of the socket. Hit me on my knees with iron pipes." Watridge groaned. "Busted my teeth." He groaned again.

"Let's take you to the hospital," Carter said. "You got a description of the guys?"

"Yeah," said Watridge. "Look for a pair of niggers wearin green GI coveralls with the sleeves cut short. One's about six feet and fat. The other one is about six three and solid muscle."

"They say anything?" Carter asked.

Dimple found a bar cloth. He wet it in the steel sink and handed it to Watridge. The injured man touched the cloth to his ear.

"That's what I want to tell you. They said pass the word they was after any cops they could catch. For that stompin which happened last night here in my place of business."

"Anything else?"

"That's all," said Watridge. "Didn't say another word. The fat one poked a hole in his sock where the mouth was. He drank a beer through it."

"Maybe he left fingerprints," Dimple said, picking up an empty beer can left on the bar.

"They wore gloves, brown cotton work gloves," Watridge said.

"You look awful," Dimple said. "You need the doctor."

"Let's move him out to the car and make our report," Carter said.

Dimple got on one side and Carter on the other. They hauled Watridge to his feet.

"Ahhhh!" the big man groaned.

"I believe they cracked his kneecaps," Carter said. "It happens that way sometimes. Try not to faint," Carter said. "Heads up!"

Watridge groaned.

Dimple supported Watridge while Carter opened the back door to the patrol car. They sat the man down then, backwards onto the car seat and lifted his legs in after him. He groaned again and Carter shut the back door. Watridge sagged in the back seat with his chin thrust forward on his chest. His body was heaving beneath his bloodsoaked shirt. The big man began gasping.

Carter started the engine. Dimple got in the front seat beside him.

"This is Carter. Got the report. You ready?"

"*Go ahead,*" came the reply.

"Two niggers did a professional job on Mister Watridge." Carter paused, referring to his notes. "Had stockings over their heads. Wore GI coveralls with cut-off sleeves. Cotton work gloves. One six feet high and fat. The other over six feet and muscular. Said for him to tell the police they are laying for any officers they can catch on account of that stomping last night at Mister Watridge's — Papa John's."

"*Got it. Those throw-away clothes and gloves might be in the alley or back of the building somewhere. Take a look.*"

Carter nodded to Dimple. Dimple got out of the car and

went around behind the building. The odor of urine was strong. A dark circle of ashes caught Dimple's attention. He stopped and felt the burnt out spot on sandy ground beneath a huge sheltering liveoak. The place was still warm. Sifting the ashes Dimple found a brass snap button and the remains of two zippers. He took these back to the patrol car. Dimple reported.

"They put gasoline on the clothes and burned them," Dimple said, holding the mike.

"Right. Then it was professionals. Take Mister Watridge on to the hospital."

Carter put on the flashing light, but left the siren silent as they headed across town toward Ormund City General.

"If it had not been for the jealousy of the judges my wife would have won Miss Ormund City," Carter was saying. "Then she had to be a shoo-in for Miss America."

The next thing Dimple knew Carter was describing a very intimate part of Mrs. Carter's physical privacy and how it felt and operated at certain times under certain ideal conditions when Carter succeeded in getting the old lady, the mother-in-law out of the house.

"I promise you, you could eat it with a spoon," Carter said. "I mean one look at that thing and you would fall outta your pants. I'm not lying, man!"

Watridge groaned.

Fear began to stir like leaves blowing and shifting against the base of Dimple's heart. For it suddenly came to him what had happened to the groaning man behind him. It suddenly came to Dimple that something was gone wrong. It was like driving a truck full speed under a low railroad bridge and remembering at the last instant, when it was already too late, that the overhead was too low, with no time even to hit the brakes.

Trying to get his mind off his fear Dimple glanced at Carter only to realize that Carter was suddenly silent and strangely pale, as though Carter too had made a discovery inside himself.

"I'm gonna be damned glad when this shift is over," Carter finally said. He turned into the hospital driveway marked "Emergency Only."

Dimple groped for the butt of his service revolver, as though to make sure it was still there.

13

POOR BOSTON

EVERY man is your brother. Every woman is your sister. Every child is your own child. All the old peoples is your parents and God is in the plan, so stay close as possible to what you know is true and don't open your mouth for a lie. I'm looking at Leroy.

Love him because there ain't nobody else to love him, but how can you take on and worry about everybody in the whole world but you have to because that is being a man and if a couple of sandwiches and some java will build him up and raise him off the ground a little then feed him and if you had as lief to feed him free for nothing as to have him pay you then he will repay you out of his heart which is worth more than anything that can come out of his pocket because we can't make it through without help. We can't die game unless we have some friends to mourn us and Leroy is good at heart because he will sit and listen at me try to tell him some wisdom.

Good-god-christ-amighty look around and they were into it and I always said one day somebody will kill Huey Bolls and the kid was on him and all over Huey like a reaping machine when didn't all of us know what Huey was up to with that kid the minute Huey Bolls laid hands to the cue stick?

It comes to me on the way over there that somebody someday is going to kill Huey and he will not be mourned because he is some kind of beast that will steal the mortar from out between bricks, that he would steal the nails out of a church and never *was* nothing but a goddamn machine squinting down a pool stick pretending to be drunk, so why *be* in no hurry? Only before I could make it over there Leroy was on the way. I hollered at him to let me handle it because somebody will only get hurt but he did not hear me and he is in it too, so then I've got to run. By now Bolls looks like he's been out in the street fighting a truck. I push him back and Leroy is swinging at the tall kid and he is connecting so I have to step in and I get a graze on the shoulder and tuck my chin and Leroy says god-damnit let him handle this tall mother that come in here and is beating on Huey and they have got up from the domino game and Huey is lying down on the floor where somebody is going to step on him and it comes to me I can kick the cottonpicking shit out of him and it will have to appear like an accident. But the tall kid bothers me and gets me off guard. He puts one into Leroy that would not have been delivered like a birthday telegram if I had not had to mind how I stepped (for the sake of Huey the cause of everything laying there in the floor where you can't even break up a sparring match for having to step around and over him) so I let Huey Bolls have a couple of accidental little numbers in his side and gave him another one close to his temple where he would remember it next week when he thought about coming in my place to hustle somebody again and just one more when he started rolling and got under the table where he should have gone in the first place. By now then Leroy was taking them pretty regular and the big kid was just warmed up like he had not even put the sugar in his tea yet and you never know how long it will take anybody to go for his steel when it gets warm that way so I kept coming in and the kid kept connecting with Leroy every time like he was delivering the mail from the post office and I'm saying "Gentlemen, cool it! Gentlemen cool —!"

And ump, the big kid has an elbow into me and Leroy goes down and I can feel the domino game behind me like a warm stove because they can take only so much of it and then they want a piece of it and you got yourself some wreckage unless you can move it out to the sidewalk and sure enough when Leroy comes off the floor he is reaching for steel and I say well then if this is how it is going to have to be so I square off a little with the big kid and he comes on like the baggage car of the Illinois-Central and I can't give him *all* my attention because there is Leroy behind me with that blade. The blade will mean a day in court so I've got to maneuver the big kid and keep myself between him and Leroy and then I trip and stumble on something and goddamn if it is not Huey Bolls rolled out from under the table again and the big kid gets lucky and shows me the color of blue lights while I'm trying to untangle my legs and kick Huey back under the slate where he belongs whereas there is nothing else to do when I get rid of Huey again but fake it a while and try to pray that I can shape the kid up a little and then put him to sleep because he is living under the dream that he is the second cousin to Cassius Clay when the fact is that he is about as dangerous as Gene Autry if you took and broke the guitar but I get me two visions of blue lights more before I can get up my nerve and courage to really hurt him because it is never any good to hurt a kid any more than you have to, so I says well Boston you are going to have to make up your mind are you a mechanic or not, and will you fix

him or not before Leroy *slips* it to him — so I let him send me
two low ones and then I stepped away and dropped my arms
and it was too much for him. He brought out his big one and
shot it straight at my head and after it had gone by I was
looking down the tube at him and I let him have a hook and it
came on him like a surprise but was still not enough so I gave
him one straight up the sidewalk and he was sleepy and it was
killing me to punish him but I had to let him have one more.
His knees went down first and then he was laid out and dreaming and I turned around and there stood Bolls. Here came the
pool cue and it broke over my head like a dry corn stalk and I
knew my head was split because blood came down like a curtain
and I said well here we are, Boston, it will either have to be
moved into the street or something must be done because the
shit beginning to act like it has to be soon hitting the fan. I was
having to wipe my eyes before I could grab Huey where I had
knocked him across the table and hotamighty he is bleeding on
it like somebody having an operation and me thinking about
the new green felt that was just put on when the table was
reworked last Thursday and it is not enough for him to break
my sticks but he has to lay on that new cloth felt and *bleed* on it
so I grabbed his feet and his shoes come right off in my hands.
I'm standing there holding his shoes and the domino game
arrives like a family of close relations and kin that ain't seen
Poor Boston Humes in forty years. I'm still holding the shoes
when some mother hugs me and another one sends me the air
mail special delivery just about one inch above and one foot
behind my belt buckle and I say well Boston you are just going
to have to open the letter and read the real bad news. I had to
go down then and make friends with their feet which is a
moment in your history which can seem like the longest time

you ever lived when you have to go down to feet city but down it had to be and I got under the table alive and I said "Well shithouse mouse" because I was still holding Huey's shoes and I says well if somebody would hand me a rag maybe I could shine his precious slippers. I think so high of Huey Bolls's shoes I got to carry them around with me for the rest of my life and then I heard some bullfrog shouting "Look out for the steel! Watch that steel, man!" so I says well here we go to the butcher shop. I heard the windows break and then out of nowhere some mothereater had a chair and was *so* proud of it. I mean like you get yourself *out* of it for a minute that way and you can see things like that chair, like what a mechanic he is when it comes to chairs because he is playing it like a couple of bass violins. You didn't have to be no college professor to see that this little stud has played with chairs and practiced all his life before the mirror. Steel just didn't hold no charms and appeals for him, didn't mean shit nor gravel if he could just lay hand to a chair and I *knew* I had to move and I *knew* I had to part with Huey's slippers but that little chair guy — here I am — Boston is under the brand new reworked pool table with blood in my ears and blood in my eyes but I believe you better not ever get so old in my business that you can't learn something new and this little fox was holding a chair school, dancing all over the territory back and forth and graduating studs twice my size and half my age — handing them their diplomas out of his chair college so fast and easy he looked like Fred Astaire's grandmaw. When he swung that chair something had to give and let anybody go up against him with another chair and this little half pint man would have the other chair and the other body on the floor so fast like something out of basketball, just that quick and beautiful like he could drive under the goal and sink one any-

[141]

time he pleased — and as for steel, well steel was not any part of it any more, once he got the party interested in chairs — once he got their attention — and just that quick they all had to have chairs and they all wanted chairs and I could have sold a dozen of them for fifty bucks each and blades and glass was falling all over the deck like rain on the pavement and to make it worse more trade was coming in off the street because I saw a dress and heard some screams and we had not had a chicken in the place when it started so I said I would have to count ten and when I came out I would have to come out running because chair boy didn't look like he was even warmed up yet and like every champion you meet he was not overlooking or ignoring anybody or anything because twice already he had waltzed over and laid it on Huey and whatever else had to be on the table by now, had laid it on so hard the whole outfit shook above me and when you shake a *pool* table, when something hits *that* hard your only peace of mind has to be that it was Huey's ass up there and not your own, and you think give me a pool cue on the head any time of the day but God deliver mankind from that motherfucking chair because even if the ideas in your mind are traveling forty-nine hundred million miles a second trying to keep up with what you never had a chance to catch in the first place, just one small look at a chair artist like that dose of medicine and you know that your *first* practice has to be perfect which is to say it is like practicing a parachute jump, I mean a lad joins or gets drafted to the Army and tells me when he come on furlough and I ask him what they got him doing and he says to me "Well I'm up to Fort Campbell or over to Fort Bragg and we *practicing* parachute jumping," and I have to think "Well if a parachute jump ain't something that has got to be perfect the first time then I'm a shithouse mouse."

So here I was in the same shape where my first practice had to
be perfect or chairboy would roll me in the aisles like a grapefruit. I hadn't no slightest intention of going up against that
chair, so I took one more deep breath and counted ten one more
last time and when he made that little twirl and knocked the
living beans out of two blade cats and a woman who thought she
had something going for her when she got her hand on the neck
of a broken beer bottle — as I say while he was giving it to them
I came out with my knees high and my head down and my
elbows on either side of my face, my hands together over my
head — I came out running and they either got out of Poor
Boston's pathway or I knocked them down and ran over them
until I looked up just in time not to butt out my brains on the
beer counter and since I could not go through it I went over it.
I got up and made it to the wall phone and had already
grabbed the receiver off the hook and was dialing operator
when it dawned on me that it takes a dime and when I reached
out where the cash register is it was not there and some cat with
a wrecking bar and a pair of pliers was working on the cigarette machine. Two chicks shoved me back against the wall out
of the way and opened the beer cooler and started taking the
cans out and I reached for the ice pick before it arrived on my
mind what I had almost been about to do — I dropped the ice
pick and gave one of them a placekick in the meat pie just for a
souvenir before I vaulted the counter. I ran out into the street
where there was nothing to do but stop and look at it the same
way you watch and witness a fire, just stand on the hot
pavement. Bleed like a hog. The windows kept breaking and
the beer was being passed out (and here comes the first cherrytop — no siren of course — just the light flashing and what you
have inside that car is two white boys who wonder why they

ever joined the city force in the first place just like I'm wondering why I ever went into the club and cafe business, because the happy times for me and them both have just suddenly ended). Somebody wants to give me a beer and I'm saying "No thanks," and he's saying well it is all going to be drank anyhow so you may lief as to have one, and when I look at him I see it's Leroy and he has a couple of beers and so we open them and then I hold them and Leroy cuts and tears off his shirttail and tries to do what he can with my head and someone gathers me gently by the arm and we cross the street, me with one of my own cold beers, one in each hand, and I see who it is that has my arm, and it is Hatcher and Little Gyp comes up to me and is wearing a white dress I never saw on her before, white hat and shoes like some little pretty angel dropped out of the clouds and saying, "Poor Boston! Poor Boston!" She is weeping. We get across the street into the shade of the grocery awning beside the pawnshop. She and Hatcher and Leroy keep trying to fix me and stop the blood some way and I'm saying "Well maybe I am a little dizzy," because Hatcher is worried, but I think God help this kid he was born with worry warts all over him anyhow, but he keep saying: "He's losing too much because you take a head cut like that —"

"Don't cry Louise. Baby it don't help nothing to cry," Hatcher says. "I can not stand it to see you crying that way, Louise."

I have to look around to see who he's talking to before it comes to me that he's calling Gyp "Louise," and then I happened to smell something and I noticed what it was that I had stepped in dog shit, so nothing was happening half way. Everything was going 100 percent.

Leroy took off his shirt and I was thinking why take off his shirt and how lean he is but he's got the muscles in him like a skinned rabbit and I'm thinking to myself this kid could be a runner (and I look across the street and the cherrytop is still giving it the whirl) and then Hatcher makes me sit down against the wall of the grocery and it comes to me why Leroy took off his shirt.

"Take my shirt," I tell them.

"Hush," says Leroy. "Be still and let's see if we ain't accomplishing business this time." Gyp helps and finally they get me bandaged.

"Leroy, baby," she says. "You got a lip fat as Rosalu Crenshaw's ass."

"If Boston could have made up his mind to stay out of it I could have wiped that stud's spoon all by myself. He wasn't nothing but just big and he wanted to lay it on poor old Huey. So when I couldn't sit there and watch it any longer —"

"When did you get so soft on Huey?" I says. "All you had to do was let me take care of it! Ain't Huey lifted your scratch enough for you to be tired of him turning you upside down and the same as holding you up by the ankles to empty your pockets over that pool table, or have I been having dreams and visions all these years? How come you so sweet on Huey Bolls all of a sudden? Did he ever —"

"Okay," Leroy says. "Maybe I went a little wild but if you hadn't came and stepped in and held me —"

"That's true. You got a point there," I says. "So call it even and tell me how I'm going to get all my beer back and pay for that cigarette machine . . ." I was looking at my shoes thinking about how there always has to be a cherry on the top of the whipcream and thinking why did they have to invent dogs on every street corner. Hatcher was saying: "Look out, look out, look out. Let's move away from here." Always worrying, and he don't even have a spot on his tie I'm thinking, so I say "Well, you kids can cut out but since it is or it was my place once I guess I will just sit where I am —" Another window broke. "I guess I will just sit here and watch them." I didn't feel like walking anyhow. I felt dizzy.

"Look out, look out," Hatcher says again and I had it already in my mouth to tell him if he couldn't shut up why didn't he go someplace else to preach, when I looked up and saw what he meant.

They had come to their decision sitting there under the cherrytop and I could tell by the fear and the uneasy paleness of their cheeks that for cops they were just about as uncomfortable as me and I was slightly miserable.

They just stood a minute, side by side like twins, looking down at me.

"Stand up," one of them said.

"Me —"

"Stand up —"

So Hatcher and Leroy reached down and helped me and when I was up the one who had spoken slapped both my hands at once and knocked the beers out of them and they rolled on the sidewalk and foamed. The other one kicked both cans into the street, while the first one took out his handcuffs.

"Man — are you arresting *him?*" says Hatcher.

"Go home where you belong," the cop said. He was trembling.

"But officer — he owns that business. This here is Poor Boston."

"You can't arrest him," Leroy said. "He's needing a doctor."

And it came to me that with my head bandaged and me sitting down like some old handkerchief head it was like waving a flag at them because they didn't want to go inside the cafe and they had to arrest somebody for openers so it was going to be me. But I have no fear. I'm not worried about it.

"Shut up," I tell Leroy. "Let the man take me if he wants me. They are breaking and smashing and robbing and tearing down my place of business —"

"Let's have some identification," says the other cop, the one who kicked the beer cans into the street.

Hatcher took out my wallet and gave it to them. I knew it would be better not to move my hands because I can see that these are just boys and they are white and they are having the fear of God loaded into them at the rate of about five tons a second, so I didn't move and they both got a look at my driver's license. "He's Boston Humes. He owns the goddamn place," said the one who had told me to stand up and slapped the beers out of my hands.

"That's what I been trying to explain and tell you," says Hatcher.

"Look, nigger," says the can kicker. "Take a walk."

"Let's go, Hatcher, baby," says Gyp.

"Because," says the cop, "we got enough to do without having advice from any of you black sons of bitches."

Hatcher and Gyp turned to leave. "I was only trying to help," Hatcher is saying. His voice has gone suddenly soft.

"Hold it," says the one standing directly in front of me. "Come back here."

"You going to arrest him?" says the other cop.

"I sure am. I already have —"

[147]

"Me?" says Hatcher. "Arrest *me?* When I ain't done one ugly thing, when I'm here doing all I can. When-when-when —!"

"Grab him, then," says the can kicker. "Put the bracelets on him."

Hatcher is maybe ten paces away by now and the can kicker yells at him to come back and Gyp is telling Hatcher something and suddenly the can kicker has his pistol drawn. He fires into the air and Hatcher takes off running.

"Halt! *Halt!*"

And probably before he knows himself what he's doing he shoots because he is keyed up like a nervous dog, the kind of bastard that you walk up to him and you happen to touch him and he's whirled and bitten the blood out of you before he knows what he's doing.

The cop fired again and I thought to myself "Hatcher tripped." So that was lucky because the shot was probably high anyhow and I thought "Well now he's stumbled and torn his Sunday threads maybe he will either run on and get lost or come back like he should have in the first place," and we just stand there — Gyp in her white dress back against the glass front of the liquor store where she jumped out of the way when he fired the first shot and me with Leroy beside me and our ears ringing and the two cops, and suddenly in the place of all the racket, the banging and the breaking, there is nothing to hear any more and they come out of my cafe but you can't hear a voice, not a sound save the broken glass that makes a crunch now and then under their feet.

Then I think maybe it is a siren, or what it is I don't know and it comes to me that it is Leroy, right beside me and naked to his belt and he has started to moan. Then he runs and Gyp

[*148*]

moves and goes after him and I'm running and my head feels like it will explode and come off my shoulders but I run too and the cops pass and get ahead of me and when I get there Leroy is down sitting flat on the sidewalk. He has rolled Hatcher face up, and he has Hatcher's head in his lap and Gyp had one of Hatcher's hands. She is gripping it to her face and they've both started moaning.

"Get an ambulance," says the can kicker. Then without waiting for the other one he runs back to the cherrytop himself, gets in, and gets on his radio.

"Put him down flat and get away from him," says the other cop. "By God put his head down flat! Stand over against that wall. Against the wall! Hands on your heads! Can't you see this man's hurt?"

I turn and face the wall.

"You saw him run," the cop says.

The sirens start. I turn back around and put my hands down because I know they won't shoot and sure enough he doesn't say anything to me. Leroy and Gyp have put their hands down too and none of us are facing the wall.

From across the street the crowd, still quiet as ever, begins to move, and the braver ones come first and then the others with cans of beer. The ambulance attendants can't get the back door open and the cops try and the door seems stuck for a while but finally the driver does something and the back doors are opened. The driver stoops beside Hatcher and reaches out his hand and opens one of his closed eyelids. He takes Hatcher's wrist.

"He's hurt pretty serious," the one cop says. "He ran and we had to —"

"You — *you* had to," says the other one. "It was you done

it — not me! And he's pretty serious, hurt pretty serious, like to say, but it was not me, Dimple, and that's something we have to get straight because — how bad is he?"

"Gone," says the attendant.

"Give him some oxygen," says the one cop. "Let's get him to the hospital."

"We'll give him anything you say, fellow. But this man's gone. He's dead."

"Let's not talk about it here," says the one cop. "Let's get him to the hospital. I think he's hurt pretty serious and if he is there will have to be a medical report."

They were putting Hatcher's corpse in the ambulance. The one cop crawled inside and folded down the jump seat and put the mask over Hatcher's nose and mouth. "Let's go," he said. "God damn it, let's get going!"

Gyp was trying to get in the ambulance.

"What the hell do you think you're doing?" says the one cop. He shoves her back. Leroy and I take her and lead her back a little distance and the sun is almost down and sweat or blood or both, I don't know, is running into my eyes and making them sting so I naturally started wiping them and there was blood on Gyp's white dress where she had sat down in it so that she looked strange when she turned away with all that blood on her little settee.

"Hatcher is dead," Leroy is saying. "Hatcher's dead . . ."

The ambulance moves away. The red lights on top flash red. The siren screams and mourns.

"*Dead! Dead!*" Leroy shouts.

Who was he and what happened and how bad is he hurt they all want to know soon as the ambulance is gone and two more police cars have arrived and the police are saying clear the street. The paddywagon comes then and some are loaded in the wagon and the cops are looking at Leroy's lip and I'm thinking they will grab him too but he runs — like a deer or a flying bird and he's gone and I look about and Gyp is gone.

Then another one of the cops — there are several now — talks to me a minute and says soon as they can clear the street he will drive me over to the City Hospital emergency room. I tell him "Thanks very much."

"How do you feel?" he says. "You want to sit in the car?" He's a somewhat older man and it seems to me maybe I've seen him before.

"Huey started it all — Huey Bolls," I say. "He could be hurt pretty bad too. If nobody has gotten him yet he's still inside the cafe."

The man let me sit in his patrol car in the front seat. Then he left and went in the cafe. He came out with two others and they had Huey. They put him flat on the sidewalk. Then the older cop came back.

"What about him?" I says.

"He's breathing." And then he drove me to the hospital.

14

CUTLER

With the report finished at last, with it riding beside him on the carseat, and the car headed out of town for Lake Maas, at last, Cutler still wasn't comfortable.

For one thing he was ravenously hungry, and lousy though the food always was at the sunbathing camp, he would have welcomed his share of it now. Already two hours late, he decided not to pause for a sandwich.

He would tough it out and eat later, he decided. A couple of drinks and a long leisurely meal with Cynthia at the Captain's Gig, a floating nightclub permanently docked on the north bank of the Meade River downtown.

He had taken Cynthia there the first evening they had gone out together alone. There was a good calypso band. They had danced. She had trembled in his arms. By look and by touch he had known she was falling in love with him and he had not wanted it but it had happened anyhow, as though somehow fated.

The assignment and the elaborate betrayal of the grocer, Alabam Webster, was a thing Cutler hadn't wanted either, and

[152]

the bluebound notebook beside him now carried a reproach neatly freighted between its covers.

It is one thing, thought Cutler, to do it for your country, for your outfit, for whateverthehell it is you serve when you enlist but doing it privately . . . privately is not the same. Privately it feels wrong, smells wrong, tastes wrong . . .

The citrus groves fell away for miles on either side of the straight, gray-black Florida highway. A faint haze of cloud drifted between sun and earth casting a grayish gold, an uncertain light which gave a strange shadow of brilliance to the dark trees and the roadside sown.

He recalled his conversations with the Negro.

It had been apparent very early that the Negro was having his "find out man" closely watched.

"You sleeping with the girl?" the Negro had said casually.

"Yes," Cutler had replied. Back then, even so recently, there had still been a hostility in the relationship. Maco had come in and out of the office. The very set of his scrawny shoulders had told Cutler the little bastard was packing a pistol under his arm. And beyond a doubt the little bodyguard could shoot, would shoot, and might even enjoy it.

Purchase Walker had also kept his bitch, a huge apricot mastiff, who napped on the oriental rug, or again, at the snap of the Negro's fingers, slowly rose, almost two hundred pounds of her, with jaws that could crack a man's skull, the bitch propping to sitting position first and then walking, lion-like, to the Negro's feet, where she would rest her muzzle on his thigh before going slowly down again and stretching out before him with a long, protective sigh.

"You adore me? You adore me, little love?" the Negro would

croon. Maco would appear. The bitch would frown beautifully when Purchase Walker spoke. It had been all, of course, just an effect, all for show, but the show was impressive and it had never failed to leave Cutler slightly intimidated, and more than slightly aware of the frailness of man, unarmed.

"You like dogs?" the Negro would say.

"We've discussed that before," Cutler would say dryly.

"Don't misunderstand me. I don't want misunderstandings. I like everything peaceful and pleasant. Back to the girl — isn't she rather beautiful, Mister Cutler?"

"Yes."

"And you a gentleman born, from Middle Tennessee." Then abruptly: "Well, let me tell you a bit about Florida. Because for being new here maybe you don't realize, maybe you don't understand some things you ought to know. Maybe you had your foxhounds before your daddy blew it? Your red coats —"

"Pinks."

"— your black hats. Then you had your setters and retrievers, I suppose."

Cutler had sighed at the slight ignominy of the moment, wanting to cross the room and break the black bastard's arrogant neck, thinking just how he would do it and feeling the muscles in his back beginning to tense. The feeling would grow until it became like nettles against his wrist. The tiny scratches that hurt worst and heal last. The man you hate; the man you have to like — for money.

And Cutler would ponder the symbiosis while the Negro preached to him. Very early in the game the Negro had come on in a very irritating, very pietistic way, preacher-like, but every inch a gangster. Cutler would be reminded of the bird that picks the crocodile's teeth. He would gaze at the Negro and

think of the scaly son of a bitch lying on the bank of the Nile
with his mouth wide open because if the birds didn't pick his
teeth then they'd rot out such that what it ended being was a
way of life for them both: the bird and the reptile, natural
enemies working together so each could enjoy the strange fruits
of such feasting.

Then Cutler would suddenly interrupt. "Look. I'm broke.
Last night I had to give him my check for $750. I let him win
again. Shit I had to *make* him beat me. Webster's got about as
much card sense as that God damned bitch."

"So you need money, Mister Cutler?"

"Bullshit," Cutler would say: thinking: (Go ahead, croc,
close your God damn mouth. See if I care) and saying: "If
you're tired of the arrangement I can tell you I'm sick of it too.
So screw it. Over and out. Dump it overboard with the rest of
the garbage. I'll go back tonight and win it all back. I'll take
him for six or seven grand which ought to last me a couple of
months, Mister Walker."

"Come, come," says the Negro then. "Come, come." He
would smile. "Relax — ah — Sergeant — I mean — ah —
Mister Cutler. The money's right here."

So you won't close your mouth after all. You do need your
teeth picked.

"Please relax and be seated, Mister Cutler. This will hold
you for immediate cash. Ton-Ton will cover your gambling
check. It only takes a phone call."

The Negro would lay the crisp stack of bills on the low,
polished table. Cutler would be forced to stand again and scoop
them up, making a quick fold of them, stuffing them in his
pocket.

"Now if you *have* a minute," the Negro would begin, and

Cutler would sit back down, still uneasy, but feeling strangely better now that the money was in his pocket. From the very beginning with Purchase Walker the money was always somewhat like taking a drink or two in the morning. Two fast ones on top of a terrible hangover. The Negro's money, once it was in Cutler's pocket, never failed of its power to warm and comfort its new possessor. Cutler could be always sure of the slow, sure comfort and the compounding sensation of corruption. For the first few weeks the job had been like a binge, like the onset of a terrifying new habit, a habit you halfway suspected you might never be able (or indeed, want) to break.

The room too would take on changes for him. Now, for not worrying, he could appreciate the fabulous colors in the rug, the Negro's fantastic tailoring, his enormous, handsome size. The whole menace and majesty of the antiques and the expensive paintings on the Negro's office walls, the menace and the majesty of what those smug white bastards over on Bayside had no inkling, would emerge for Cutler again in shining daylight clarity.

Over on Bayside, he would think. They lean over and putt. Pick up the ball. Get in the electric cart and ride to the next tee and talk about a contribution to the Republican party, the new broad you're screwing, the wife's new car, Paco's sailboat and how the hell did he ever afford it and all the while, and they never over on Bayside, they never seem to realize that the two richest permanent residents in your town happen to be a white hick grocer nobody wants to catch himself dead shaking hands with — and a half-Cuban nigger.

Even if they were to glimpse it or sniff it, ninety percent of the time they would not know what it was. A hundred percent of the time, even if they did know, the answer would be that they knew there was nothing they could do about it anyhow.

Cutler had been telling himself the same thing. That like whoring and soldiering, ancient as man himself, nothing really has changed. Nothing has really changed, tell yourself, since the Middle Ages. Nothing — give or take a few words, a couple of terms.

The Negro didn't merely represent power. He was power.

Accordingly, Cutler would open his mouth and say: "I'm listening."

And the Negro's voice, gone soft again:

"When I was a child there was opportunity to visit inland, back in the scrub, beyond the groves where my mother's people come from. I mean after they were chained and brought here by the Spanish. Where they come from recently, I want to say. There was opportunity to visit. I carry my mother's name, you realize. Which is not saying I'm a bastard. I'm a bastard by your definition, but taking the mother's name, you see, it's more a tribal, African custom."

"Matriarchy —" Cutler would say, wondering at the man's intelligence; marveling at how starved he was for conversation. "Because they didn't know what caused children," Cutler had said. The Negro had been enormously pleased. It was, in fact, the first opening of real rapport between them.

"Now, you got it!" Purchase Walker had snapped his fingers. His eyes had widened. "I was making a point," he had said, pushing the bitch back down and the bitch looking surprised and hurt for having responded to the snap of her master's fingers. He had snapped them again, and the bitch, flat on the floor again, had merely twitched her ears. "Dogs!" said the Negro.

Cutler had smiled.

"Back in the scrub Mister Cutler, the hogs run wild. The pigs. So if a man wants his hogs he has a special animal. It's a

catch dog. This is a Florida-something you have to understand."

"Catch dog," Cutler said.

"You never heard of it."

"No."

"Then listen how this dog operates. This dog finds the pig,
then he barks, and next he grabs it by the ear. He catches on
quick." The Negro had made a motion with his hand. "He
holds that ear once he's got it. And that's how the catch dog
earns his living. That's why the man feeds him. Get the point?"

"Most interesting," Cutler had replied politely.

"The fascination of it," the Negro had said. "Catch dog does
his job and everybody eats barbecue."

"Everybody but the hog," Cutler said.

"Right! You got the message now. I believe the message
faintly begins to reach you. Take this dog here, she descends
from the households of kings. In the dog kingdom, the mastiff,
he's the king."

"The head nigger," Cutler ventured.

Purchase Walker burst out laughing.

"Now you dig!" he cried, slapping his big thigh. "And just
because your people owned my people? That means nothing
today, Mister Cutler. Because look here who's working for
who!"

They both laughed.

"The overdog and the underdog? Man, they've started to
swap places and roles." Then the Negro was calmer. "It's
funny," he said.

Cutler smiled. "You're a wild son of a bitch," he said.

"That I am," the Negro nodded. "That word *wild*. I like
that word. And that mastiff — I like that dog. The Romans put

[158]

him in the amphitheater — he went up against bears, he went up against lions. He went up against anything, any odds, and he prevailed. The British even preserved him down to modern times. Guess what for."

"House guard," Cutler said.

"Wrong, all wrong, Mister Cutler. You misunderstand the British."

"Then I give up," said Cutler.

"The mastiff was preserved for one purpose only."

"For what —?"

"To catch men, Mister Cutler. Poachers, thieves and felons. Serfs, bad guys, slaves, welchers, anything or anybody. Like somebody with a big mouth he can't keep shut. Somebody who talks when he should listen. You dig?"

"Wild," Cutler had said.

"So thus far what do we have? Mister Cutler? On Cousin Alabam Webster? Okay, he's a nudist. Fine — but you can't use it. Not in Florida — not around Ormund City anyhow. Old shithead's a sunworshiper — so what? He's got a weakness for a certain nice young lady nudist girl, the old hog does. The catch dog takes her to bed — maybe even falls in love with her. Me —? Do I know? Do I care? But I'm asking myself about this weakness of the hog for the young girl. Can we use it? That's what I keep asking myself. Now I'm asking you."

"It's very doubtful," Cutler said. "In fact — it's out."

"In real life, Mister Cutler. It is the man who meets the payroll that makes the decisions. Not the other way around. So when you start meeting my payroll you can start directing traffic. Let me just ask you again — can Cynthia be used?"

"No —"

"Why not?"

"Because in the first place she wouldn't allow it — and in the second place I wouldn't allow it. But putting that aside, Alabam Webster's not that great a fool."

"I underestimate him?"

"Yes. And I'm saying you had better not."

"I only feel this way briefly. Only once a week on the average. Just one more point and then feel free to leave, Mister Cutler. I know your work has urgency about it. The hog's out there in the scrub and we both need him."

"Yes," Cutler had said.

"Then what we want is the business information. All the dope. Where the corn goes in and how the meal comes out — Kutrate."

"That's the right tack," Cutler had agreed. "Some of it I have already. The rest may not be so easy to get. It may take time. He's close-mouthed."

"I'm sure," the Negro had said. "But you're the best. Get the rest of it. Get all of it. Grab it quickly — and be sure, just before you do, be sure to bark so I can hear you."

And it was there, then, the common bond between them. They were both out to nail an agreed-upon victim. Catch him, gut him, and nail his hide to the wall, Cutler thought.

He glanced at the finished report lying beside him on the carseat. Maco had never again entered and re-entered the room when they talked. Cutler had never laid eyes on the mastiff bitch again.

"I'll deliver it all," Cutler had promised.

"I believe you," Purchase Walker had said. "Three of the six most powerful words in the world," the Negro had added.

"The other three?" Cutler had asked.

"I love you," said the Negro. "Put those six words back to

back and you have something you can lean against when the going gets rough. Good luck with the girl—if it turns out she's what you want."

"Thanks," Cutler had said, leaving.

"Goodbye," came the Negro's voice in the hallway behind him.

"Goodbye," said Cutler aloud and the word seemed to vanish into the slipstream of the wind shuddering past the windshield and roiling behind on the roadway. He slowed now and went left on the narrow, winding road that led him deeper and deeper into the groves.

Meanwhile he began preparing himself for the undress masquerade, for Lake Maas. He stopped at the iron pipe barricade gate, got out and opened it, drove through, and got out again and closed it. Driving down the usual line of numerous Sunday afternoon automobiles, he saw Cynthia's blue Chevy and parked behind it in the shade of a moss-bearded live oak.

He got out and reluctantly, slowly, removed his clothes. Then he put on his worn Topsiders, tucked a pair of rolled up Bermuda shorts under his arm, threw a towel over his shoulder, and set out for the main recreation area considering the intellectual garbage dump, the phony Puritan-exhibitionist double-thick mind of the average American nudist. Gnats were already swarming at his nether parts.

When he was more than half the distance to the weathered central dining hall he remembered Cousin Alabam Webster's summation and introduction to the place:

"For every good looking piece you'll gander at out here or any other nekkid place for that matter you'll have to see a hundred and nine — count 'em — that will make you wonder why in thunder God ever built 'em in the first place. Unless you like men of course, I have a notion myself it's a great deal of queers among them. But where I'm concerned how else could you see so much so cheap?"

Thus had the creator of bargains described a bargain, thought Cutler. And at least the grocer was honest with himself. When he came to Lake Maas he came strictly to shoot squirrels. Cutler smiled at the notion.

Just ahead he saw a marvelous piece of tail coming his way. She was followed by a child, a little boy of six, and a big, ugly, stocky-looking man.

The woman was perfect — teats, belly, face, clean beautiful smile. She knew it of course. They all three knew it. The husband, proudly bringing up the rear, wore a ludicrous blue fishing cap. He looked to be about forty-five, a well-weathered victim of life wearing a tattoo on one arm, with a great slouching beer belly hanging down in front, slovenly varicose veins, and for dessert, a crookedly yellow-toothed smile.

Lookee how beautiful! said her elegant face.

Lookee how lucky, said the expression of the hulk behind her. *This broad, this delicious lay is mine — all mine. Just look.*

The kid, Cutler imagined, was probably busy thinking up ways to explain to his friends where he had been all day Sunday. He looked like a decent kid. Obviously he was pondering something.

The club was strictly for whites. It barred Negroes. Naturally. But so did golf clubs. And I don't mind. Nobody minds, really, Cutler thought. Negroes probably least of all, he thought, remembering Purchase Walker and thinking for an instant of the risk he (Cutler) ran, leaving the report where it was, in the front seat of his unlocked car.

"Hi, Rann!" the great hairy-chested husband shouted.

And Cutler was thinking how perhaps a Negro wouldn't have anything he would have to prove in this strange way. The Negro appreciated his clothes, knew the value of decoration, had the eye for color and the heart for fun and for sex in a way most of these poor hapless middle-class bastards would never once in their whole formless lives, grasp or understand.

The wife stopped. "We're friends of Cousin Alabam's. Last week? Remember? I'm Nancy, that's Mike. And this is our little boy, Tommy," said the perfectly built wife.

"Nice to see ya again, Rann," said the husband. "Sure a hot un. Just gettin here?"

"Yes," Cutler said. "I'm late again."

"Oh, the food was just great today," Nancy said. "Just great, wadn't it, Tommy?" She looked down at the child. She had a shrill, nasal voice.

"Uh-huh," said the child.

"Say ma'am to your mama, boy!" the big husband growled.

"Ma'am," the boy said sullenly.

"Oh, you missed a great meal," said Nancy.

"Too bad for me. Seems I'm always missing out," Cutler said, wondering as it seemed he had a thousand times before why all of them always got so excited over the lousy chow. Maybe they liked it because it was cheap. Buck and a quarter for all you could eat — family style. "I sure hate I missed it," Cutler lied, aping the quality of their rundown lingo.

"Sure is hot," Nancy said, turning sideways to raise one manicured hand, shading her light blue eyes and giving Cutler the not unwelcomed benefit of a perfect profile view. "Hot as tar, of course. But I like it," she added.

"Yes," Cutler agreed, wondering why it didn't bother him to

lie. "It's beautiful." The gnats had settled on him. He could feel them.

"Cynthia and Alabam was sure lookin for you," Nancy said. "Saved you a place at their table."

"Then I better go find them," Cutler said, and with a smile for the little boy, who had not changed, and walked on and it was as though he could hear the thoughts rushing and colliding everywhere, all about in the shade and sunlight.

Lookee — look at me!

15

COUSIN ALABAM

Edison Thomas Alabam Webster. Me. Cousin Alabam sunning. Daydreaming like a fence lizard on a gray rail far away home in Tennessee when I was a kid. Down here faraway in Florida and the lake nearby at my right hand and the volleyball court to my left. Cynthia there leaping and jumping. The young men all leaping and jumping with her, hitting the ball and the sun coming, sliding like melted gold, falling like pistol shots straight down, pouring over us, pouring into me; a pressure, a throb, a golden pulse.

Eyes closed. Back home long ago. See the lonely fence lizard showing his money. Eyes and sunshine again. Naked bodies leaping, dancing after the ball.

Comes a little yellow plane now sailing down, soaring over the brownstain water, the secret springfed lake. Down he drifts dodging cropsdust style low between the grandfather mossbeard cypress trees standing a long circle about the lake edge, the old trees like waders suddenly frozen there and the plane like a yellow moth skimming down between and the trees like brown stone pillars set standing on that glasshard, that windless looking watersurface. As though they were set there ten-thousand-odd years ago, left so to stand and be forgotten. The little plane comes buzzing straight in over the tea-colored water, straight over the weathered, silver-gray swim raft. All that trouble just for a peek at the scenery.

It is always the same. Some little Sunday pilot risking his neck to see man and woman naked as they were born. In the raw natural state; Adam. Eve must have looked like Cynthia.

Will I ask her today? Or won't ask her or would have already asked her but for that nigger kicked in the head. For when I heard it the news went off in me like a timebomb and set me trembling. Kicked in the by God head, handcuffed and helpless. So right on down I went to the newspaper. They didn't like it, being reminded of the advertising budget for both Kutrate stores. But as I told them, that alone entitled me. I told them I says by God. Maybe you don't have any civic pride? You want Ormund City ripped down brick by brick? Because then if as I understand you, you don't *care*, then *put* it on the front page and print pictures of blood coming out of all seven holes in his head, mouth, eyes, ears and whatnot and pictures at the hospital. Do it then!

"Freedom of the press," says he. "Duty as a voice . . . conscience of the people."

Since it was obvious *he* was no help I walked into the publisher's office. "I knew your daddy," I says. "He would not have let this on the front page and if you love this city," I says. "Do you by God love this city? Love your community?"

"Mister Webster." Like a scared boy who never asked for the job. But now he's publisher.

"Son, I'm Cousin Alabam to you. Cousin Alabam."

"This is terrible," he says. "The wire services get a carbon of everything they write out in the city room. A new police reporter, Kimmons wrote it, covered it."

And I says yes everyday you live you'll be sorry if you live to be a thousand you will regret the hour you let them front page this two-bit hooraw. And don't misunderstand. I am not down here as your biggest advertiser. I'm down here because I knew your daddy. I am here as a citizen of Ormund City, Florida."

"That other handcuff shooting. The killing," he says.

And I says sure but you wouldn't have to mention that again would you.

"Well," he says. "But handcuffs. It ties in."

You trust the mayor? Call the mayor. Go ahead, I says.

His secretary got the mayor on the phone. The mayor talked to him. When he hung up from talking to the mayor his eyes were gone limp. He looked ten years older.

"How could it get so bad so quick?" he says.

I says it has always been bad. I told him it has always been a keg of powder. All the time I'm wondering how he could grow to manhood and still know so little about his own hometown. And him acting like he never saw a nigger. Like he didn't know what a nigger was. His mind was trying but he couldn't grasp the fact with his mind.

"It can't. It won't happen here," he kept saying. His eyes went limp again.

I shook my head.

"Okay. All right," he says. "We *won't* mention that other one. Get Dave in here," says he to his secretary, the somewhat older woman that worked for his daddy before him. She goes out. In comes Dave, the editor.

"We don't tie in the other killing."

[*167*]

"Then I quit," Dave says. "I work for newspapers. In fact if I have any say-so we will *all* quit. Write your own God damned copy."

"Dave, please. Will you just listen?"

"It's thirty — no, it's twenty-five minutes before the bulldog goes down," says Dave.

"Dave, something's at issue here."

"You're God damned right. Integrity —"

I clear my throat. "If you'd like me out of the room I'll go."

"You?" Dave looks at me. "Did you? Who put this little son of a bitch up to this? You did? Mister Kutrate Meat Market."

In comes the advertising manager followed by the publisher's secretary. She, at least, is calm.

"We can't run that story front page. You can't have those pictures. This is a morning newspaper. We can't turn a subscriber's stomach at the breakfast table," says the advertising manager.

"*You* are a son of a bitch," says Dave.

"Cut it out!" says the publisher. "Let's *read* the story. Let's all read it."

In walks the mayor. They all try to read the story. They pass around the pictures. The prints are damp and smelly. The pictures stink.

"I don't see the news value," says the mayor. "Arrest Watridge — or whatever his name is and you haven't accomplished anything. I don't see how it can help anything. Arresting him. How about you Cousin Alabam?"

"I'm here as a citizen," I says. "And I don't see how it can help anything. But then I'm not the editor. Dave's the editor.

He's the judgment and the experience around here. He's the one hired to make the decisions. Isn't he?"

"That's true," says the publisher.

Dave picks up the phone. He gives the order. They stop everything. Meanwhile the mayor adjusts his handkerchief. A boy walks in with front pages. Everybody gets a front page.

"Get out of here," Dave tells the advertising manager. "You," he says. "Before I kick your fanny get out of here." He makes a move. It is obvious he means it. Dave will hit him.

"You need me I'll be downstairs," says the advertising manager. Out he goes, quickly.

"I want Fred in here," says Dave.

The secretary runs out. In comes Fred, the managing editor.

"This is too God damned strong," Dave says. "How about it, Fred?"

"Well that's my feeling too," Fred says. Now the room smells like newspapers. When the door opens you can hear the machines — the wire services — in there chat-chatting. The secretary closes the door. Fred studies the front page. "I could see it on page two or page four. But I wouldn't give it a righthand page. Above the fold would be okay — I mean if you're asking my opinion."

"That's what I'm doing," says Dave. "Sum it up."

"Well, here you have a plain, simple complaint. They arrest a drunk but who has any facts straight? Watridge says one thing. The kids — they're just inexperienced kids — your police tell something else. The Negro can't talk — Christ he's drunk on God knows what. He drinks spode. He's in the recovery room at Ormund City General getting intensive care."

"What's *spode?*" says the publisher. "Drinks what?"

"It's something they boil and mix. They make it with varnish thinner and wood alcohol," says the managing editor. "It has everything but peanuts in it. To drink it they mix it with soda pop. Spode."

"Who mixes it?"

"Certain Negroes. They're like specialists. Call themselves 'good-kind men.' The ignorant bastards like this one Watridge kicked, they believe a 'good-kind man' is an alchemist capable of mixing something that *won't* kill them."

"Spode," says the editor.

"The stuff destroys their brains. Finally they take an overcharge. The big dose kills them."

"Spode," says the mayor.

"The Negro was drinking spode. Already drunk he walks into the Watridge Grocery, your combination bar and grocery down on Woodyard Street. He's got wine he bought earlier at the Central Kutrate —" The managing editor looks at me as if wondering if I'll give him away, that it was him called me in the first place. "He proceeds to drink supermarket wine in Papa John's."

"I'm lost. Wait a minute," says the publisher. "That *other* place."

"Papa John's is the *old* name for the Watridge Grocery."

"Well," says Fred. "He's drinking wine bought another place. Drinking right under Watridge's nose. The Negro even calls the wine to Watridge's attention. Got it cheaper says he at the other place. Watridge phones the boys. The police come down. Handcuff him. About then Watridge —" and Fred shrugs. He's a stoop-shouldered, a gray little man, white shirt sleeves rolled halfway to his elbows. "Watridge sees his tormentor about to leave, loses his temper. He stomps him. Stomps billy hell out of him. That's one version, probably true. Another version is that he fell, that the Negro fell when the police tried to put him in the police car. That he fell again when the boys took him out of the car at the hospital. Also probably true. With his hands cuffed back of him no kind of fall could do him good. Witnesses, all except the police, witnesses say Watridge stomped him."

"Is he going to live?" says Dave.

"Yes," says Fred. "I see it as page two. He will pull through okay."

"You can't kill 'em," says the mayor. "Knock 'em in the head with a sledgehammer. They won't die. Cut out their hearts. That's what they do to one another. Otherwise they won't die." He's fingering his handkerchief. Dave gives him an irritated look, like perhaps the mayor is some kind of fly buzzing around in the room, something Dave has not got the time right now to swat.

"Page three, above the fold. Kill the pictures," says Dave.

The managing editor nods. "Then, putting the story together the kid — Kimmons — harks back. Like the good police reporter he is, Kimmons refers to the handcuff slaying. That was police recapturing Negro suspects handcuffed together. Not really the same thing, eh? Unfair comparison, maybe? That's just my opinion."

"Cut that too," says Dave. "But page three above the fold. I want the story where people can see it."

"All right," says Fred. "Page three." He walks out carrying his front page. The mayor adjusts his handkerchief. Dave looks my way. He picks up the phone and dials three numbers. "Fred? Also cut any mention by name of the Kutrate store."

"Thanks, Dave," I say.

"That's right, Fred, cut that too." Dave puts the phone down. "Unfortunately Kimmons's story has already gone on the AP wire."

"Well," says the mayor.

"Kimmons may quit," says Dave. "He will want to quit."

"Dave," says the publisher. "Dave?"

Dave walks out. The machines come through chat-chatting again. The door shuts after him.

"He's a crackerjack. Good man there," says the mayor.

The secretary comes back. "The governor," she says.

"Oh, God," says the publisher. "Where's he calling from?"

"Palm Beach."

"How could *he* get it so fast?" says the publisher.

It dawns on him. He looks at the mayor. "He's got a God damned wire service machine hid in a closet downstairs from his office in Tallahassee. The staff must have got it off the AP. Phoned him."

The publisher sighs. He sits down at his desk. Finally he picks up the phone.

"Hello? Speaking! Well frankly Governor we played it down. Yessir. We held the bulldog and looked at it again. Decided page three was the place and no mention, no tie-in of the earlier handcuff shooting. That Negro killing. Yes. Yessir. A responsibility. Yes. Of course there's no way of our knowing what other newspapers in the state. Out-of-state, nationally? Well of course that's unfortunate, of course, but as you know — Governor as you are aware — copy goes from the city desk to the wire services editor. He puts it on the wire. Sometimes instantly. A carbon copy. Not what we publish necessarily. What the man, what the reporter writes. Yes. Yessir. Industry. And citrus. A responsibility to . . . yes, and we did every-

*thing we could. I could speak to Dave about it. Our editor.
Could speak to Dave. Tensions — yessir. I wouldn't go so far as
to call the — wouldn't call Meade County a troublespot! No
more than any other Florida county. It may hurt Ormund
City. Yes. It may hurt Florida. Statewide code — press code?
Well. Ah — Sure. We can talk about it."*

The mayor looks at me. I wave at the publisher who is still
gasping into the phone, and I tiptoe to the door. I walk out and
down to the elevator. The machines chat-chatting . . .

The yellow plane circles, turns, and comes buzzing in low
again. On the swim float the folks wave. They pause on the
volleyball court. Cynthia waves. Will I ask her today or not?
The answer is except for last night. Last night upset me so.
First the nigger business. Then the newspaper. Then Cutler
has to leave early and Cynthia has to leave so I never got
around to it last night. But today. If only Cutler would get
here. If Cutler gets here then. If he gets here inside the next
thirty minutes?

I look at my watch. I decide then. I will ask Cynthia today if
he gets here in thirty minutes.

I have almost given Cutler out. Hilda, the old German dame
in the chair next to me, Hilda is reading the *Ormund City
Times,* the newspaper, and her diamond rings and her sun-
glasses, her operation scars, the sunglare on her newspaper and
she always has to sit next to me, why I don't know. Her scars.

Some doctors will cut anything that will set still. Then the
rest of the population has to hear it told. Because Hilda set still
for some Slash Gordon, M.D. but I say if that happens to be
their business. But the first thing they ought to begin, on a rich
old grandmother like Hilda they ought to started with Hilda's
tongue and then go on and took out whatever they pleased —

appendix, gall bladder, female organs. First thing just prop her jaws open. Take the knife to that everlasting tongue. Then the rest of us would be home free.

Instead usually they start at the opposite end. Hilda has got the correct title of every slasher starting with "proctologist." That was ten years ago. Why I remember is because I had not been long in Ormund City and had just joined the Lake Maas Resort Club. Merely looking at me Hilda remembers, her first operation, the butt cutting.

So I never really look her in the face and always Hilda pulls her chair close to mine. Every last weekend and I'm always looking over her or under her, never at her, and she sprays on bug repeller to calm her gnats. Gnats love Hilda and if I was in Miami all the way down in Dade County I could smell that repeller she uses. From here to Miami and back and Hilda's gnats then naturally move over to me, to my hairs because if they can't have Hilda then they'll take me. That's a gnat for you even though Hilda is their first choice. Gnats, airplanes and what next. Gnats and doctors neither can resist Hilda and careful not to look at her I ask her what's new in the papers.

"Awful, terrible. Knee-ger fightink," says Hilda. She's clucking over page three.

"Just a saloon brawl," I says.

"Not good," says Hilda.

"What else?" I says.

"You —" she says. "Selling a one pound of Folger's for *nine* cents, Kossin Elebim?"

She always reads my ads. "That's with twenty-five bucks worth of groceries," I remind her.

"But nine cents. You go broke," she says. She's going over our Sunday ads, shaking her head.

Like everybody outside of my business looking in, they all think I have to be going broke and if I were to tell them we average 16 percent markup on groceries, 20 percent on meat and fish, and a bit higher on produce, hell fire they wouldn't believe it because hell they don't want to believe it. All they can see is the loss leaders like a twenty pound bag of charcoal briquets for 69 cents and suddenly every white woman in Ormund City is waiting for the Bayside store to open come Monday morning.

A hundred and fifty specials a week and they come in droves. They swarm, and I'm thinking this when Cutler appears.

"You had me starting to wonder," I says.

Because he never talks about his work except to hint that it's secret, Cutler has nothing to say for a while. He sits down.

"Me and Cynthia saved you a seat at dinner," I says.

Rann nods. "Sorry to miss it," he says. He closes his eyes. He's always so calm. Watching his face brings me a sort of peace — the long nose, the strong jawline. He has something people like, something in the way he looks, how he talks and acts. He makes everything tranquil. The Marines or something must have educated him that way. I don't know.

"It was sure a wonderful feed, Rann," I says.

His eyes open just a slit, like a dog's.

"The work you do. All those late hours. Being on call that way."

"Yeah." He sighs. "It's a bitch."

"So finally you come, Rann?" says Hilda. She stands up.

"Finally," Rann says. "How's yourself?"

"Good," she says. She rattles the newspaper, folds it, and lays it in her chair. I have a view of scars. She stretches. "Time for sauna," she says, and off she goes. "See you later?"

"Yeah," says Rann.

[*175*]

I let her get gone a ways. "Listen, Rann."

"Yeah?"

"Cynthia," I says.

"Getting anywhere with her?"

"Today just after lunch down in my trailer I kind of kissed her on the shoulder," I says, remembering. "But I didn't ask her to marry me. I — it didn't seem like the right time to do it. If I don't get her soon I don't know if I can stand it or not."

"I'm not worried about you," says Rann.

Cynthia comes walking over. "Well," she says. "Finally." Her body glistens with sweat. She smells wonderful. She wipes herself, using Rann's towel. "Look what the cat dragged up," she says.

"Uh-huh," Rann says, not moving a muscle, not opening his eyes.

"Rann's asleep," I says. I wink at her.

"He looks dead to me," she says. Rann reaches for her and catches her by the hand.

16

CYNTHIA

Watching the two men on the raft — Alabam and Cutler, Cynthia lay half listening to them; half not-listening. She let her thoughts wander; yet she was all the while conscious of Cutler's questions. Cutler was carefully double-checking facts contained in the report he would hand to the Negro this afternoon . . .

"Your average store," Alabam was saying. "Has twelve to seventeen butchers in the meat department. A Kutrate employs sixty-three . . . sixteen thousand tons of meat each week . . ."

In the months she had known him the grocer had told her all about himself, how he was born on a swamp cypress kitchen table in a rented cabin in the midst of rented land.

Behind the woodstove in the cabin kitchen there was the cat named Sophie Jo minding her litter of kittens. In the barn stall the coonhound bitch, Honeybelle, lay with fat puppies squirming and climbing over her. And in the barn lot where bitterweed grew thick, pigs of every size wandered, from the smallest clear on up to the big red boar.

"Six hundred people work for me, Rann. Out of that number

there's exactly six niggers . . . up front where it shows, on your checkout registers . . . one black gal will do wonders to keep the mixicrats off your neck." The grocer's voice was like a soft buzzing. The wind swept across the lake. A cloud passed briefly over the face of the sun and the pressure of its heat withheld itself an instant before it returned, full force, on Cynthia's outstretched body. She must plunge in the water soon, to cool off, but not yet, she thought.

Alabam had told her how his maw carried a heavy club fashioned from a mock orange limb. If the mean old boar looked at her cross-eyed she gave him a quick bloody nose. She knocked him sprawling. Let the pony try to nip her (that pony was a sight about nipping a person the moment their back was turned) and she would whirl and crack the pony between the ears. Down the little beast would go sometimes, down on his knees.

The kind of woman Alabam's maw was. She got her boy his first job in a country grocery store because she wanted better than a rented cabin and rented land for her child. And for a bed the boy slept on the grocery counter at night. Mornings at daylight he swept out and either lit the stove or set the overhead fans going, depending on the season.

Then on to a larger town, a larger grocery, and finally into the Army where they quickly found a place for Alabam in the quartermaster corps because he knew the grocery business, from meat to produce, from soup to nuts. And once out of the Army he got the job in Memphis as assistant manager for one of the chains. Then he was made a manager and took it on himself to experiment with loss leaders. Sales at the Memphis store doubled in six months. The district manager took notice of him. The chain started shifting him from one "problem" store to another . . .

Cutler laughed quietly at something the grocer had said. *Look at me. Look at me.* Cynthia thought, willing Rann to look at her. Rann was avoiding her eyes. *Look at me!*

"The niggers bother you very much?" Rann asked.

"Every couple or three months," said Alabam. "Father Ned and maybe the nigger doctor or another preacher."

"Father who?"

"The God damned nigger Episcopal preacher. Oh, I kinda admire him. He's some persistent nigger okay."

"Look at me," Cynthia thought, watching Rann. She moved her legs.

"The meat operation. Yeah. That's where the balance is — end cuts to the nigger store. Center cuts to the high class white trade over on Bayside . . ."

Look at me.

"Divide hogs the same way — nigger cuts, white cuts."

The grocer, who rarely took his eyes off her, was not looking either, she saw. *Shouldn't tease poor Alabam,* Cynthia thought.

Closing her eyes she saw in her mind's eye the grocer's rough finger, that habitual gesture, the finger touching the flint-hard farmer's jawline, stroking the steel gray sideburns which he wore long, like a cowboy's. *I'm a bitch to tease him.*

Waiting for Rann she had sat next to the grocer at lunch, watching Alabam gorge himself on ham and field peas and roast beef and fried chicken, swilling down glass after glass of iced tea. Cynthia, thinking only of Rann, had pretended to eat.

And here was Rann, betraying the grocer, Alabam. It came to her as strange that Alabam was a man who had been pulling a loser out of the kinks in Miami just a few years ago, running ninety loss leaders a week, working twenty hours a day, half-soling his shoes, pinching to bank every possible cent.

"Not trying to bore you or nothing — anything — to bore you, Rann," the grocer was saying. "But anytime you want, you and Cynthia might want another tour of the Kutrate like we took last Sunday? I mean if you are interested. Because as the little boy says of course Kutrate, why it's my whole life. I never done — did anything else but work in the food industry since I was a kid and left the farm. So I could talk about it from now till doomsday. You sure missed a feed today, Rann. Didn't he Cynthy?"

She nodded as it came to her *why* Rann had so cold-bloodedly maneuvered Alabam into taking them all three on a tour of the Bayside store just Sunday a week ago.

Feeding on Alabam, she thought. You bastard. *Look at me, Rann.*

He looked then. She felt it go all the way into her arms, wanting him all the way to the center of her bones, wanting nightfall somehow to rush, thinking: *The nights are too short. And the days are too God damned long. I love you.*

Cutler frowned. *Not that way. Don't look at me that way,* he was saying, by the frown, the look on his face. *Not here.*

You bastard, she thought. *I love you.*

She stood up and plunged into the cool, springfed waters of Lake Maas.

17

PURCHASE

Hell — more than Purchase ever expected — was broken loose. First the priest phoned from the hospital. Next he appeared in person interrupting the watermelon feast. His voice betrayed shock:

"Watridge beat to a pulp. Hatcher shot to death. People moving in the street. I've tried to talk to them. Now you must try," Father Ned was saying.

Ton-Ton sat weeping. Miss Sula sat dry-eyed, expressionless. Now and again the older woman sipped from a straw stuck in the melon on the table in front of her. Beside her Maco was playing solitaire. The cards clicked.

Purchase paced the room. The priest's eyes followed him.

"It's as though I predicted it," said the priest. His skin looked like dry bark. "As though it was destined before I knew Ormund City existed. They shot him down."

"How come it to happen?" Miss Sula asked.

"Who knows?" said the priest. "A squad car answered a call from Watridge. The police say they've been threatened. Two Negroes beat Watridge so horribly . . . I rushed to the hospital. They let me speak to him . . ."

"To Watridge?" Purchase looked at the priest.

"He cursed me. He accused me. I see now that you couldn't have protected the man. I understand now that everything was — is destined." The priest sighed. "Until today I only suspected it now and then. Now I know for a certainty —"

"Sure," said Miss Sula. "Everybody know that. It's wrote down in the book that what is to be will be."

"Hush, Mama," Purchase said softly. "They're in the streets. Many of them?"

"A great many," the priest said. "I never thought I'd fear my own people."

"God damn you, why *didn't* you stop it! Why *did* you have to cause it?" Ton-Ton burst out. "That boy — you *killed* that boy!"

Purchase stared at her. "Hush," he said.

"Don't blame Purchase," said the priest. "It was wrong of me this morning to believe he could have prevented it — and you must not blame him."

"He is the cause!" Ton-Ton said.

"No," said the priest. "No, my child."

"You best hush talkin that way, Ton-Ton," Miss Sula said quietly. "You just upset. You *know* Purchase had nothing to do with any of this. Just like me. Just like Maco. Just like the preacher here trying to tell you."

"I must do something. The mayor asked me to phone him. I don't know what to do," the priest said.

"Maybe they won't wreck things. Maybe just moving into the street will be enough," Purchase said.

"I must go where I'm needed," said the priest. "I must find where I'm needed."

"Tell me about Hatcher," Ton-Ton said.

"As well as I can piece it together there was a fight at Poor

Boston's. The police came. Boston's cafe was wrecked and looted. Hatcher and another boy were trying to assist Boston. The police started to arrest Boston because he was bleeding. Hatcher tried to explain. The police had just seen what happened to Watridge. They turned on Hatcher. The boy ran."

"Why would he run?" Ton-Ton asked. She had stopped weeping.

"Because he didn't want an arrest on his record. Because he was clean, I suppose. He had no right to run, of course. No one has the right to run from officers of the law."

"But the law has no right to kill a boy just because he runs!" Ton-Ton said.

"The boy who shot him was such a lousy shot he couldn't have shot him on purpose. He fired once in the air. They say Hatcher had stopped. Some say he had. That his hands were raised in the air when the boy fired the second time. Hatcher went down, bleeding from the mouth. The girl was with him —"

"What girl?" said Miss Sula.

"A girl — I don't know. They intended to marry," the priest said.

"I don't believe in marriage," said Miss Sula. "Married folks just fight. I said I never wanted to marry no man and spend the rest of my life fighting him. Mens and womens don't have no business marryin if they love one another."

"That's me too," said Maco. "Marriage is for the bees."

"It wasn't destined," said the priest. "All my past life must have been lived for the revelation of this day. Yes, it was. At first I saw through a glass darkly. Now, clearly, I see his face."

"Whose face? You see Hatcher's face?" Maco asked, not looking up from his cards, the cards clicking in front of him. The little man's fingers were like twisted stems.

Maco can't understand, Purchase thought. Mama and Ton-

Ton understand, but Ton-Ton can't accept. The priest wouldn't believe the truth if you told him. He wouldn't know truth if it ran over him in the street.

The priest was talking to himself.

"I've seen the face of God," he said. "I used to think God was the love of Jesus Christ for mankind. Perhaps I even believed it. I tried to believe it."

"You want to lie down a while? Father Ned? If you feel weary there's a spare room," said Ton-Ton. She went to the little priest and took him by the arm.

"No," said the priest. "No thanks. I'm all right." He removed his glasses. "It's true that I've suffered the impact of a religious experience." He took out a dirty handkerchief and wiped his eyes. "But I've survived it. My only mission now is to go where I'm needed most. I must talk to Hatcher's mother and find the girl. The girl must be somewhere screaming herself hoarse. I don't even know her name."

"Louise Hollan," Purchase said. "He was a smart boy all right. He was a good kid. He had some possibilities —"

"God damn you to hell," Ton-Ton said. "You can stand there and say that. God damn you. Before now I never knew what you were. Well now I know what you are —"

"My child, you must promise me to wipe this unreasoning malice from your heart," the priest said, interrupting her. "This is the natural reaction from your grief. One always wants to blame someone else. Sometimes the person blamed can be very close. Don't say things you'll regret. Promise me you will not leave your husband — excuse me. I keep thinking of you as married."

"They don't believe in it either," Maco said. "They are like me and Miss Sula, preacher."

"Promise me never to leave your friend —"

"My employer —"

"Your employer —"

"This whoremaster, this murderer I work for —!"

"I must go but I can't leave as long as you are so over-wrought, Miss Ton-Ton," said the priest.

Ton-Ton sighed. "Go on. I'll hush. I'll never mention it again. I'm caught anyhow."

"Lady-gal, anytime you want to cut out from here and leave please be my guest," Purchase said. "Go!"

"Now he's tellin jokes," Ton-Ton said.

Miss Sula took another sip from the straw and cleared her throat. "This ain't leadin nowhere — ain't no time for quarrel-ing. Let the preacher leave and get going on his business."

"Yes, let Father Ned depart in peace," Purchase said.

"I'll show you to the door," Ton-Ton said, taking the little priest's arm again. "Be careful. If there's trouble don't get hurt in the streets."

"Everything is destined," the priest mumbled. Ton-Ton led him away. "Destined," came his voice from the hallway. A door closed. Ton-Ton returned.

"Everything I touch turns to shit," she said.

"You have to learn to separate yourself," said Miss Sula. "Business have to be separated from the heart. What my boy has did come under the order of business. He didn't kill nobody. He didn't beat nobody up. He only tended his business. You love him don't you? Lady-gal, you do love him, don't you? Course you love him! You love him so much you could kill him. I see it sticking out all over you like fiery pins."

"Sets on her shoulder like a pet monkey I knew once," said Maco. "This Cuban name of Chavez had a monkey on a chain. Drop a penny? That monkey would dance just like a man. Chavez played the French harp and would dance too. I bet they collected fifty cents a day between them, dancing and picking up pennies. It was big business down at the Woodyard. When business got slack the monkey rode that Cuban's shoulder."

"So he did," said Miss Sula. "I recall that."

"Love sets her shoulder the same way," said Maco, nodding at Ton-Ton.

"She's wantin Purchase to slap hell out of her." He chucked a card down. "Or somethin," he said.

"Have a sup of melon. You ain't hardly touched your straw, Ton-Ton," Miss Sula said.

Ton-Ton was trembling. "Sit down, Lady-gal," said Purchase. "Do like Mama says."

Ton-Ton sat down but made no move to take the straw in her lips. "I might tell a long story to the grand jury," she said. "I might sing my head off one of these days."

"Wrong again," said Maco. "You might blow your head off but you won't sing it off, will she, Miss Sue?"

"Let her alone," said the older woman. "She's coming in contact. In every business sooner or later you have to come in contact. The same with your life. You have to come in contact and it happens always to be painful. Lady-gal is strong enough to get over it."

"You got nice clothes," Purchase said. "Nice automobiles, perfume, jewelry, credit cards —"

"Gin and watermelon," Ton-Ton said.

"You could be dancing in a go-go cage and covering your back with your tail," Purchase said. "Or you could be teaching school or working in some bookkeeping department in a bank.

Sometimes, Lady-gal, sometimes when I look at you I tend to forget you got all that college education inside you. Because you're so pretty. Don't you want your melon? You gonna let Mama drink it all and get herself drunk?"

"God — even the priest," Ton-Ton said. "Even that poor bastard. He's out of his mind —"

"No, baby, he coming in contact too. But he haves to come a different way, don't you understan me?" Miss Sula said. "Drink your melon, baby. Suck your straw."

"Maybe somebody around here needs a bottle with a nipple on it," Maco said.

Ton-Ton looked at him. The cards were snapping down again. "One more pop out of your bill? Just one more? And I'm going to open your neck at the bleeding place? So listen at me, you sawed off stack of shit. I didn't get this far in the world to take it off you? Now I want you to tell me something — *do* you understand?"

"Yes, ma'am," said Maco. "I'm sorry."

"Maco don't mean nothing," said Miss Sula. "He just speaks to hear his own talk. You know that."

Ton-Ton took the straw in her delicate fingers. The phone was ringing.

"Want me to get it, boss?" said Maco, never looking up from the cards.

"I got it," Purchase said. He reached for the phone. It was his cab dispatcher. From the calls he was getting, the dispatcher said, there was going to be trouble. What to do about the cabs? Call the units in and put them on the yard?

"Leave them out. Tell them I said business as usual."

The dispatcher hesitated.

"This is *me*. I say business as usual."

"Right . . ." The dispatcher said some units might get lost or damaged.

"Yes, and if you call them all home and concentrate them in one place we could lose all of them. Pass the word that every man stays on the job. I want the name of any man who leaves his unit. Tell them I said I'm going to take names. If what I think is going to happen does happen then I want them out where I can call them anytime I want to and get a *yassuh*. You tell them that, and tell them that when it starts I'll be on the radio myself some of the time. Ease it over to them that I said if they desert a cab it won't be just a job they'll be out of. Put it in language they can understand. And this is *me!*"

Purchase slammed down the phone. "I think I got him, Mama. I smell him!" he said.

"Don't take nothing for granted. Stop the ratholes. Hem everything up 'fore you wade in after him. If I know Cousin Alabam he ain't gonna be easy to catch out," said the old woman.

Purchase was pacing and swinging his arms. "A shrewd grocer makes his fortune somehow with an operation consisting of only two stores. Turn that over in your mind."

"Yes, I have asked myself," said Miss Sula, nodding.

"Then he comes along and starts crowding me. *Me!* When I *never* had from very early in life anything but the decision that the needs of man in Ormund City were three in number. Women, gambling, and a way to get places."

"Because he's got to have wheels to get where the gals and the action can be had," said Maco. "Mankind got to have shot and he got to have action or Saturday night just may as well be took off the calendar."

"So I set out to control the taxicabs? *Years* now I've owned both companies. Yellow for whites; Blue Top for colored.

Everything sewed up. The whole bag, and here comes Alabam Webster — like a stink. Suddenly he's everywhere befriending people. Ingratiating himself with Paco Perrone. *Me.* I stuck that wop in office."

"True," Miss Sula said. "But he can be removed."

"So he stands by and lets Cousin Alabam move in on my territory? What the hell did this city need a new cab franchise for? Here comes a God damned grocer and out of a clear blue sky he gets a cab franchise and buys a hundred and eleven brand new air-conditioned cabs. *Air*-conditioned! Was there ever an air-conditioned cab in this city before he did that?"

"Never," said Maco, snapping down a card.

"So I have to buy two hundred new *air-conditioned* cabs just to meet the competition and stay in business."

"Two hundred-and-fifty-six," said Ton-Ton. "Get it right as long as you're determined to get it, Mister Studhorse. I believe Doctor Stinkfinger has started himself on a tirade against the poor old honest grocer. We got a nigger-style vendetta on our hands. Pretty soon we gonna have a war in the street just to satisfy the big studhorse."

"It boils down to a simple equation of self-defense," Purchase said. "Well, now I have it. The way is found. Something subtle and powerful as magic. Fear is like an edge of sharp steel."

"What you planning?" Miss Sula asked.

"If Cutler's find-out papers read like he says they do? That's the last question that rests on my mind. What time did he say he was coming?"

"Sometime this evening," said Ton-Ton. "You know Cutler, Mister Studhorse. He never gives a time of day. He's always late."

"You found him and hired him," Purchase said pleasantly.

"And he's done the job I hired him for — unless he's been lying. And I don't believe he's built for lying. Gambling, yes; lying, forget it," said Ton-Ton. "He likes to go by the rules. I wonder what he'd say if he knew about Hatcher."

Purchase turned on her. The back of his neck went numb. "Never mention that again."

"Yes, lover. That's blood under the bridge. All right — I won't mention it. I'm in on it too, after all. Laying it on Watridge — that pulled the trigger."

"Now you thinking in the sensible way," said Miss Sula. "Don't the melon taste good. If we had us some deviled crabs they'd go good. I might send after some crabs and devil 'em tomorrer."

"He couldn't be leaned on in the ordinary way," Purchase said.

"Who?" Miss Sula asked. "Son, why don't you sit down and quit walking up and down like a tiger?"

"The grocer," Purchase said. "Because he's fully aware. He's too smart for anything strong-arm. Lean on him that way and do time in the pen because he *knows* a third cab company has *got* to be like a thorn in my side. So leaning on him, or anything else like that —"

"He wants to say murdering him," Ton-Ton said. "But Studdybuck ain't got his guts where his mouth is, Miss Sula."

"Killing is old-fashioned," Purchase said.

"You know a killing here in Ormund don't cost no more than a good lay? I thought about that yestiddy," Maco said. "You want somebody killed? Lay down a fifty and you will come up with *change* in your hand. I hate to see it go down that cheap where just anybody can have you laid out for chicken feed."

"I never knew it to be any other way since as long as I can remember," Miss Sula said quietly. "Far back as I can remember all you had to do was raise your eyebrow. But I say Purchase is right about Cousin Alabam. A man like him is a different hunk of cheese. He's *made* out of something different. That's why it was right of Son to study him. Put the find-out on him. Listen to him and learn how he ticks and tocks. Take somebody big that way and no kind of ordinary stuff will take him down. Ton-Ton was right when she advised to study him."

"That's gonna put a big star in my goddamn crown," Ton-Ton said. "Order some flowers sent to the house."

"Me?" said Maco. "What house?"

"I want a hundred dollar arrangement. No name — just a hundred dollars worth of white orchids or something. Something *real* nice."

"To what house?" Maco said.

"The Hatchers."

Reluctantly Maco abandoned the cards. He went to the phone.

"That's nice," Miss Sula said, nodding. "Nice."

"Cutler ought to be here," Purchase said.

"Yeah," said Ton-Ton. "I remember during the first weeks of his employment. That impudent way he had to ringing the door chime? Like he was God-a-mighty just blown in from St. Louis. Got Stud in an uproar everytime. Stud was gonna kill his find-out man because he was impudent. Didn't treat Mister Walker with proper respect. Didn't bow and sweat in Mister Walker's holy presence."

"Shut up!" Purchase said. "You know I always spoke softly and kindly to him."

"Because you had to have what money can't buy from people. You have to have his loyalty, his friendship. It was vile," Ton-Ton said. "It was nasty."

"It was your idea," Purchase said. "And it worked. Today

[*191*]

we get the papers and there's going to be fulcrum enough and prize pole enough to get a purchase on Cousin Alabam Webster and move him gently — *but oh, it's got to be gentle* —" Purchase said in a whisper. "*Gently* out of the taxicab business!"

"Son, calm yourself," Miss Sula said. "Drink your melon."

Maco returned from the phone. "Ordered your flowers," he said. He picked up the cards.

"Purchase can't sit down," Ton-Ton said. "He wants his hands on the find-out papers too bad. And to tell the truth, you know I'm interested myself?"

"Sure," said Miss Sula. "You just came in contact, that's all. You going to make it, Lady-gal. You got all the stuff it take. Breathe deep breaths and think about how wisely the trap was laid. Think how lucky for us that it's sprung like it is. If a few people get hurt and killed along the way why that's just part of it! You have to let persons lie *easy* in their graves and only your mind can do that for you. Everything is working out lucky for us. So be thankful!"

Ton-Ton nodded. She left the table and came toward Purchase.

"What's wrong, baby?" she asked.

He put his arms about her and she snuggled into his chest with her own arms crossed.

"Want to play?" she whispers.

"Now?" he replies, close to her ear.

"Maco and Mama can mind things."

"*You* wanna play?" he whispers.

"I need to," she says.

"Mama, will you excuse us?"

"Yes. Makase and mend your differences. Go make up and

when Cutler comes I'll let him in the door and call you." Miss Sula smiles.

"Lovebirds," says Maco. "Always got to sit close together."

Purchase closes the door, shutting away Maco's voice and the snap of the cards. He opens the door to the bedroom and she's already there. The dress comes over her head. She kicks her shoes off and comes toward him. His nether gorge goes down. He feels his heart pound.

"My nerves been tight as a drumhead," he says, and so saying, kisses her.

She accepts the apology.

18

CUTLER

THE tarpon hang like martyrs. Gills flared in death, they hang in pairs beneath a neat open shed just off Bayside near the sport fishing docks on the west bank of the Meade River, in full view of traffic flowing toward the main business districts.

As he always did, Cutler slowed down for a look at the fish. Beside him in the front seat Cynthia held the loose-leaf notebook in her lap. From time to time he felt the touch of her fingers laid gently against the back of his neck.

Each caress became a reminder and a promise. Everything that retarded a moment of their coming together was strange, delicious torture, and their passion changed the appearance of the world. Anything sad was enormously pathetic. Any ridiculous thing was so comical they laughed themselves sore. It was as though their coming together as one flesh somehow magnified everything in all the world about them.

Where the river lay catching the reds and yellows of a late and descending sun, it served as background for objects, one after the other. There was a lonely, stark and structured piling, perhaps a last reminder of the banished sailing ships; there was a heap of stones. There was a row of fronded cabbage palms; there was a feathery stand of bahaia grass and all these things went drifting past the vision of lovers such as Cutler and Cynthia, who saw everything as with a single eye; vivid slashes of color went casting against the azures and cordovans of the shifting river surface. And the river was here and there dappled with drifting rafts of green water hyacinths. And there was a flash of oleander and a stretch of perfumed jasmine, and a sudden appearance of blooming exoria was like a silent, outfolding explosion.

Once over the bridge and into the more crowded districts there was a sea change. Buildings seemed to brood behind a multiplication of painted, imprinted words making mawkishly lusterless demand upon indifferent senses — a port city, a sport city, a squandering city where goods were manufactured and services advertised, offered, and rendered. A churchyard here and there spoke quietly for religion or was tricked out with a gaudy blue neon sign, as though God, even, had in some wise been lured into this sprawling life of trade and he was plying it with a cunning array of spiritual merchandise.

Everything was funny and everything was lovely for Cutler and Cynthia.

They passed the broken fireplug and the wrecked automobile and the sweating city utilities employees wearing yellow hard hats. There was a wrecker preparing to tow the stricken automobile away and there was a man directing traffic around the broken plug, standing in the wet street and waving his arms, and there was a solemn mob of Negroes standing on the sidewalk, watching.

Cutler was busy explaining that he was not a nudist. Never had been one, not really. He had joined the Lake Maas Club simply to be closer to Alabam Webster.

[195]

"You had me fooled. Here I was thinking you enjoyed it — the sunbathing, the cardplaying, the swimming and volleyball," Cynthia said. "Now *I* can confess."

Cutler wanted to know what her confession might be. "I never saw quite as many people on the sidewalks before," he said. "Strange . . ."

"I'm not a nudist either. I had tried everything else, so when a girlfriend suggested it — her name was Marge Miller and she got me to join and then she met a man and married him. I never saw Marge again — I joined. I wanted to meet a man. Well," she said. She laughed. "No more hauling my drawers off in public. I met my man."

"But to keep me happy you'd have kept making the scene at Lake Maas." Cutler laughed.

"Yes." Cynthia pretended to pout. "You're sneaky," she said. "You deceive little girls." And then: "I love you, Rann."

"Yeah," Cutler said. "Well, let's get fifteen hundred bucks from the nigger and I'm ready to leave Ormund City."

"When are we leaving?"

"The sooner the better," Cutler said. "I've got a plan. I'm going to be decent and respectable. I'm taking you home to Tennessee."

"What changed your mind?"

"I have to make a decent and respectable living so you can have decent and respectable babies."

"What's wrong with living this way — gin rummy, golf, fishing, stealing secrets —"

"Yeah," Cutler said. "You got it added up. I can see you're ahead of me. So many jiggs on the street. I can't figure it."

"It's the heat," Cynthia said. "They come outside to breathe."

"Maybe," Cutler said.

Making a sharp turn off Central and doubling back up Woodyard, Cutler swung the car into the alley behind the 312 Club and parked it.

"I'm coming in with you," Cynthia said. "May I?"

"Of course," Cutler said. "I want you to meet my friendly employer."

He got out and went swiftly around to her door but she was already out. "Where to?"

"This way," he said. They crossed the alley.

"The odor," she said.

"If you never smelled it the reason is simple. You were never down here," he said. "It's the Woodyard."

"I was born in this city," she said. A note of fear crept into her voice.

Cutler took her arm. "Cool it," he said. He rang the bell.

"I don't like this. Listen! Rann?"

"It's just a siren," Cutler said. He pushed the bell button a second time. The door opened.

"Come in," said Ton-Ton. The Negress wore white stretch pants, yellow high heel shoes and a dark blue polka dot silk blouse.

"Cynthia, this is Miss Ton-Ton. Cynthia and I are engaged."

"Pleased," said Ton-Ton. "Mr. Walker is waiting. You're right on time. For once."

"Yeah," Cutler said.

"How do you do?" Cynthia was saying nervously. "Your name again?"

"Ton-Ton," said the Negress in a softly melodious voice. "While the gentlemen talk perhaps you would like a sip of something cool? Mr. Walker's mother is visiting."

Cynthia looked quickly at Cutler.

"I'll be a few minutes," he said.

"Yes," Cynthia said. "Something cool. That would be nice, thank you."

The siren, meanwhile, came nearer.

"We had our troubles today. Now maybe there's a fire. This way, Miss Cynthia? The boss is in his office," said Ton-Ton. She led Cynthia away.

Cutler entered without knocking. Purchase Walker was smoking a cigar. The radio beside him was sputtering. He turned it off and glanced at his watch. He wore a yellow shirt, the same shade, a match for Ton-Ton's shoes, Cutler noted. It was silk. The loose sleeves were rolled halfway to the elbow, showing the Negro's bare, powerful forearms.

"Always on time. Never early. Never late," the Negro said sarcastically.

Cutler put the blue notebook on the desk. Purchase Walker opened it, turned it around, and began reading. "Square footage, physical layout, machinery, employees, monthly gross . . ."

Cutler sat down. "Cigar?" said the Negro.

"Thanks." Cutler took one. "Cuban," he said.

"Yes," the Negro replied. "*Always.*"

Purchase Walker scanned the columns using his index finger for a guide. He drew gently at his cigar. "Excellent, excellent," he murmured. "So far excellent. I have to let Ton-Ton read it. Ton-Ton has a business head."

"There's something else," Cutler said.

"What?"

Cutler mentioned the spoiled meat operation.

"Without really knowing whether it *would* interest you," Cutler was saying. He watched the Negro's jaw drop. He watched the Negro suddenly smile. "The bacteria count *is* rather high by the time the meat gets to the Central store. They process it with chemicals and mark it down for quick sale."

"This is a *fact*."

Cutler nodded. "Absolutely."

"Ahhhh . . ." The Negro bridged huge hands in front of his face.

"An occasional sickness? Maybe even a death if an old person or a young child say, got hold of Cousin Alabam's marked down meat? When we talk in terms of a small herd of beeves butchered every week for an operation like Kutrate, we're talking about thousands of Negro customers pushing their carts down that long meat counter at Central," Cutler said.

"I was listening to police calls when you came in." The Negro laid a hand on the radio. "You got me just *what* I needed, just *when* I needed it."

"Police calls?" Cutler frowned. "There seem to be a lot of people on the sidewalks."

"There *are* a lot of people out there. Yes, a lot of people and a lot of rumors —"

"What about the sirens? My girl is with me," Cutler said.

"A *lot* of sirens," said the Negro. "How much was your bonus? I've forgotten."

"Fifteen hundred was our agreement."

"I'm adding on a little. I'm going to sweeten that a little bit."

"Since my girl is with me I'm not anxious to hang around this time," Cutler said.

"You're safe," said the Negro. "Just let me get Ton-Ton. This is *the* girl, huh?"

"I'm going to marry her," Cutler said.

"Good." The Negro smiled. He was all smiles now. He brought his hands together with a loud clap. "You got yourself a wife in the bargain. All that money and a nice wife. Membership in the Lake Maas Club."

"*That's* over with," Cutler said dryly. "The Lake Maas act is a thing of the past."

"Just let me get Ton-Ton," said the Negro, getting up from the desk. He went through the heavy polished door behind the ornate desk.

Cutler sighed. There came the dull thump of an explosion somewhere outside, somewhere on a distant block, how far away and in what direction exactly there was no way to tell. The office was windowless. *You're safe here.*

Cutler stumped out his cigar in a green cutglass ashtray on the Negro's desk. He sat back down. There was a siren, more distant than the first. The silent door swung open. Ton-Ton appeared. She wore glasses with white frames. Purchase pushed a chair up to the desk. She sat down. The Negro sat down in his own chair. The two of them began reading. "Here," said Ton-Ton, nodding. Purchase Walker nodded. "And this." She turned a page. "Good, very good!" Ton-Ton said, showing her teeth.

She looked up at Cutler. "Construction is definitely underway on the new stores, these locations in Florida and Alabama?"

"Yes, definitely," Cutler said.

"How about it?" Purchase Walker said.

"This is what we need," said Ton-Ton. "This *and* the meat operation."

"Let me open the safe then," said the Negro. "You prefer fifties or hundreds?"

"Cash," Cutler said. He smiled.

"Would you be interested in other assignments?" said Ton-Ton.

"Not interested," Cutler said. He could hear the safe opening in the back room.

"Why? If you don't mind my asking? Because I have to say you make a damn swell find-out man. We need information? You need money?"

Ton-Ton made an eloquent gesture of bargaining with her slender hands. Purchase returned and laid a stack of bills beside her on the desk. Licking her thumb Ton-Ton recounted the money quickly. Like a bank teller, thought Cutler. Like a God damned lady bank teller. "Two thousand, Purchase?"

"I decided to sweeten it," Purchase Walker said. "We might need Mister Cutler again."

"He just told me he was not interested in other assignments," said Ton-Ton.

"Uh-huh, and he's quitting the cards and the dogs and the ponies too, I bet. Turning over a new leaf. Getting himself married."

Standing, the Negro slipped the money in an envelope and handed it to Ton-Ton. She came around the desk.

"Thank you," Cutler said, taking the envelope. He opened it and folded the bills and stuck them in his pocket. They felt warm, like a comfortable drink of bourbon at sundown, like a fresh hand at bridge with a good partner across the table and a gentle murmur of voices from the club bar. Like dance music playing in yet another room, beyond, where people at this hour would be dining, enjoying life, and witnessing the sunset, watching darkness rise beyond the sailboats like a live shadow, rousing from the placid sea and striding ashore.

"We'll be going then," Cutler said.

"It might be safer — just a suggestion," Ton-Ton began, "if you were to wait a little, until *good* dark."

Purchase had turned on the police calls.

"Good dark?" Cutler said. The radio stuttered.

"People on the street wouldn't be so likely then to see the color of your skin? Your color?" Ton-Ton said. "I'm thinking of your girl."

"Shouldn't have brought her," Cutler said. "If only I had known . . ."

"You had no way," the Negro interrupted. "No more than me. Who would ever dream it would turn out this way. I kept asking myself maybe two years or more now why would I *want* trouble in these streets?"

"You mean to say . . . " Cutler brought himself up short. The realization came at him as though from a distance, like a wind sweeping suddenly into a dark corridor. The Negro was nodding.

"That's what I mean to say . . ."

"But the casualties," Cutler said. "The *casualties!*"

The Negro nodded. "It bothers me too. But I had to make a choice. Either cool it or go ahead and heat it up. Either make my play now, while I have the opportunity, or let the opportunity pass. Wait a few months and lose more time while my enemy gets stronger." He shook his head. "No," he said. "You had no way to know. I had no way to know." He paused and looked at his cigar and then at Cutler. "Dusk is due to fall — to settle in a little while. We can offer you a drink meanwhile. That is if you'd enjoy a drink. Ton-Ton is correct. It will be safer to leave after dusk."

"I'll be God damned," Cutler said. "Then you mean to heat it up?"

"I'm going to heat it up. I *am* heating it up," the Negro said.

"Shall I call the young lady? All right?" said Ton-Ton.

Cutler drew a deep breath. He nodded. "Bourbon on ice," he said.

Ton-Ton left the room. Purchase Walker meanwhile had reached for the phone.

Cynthia came in and sat on the arm of Cutler's chair and rested her fingers lightly against his neck. She held a glass. "Something with rum," she said. "I've been talking to Maco and Miss Walker. We're staying a while?"

Cutler nodded. Ton-Ton brought his drink. "Thanks," Cutler said.

"Black rum and soda for me," said Purchase Walker, placing his hand over the mouthpiece of the phone.

Ton-Ton made a face. "He drinks *that* and it makes him stink. He drinks that and I have to drink it too. He drinks it just to anger me. Tastes like iodine!" She slapped Purchase Walker's shoulder. The Negro smiled and continued murmuring into the phone.

Cynthia laughed. "When are we leaving?" she whispered. Her hair brushed Cutler's cheek.

"In a few minutes," Cutler said.

"I want you," she whispered. "I've waited all day. And besides, I'm hungry. This stuff is going to my head."

"Relax," Cutler said. "I'll see that you're fed."

"By God, you better," she whispered. Her fingernails stroked his neck. "You're going to have a drunk broad on your hands."

"Good," Cutler said. "Just what I've been needing all day long."

"Here's your drink Buster Brown," said Ton-Ton, return-

[*203*]

ing. "I don't know why Buster Brown has to spend all his life gassing on the phone. His phone bill is like the national debt. Okay, Buster Brown, hang up and drink your lap. You got company, man."

She perched on the side of the desk. "You know, woman to woman, dear, this Purchase Walker, he's got just about the biggest, blackest bastard — he's the meanest, ugliest son of a bitch that ever tore pants. I don't know if that's much of a message but it's all that comes to my head right at the moment." Ton-Ton raised her glass, took a sip, made a face. "Iodine, baby. Iodine. God!"

Cynthia laughed.

"Tell me, honey," Ton-Ton continued. "Why you want to marry that guy beside you? Don't you know he's dangerous?"

"He's making me," Cynthia said. "Making me marry him."

"She-it, darling. And I were you before he'd make me do that I'd kill him. Baby don't you know it's all right to live with him — but marriage? Marriage is for the bees. Let the queen bee marry and spend all her life laying eggs if that's her pleasure. But honey don't you know marriage to men like these — that kind of hook-up is fatal?"

"He's making me," Cynthia said. "I'm going to have his babies."

"I suppose if you must you must. I might have some of this stud horse's pickens. But baby, I'll never marry him. Once I did that he'd slip through my fingers like dry desert sand. You know the difference in desert sand and beach sand, hon?"

"No," Cynthia said.

"Well, beach sand is all jagged particles. Every kind of broken shape. Desert sand is a collection of little spheroids. The wind makes the one. The ocean makes the other."

[*204*]

"I never knew the difference."

"Yes," Ton-Ton said. "I learned that in college. I went to college and that is ninety percent of the reason he keeps me around and feeds me turnip greens and peas and hog jowl. He feeds me nothing but pure soul food, trying to make me fat. Every man wants to destroy every woman, baby. Yes, I got all that in college and you see here how I live, talking to myself while Buster Brown talks on the phone. Drinking by myself and working for this God damn gangster. Your fella, he's smart to move out of this game. Make him get a job outdoors somewhere. Let him run a boat dock or guide the tarpon fishing or teach rich chicks sailing or golf. Riding. He knows all those games and more besides."

"How do you know all that?" Cynthia said, amused.

"How? Honey we ran a check on him ourselves. That's half what we do most of the time. Check 'em up; check 'em out. Hire 'em, fire 'em, harum-scarum. Buster Brown here would like your man on a permanent basis but your man is wise. He's on to it."

"Prison never had any appeal for me," Cutler said.

"Now he's talkin," said Ton-Ton. "He's makin sense. The fuzz will never lay hands to Buster Brown. But anybody else in his red-ass organization?" She snapped her fingers.

Purchase Walker hung up the phone. "You're talking too much," he said.

"Drink your lap, stud," Ton-Ton replied. She winked at Cynthia. "Did I make your lap strong enough, Buster Brown?"

"Okay, I've told you."

"He's laying a threat on me. Hear that? When you walk out that door he might just try to slap his little woman around. But honey, I got knees for him. I know where his God damn

manhood has its residence, in two big round apartment buildings. The last time he couldn't walk for three days."

"She's turned on," Purchase Walker said. "She likes you."
He sipped his drink. "I believe now would be the strategic time
for your departure," he said.

"See how he wants to run you off? He's afraid I might have
two cents worth of fun. He's all work and no play here lately. I
might have to visit him with my knee again if things don't
improve around here."

"Seriously, it's time."

"We enjoyed the drinks," Cutler said.

"We obviously enjoyed your visit very much," said Purchase
Walker. He stood up.

"Quite an animal ain't he?" Ton-Ton said.

"Mister Cutler, if ever you should change your mind a job
will be waiting for you here."

"Thanks." Cutler reached for the Negro's hand and shook
it.

"But no thanks," said Ton-Ton. "He's got good sense.
Mister Cutler is a sensible man. He's going to find something
outside. Something happy that will fit himself and this pretty
foolish kid that's marrying him because she thinks she must.
Well, honey, good luck."

"Good luck," Cynthia said.

She leaned against Cutler's arm. Purchase Walker opened
the alley door for them. Cutler opened the door on his side of
the car and let Cynthia slide under the wheel. She sat very
close, with her hip riding against his. She kissed his ear.

Catcalls and whistles fell into the wake of the automobile.

"Why drive so fast?" she whispered.

Poor bastards. Poor black bastards, Cutler thought.

"You wouldn't understand even if I had time to explain," he said.

"I told you that rum was getting to me," Cynthia giggled.

There was a rail spur ahead curving out from between a line of warehouses. A group of Negroes came stringing across the pavement beside the rail spur and Cutler slowed down to let them cross. As he did so they stopped squarely in front of him and faced the headlights. Cutler hit the brakes. The windshield seemed to explode in his face. The engine choked out.

Half blind, Cutler reached for the ignition-starter. The window beside him smashed. The door opened. Blood came like a curtain over his eyes.

Instinctively Cutler snatched the keys, breaking the chain, taking the other keys in hand and leaving the ignition key still in place. He tried one last time to start the car and was yanked bodily off the seat. He heard Cynthia's shriek.

The keys were his weapons. He slashed out and was rewarded with a groan. That's one, he thought.

He went down, protecting his vitals. They were kicking and trampling him, but not seriously as yet. He caught a leg and slashed it. The victim screamed. The crowd moved. He felt something blunt strike his head. Now suddenly several of them sat on him.

Wising up, he thought. The blunt something struck his head again, near the temple. Then it was pressed to the back of his neck. "Shoot! Shoot the honkie bastard! Pull the trigger, man! What's the matter with you! Here, gimme that heat! I'll do it to him!"

Inexplicably though, the gun moved away. The car meanwhile was also being beaten. Glass kept smashing and scattering to the pavement like gravel.

"Hold her! Hole dat white-ass bitch! Give her some of dis here!"

"Give it to her!"

"Put it to whitey's woman! Shove it to honkie gal!"

Cynthia's screams, regular at first, were now at intervals, hoarse, and hoarser still. Cutler heaved with all his strength. Now someone stomped his hands. He shifted. A kick caught him in the side. They were trying to roll him over on his back. Once over and I'm dead, he thought, thinking deep in the twilight of his consciousness. Dead. To have come through so much and to go out this way, he thought. To find something, to hold something at last, and to lose it? Now?

For an instant he seemed to glimpse the river again. He saw the flash of an evening sun stabbing it like a golden sword and from somewhere bells seemed to be ringing, deep cathedral sounds, tolling and lulling him toward a dream of trees and meadows wherein he hovered and was at one with and a part of everything that was, that is, that will be . . .

19

GYP

I shut the door on her mouth and crossed the porch and three door up at Hatcher's they were passing in and passing out of the house in their Sunday clothes and I heard some woman weeping. They were bringing food and some flowers when they could not understand the facts that he wasn't, was, and ain't and that no amount of flowers and food and Sunday clothes is going to put him back on his feet, back to *was*, and anyway he lived a long time, Hatcher was up in years. Nineteen — that ought to be long enough to satisfy anybody, but that woman went on and on weeping and gargling and I said to myself if somebody would explain to me how that's done when you lose something like this, that you can weep and holler and gargle and help anything that way when he never even called you Louise? *You* can carry on *that* way?

Or take it another way that Leroy never had to tell him nothing about the blood and the syph and the clinic and Hatcher went on out without never knowing he even had it. So far as he ever knew, everything I gave him was good and clean and I gave him everything good that I have got and so he got it all, all he could take, all I could give and some that maybe he didn't want because he didn't know nothing about it but I gave him that too and I would not give that part of me to another man and I will never give that part of me to any man again. So Hatcher, my dear Hatcher where he went, where you are my dear you got that going for you that what I gave you, part of it anyhow, was what I never gave any man before and will never give any man again and if you can hear me listen and know that *that* is yours forever little Hatcher dear wherever it is now, wherever it is he went back to; where he was before he got born. He had something nobody else ever will have from me again and maybe some time ago when I thought about it I was deciding inside myself that some part of me had to be saved for the man I would love if he ever happened.

I could hear her gargling all the way to the corner. Then I heard something else. Nobody had to tell me. It was shooting down in the direction of Boston's over where Leroy stay at in that neighborhood and then I saw the car stop and I heard the store window break like some kind of glass waterfall and they were coming out through the window with guns and it come to me I might not have no easy time to win my bus ticket tonight. Tires hollered. They drove away. I crossed over. There lay the window busted big as bull cock and the night light inside at the back of the store burning. A couple of kids come by me. They skipped inside and started looking around. They started after the drum set behind the unbusted window, taking it apart. I stepped in and went to where the watches were but it was locked and I was wondering what to do. There was a guy getting a gun and some shells for it. I tole him it was locked. He hit it twice with the gun and broke out the glass. I reached in and got the one I wanted. I had already looked at and thought about it for layaway. It had little chip diamonds on both sides the face.

When I started out women and kids were everywhere all over
the place grabbing and hollering and snatching a couple of
little portable teevees back and forth. Since I wasn't carrying
nothing but my purse and the watch was in it they didn't have
eyes for me. The boys had the drum set out of the window, all
except for the bass.

I got to the alley and took off my old watch and threw it
away. I slipped the new one on and ran down the alley. Another
car was stopped down there. I could hear them breaking the
windows and Jesus C. Christ I thought if this is not the most
wonderful esso bitch of a night that the sun ever went down on
yet, if this ain't and there the beginning of it all was when you
sat down in his blood and never knew what it was you had set
your sweet ass in and when I got to the end of the alley they
had already set that esso bitch on fire and so I said to one of
them why set the esso bitch on fire and he says well don't the
firetrucks need some business too? Do the police need all the
business? And the other one said he was going up on the roof
and hunt pigeons, he didn't know, maybe *some* cats would
rather stand in the street and get laid for a nickel but he was
going to climb while the climbing was good. He was going to
save his five bucks, he said. So I ask the other one. I said why
you want to burn the esso bitch? And he said this was the Jew
and the checks were all in there and if the checks got burnt up
then the Jew couldn't collect for nothing since he would have no
more paper on anybody. 'You never signed no check here?' he
says.

'Never had no money in the bank to sign a check for,' I
says. He wasn't no bad stud. He had a black hat with a pink
hatband and he had a pink shirt.

'Which is the whole point,' he's saying. 'Nobody *I* know

has got money in the bank to sign a check for but when you want his credit he has you sign a check—see what I mean? You sign a check and then if you don't pay him he can put your tee-tee in the pen for *several* God damn years because you passed a bad check."

I says, 'But he never asked me to sign no check and I been buying from him for cash and on the layway.'

'Yeah, baby, but you ain't old enough, because you have to be twenty-one before the check racket will operate against you.' He took shotgun shells out of his pocket and loaded three in the gun. 'I got to get on the roof, I guess. Because if they come trying to put it out we done started this mother all for nothing. So we can't let them put it out—'

I says, 'But you ain't going to kill the firemans just to get the place burnt to the ground.'

He smiled. 'Well, I *mean* to shoot over their heads. Now what anybody else will do I don't know. Move the car, Eddy!' he yells and the car moves off and he says to me, 'Now you scram out of the way, kid, because I hear them and they may be coming this way.' He left.

I ran up the street and I thought well the poor old Jew has had it and Mama's layway shoes and my layway coat and her papa's layway and all that esso bitches threads that she feeds and gets drunk and dates with — all the layway in it that I been paying fifteen a week for that's gonna get roasted. Anyway I had the watch.

The firetruck came around the corner. I got back close to the wall. The firemen jumped down and started hauling on the hose and running for the fireplug. The cats on the roof opened up and it roared in the street like cannons and two firemen dropped the hose and two crawled under the truck and the one that must have been supposed to drive was like he didn't know whether to go blind or shit b.b.'s and he got in the driver's seat and then climbed back down and got back up there and the ones under the truck were yelling for him not to run over them. He finally cut the engine and ran across to the phone booth and then after a minute he came out and ran back to the truck and crawled under it with the rest.

The shooting calmed down some and I said well maybe I better move on because they might aim over your head and hit your drawers and then you wouldn't have to sit in no borrowed blood, so I ran another block and watched them unloading a liquor store.

.'Somebody put the hurt on Watridge,' says one.

'Wonder who?' says the other. They start laughing.

20

THE DOCTOR

THE first inkling the doctor had gave him no full measure of warning as to what was to follow. The first patient was a colored female age sixteen with multiple beer bottle lacerations of the breast, neck, brow and cheek. When the doctor suggested that she be taken to Ormund City General, or failing that to the nearer but substandard Negro hospital, Patrick Memorial, her companions expressed a curious bewilderment.

"We not for certain to get there," said the most forward of the three. "We not for sure."

Just then the doctor heard the sirens. A strange prickling of the nerve ends coursed the skin at the back of his neck along the joint between spine and skull. His first thought was of his daughter, Elizabeth Anne. For a wild moment he imagined that she was out of the house. Then it came to him just as suddenly that she was in the next room watching television with one of her high school friends, a girl whose father worked at the Ormund City Body Shop.

"Then let's step next door to the clinic," the doctor said. The girl was dripping blood on the kitchen tiles. He felt her arm.

She was going into shock. "This way," he had said. Then he shouted for his wife. When she appeared she (almost as an automatic gesture) got the mop kept for such occasions. She began wetting the mop under the kitchen faucet, preparing to clean up the blood, and he paused at the door, still holding the wounded girl's arm. "I believe it's big trouble," the doctor said.

She looked at him from the sink. A siren howled by in the street. Tires squealed at the corner. Then came a sharp sound, like a blowout, an instant later a large thump. The doctor knew the later sound, an automobile collision. One of the girls — not the wounded one — began to moan.

The doctor turned. He took the Sunday *Ormund City Times* from the kitchen table, and spread it carefully on the floor. "Lie down," he told the wounded girl. "Put her flat on the floor."

The girl did as she was told. The three teenagers with her, the two girls and the boy, helped her down. They stooped, squatting beside her.

"You be all right now," the boy was saying. "We got the doctor now."

"We taken her nex doe to de clinic?" one of the girls was asking. "Doc?"

The doctor went to the closet and got his fishing coat and covered the girl lying on the newspapers.

"Keep her still a moment," he said.

His wife was mopping the blood. A hand-like groping of terror commenced reaching into the doctor's throat. He fought it back, reminding himself. He was the only Negro physician living in the district. Another siren passed. Firetruck, he thought.

"Fill the bathtubs," he said.

"All right." She was still mopping. It was a rich quality she had. Small things could tear her nerves to pieces. Yet when the chips were down she was calm as stone.

"Fill the tubs and the sinks. Let the girls help you. Draw the blinds. Fill any pots and pans, tubs, buckets. Check the windows, lock the doors when you leave and bring along the keys. Don't lock us out. Tell the girls to stay just where they are. Call Mrs. Cunningham and tell her Dinah must stay here. Tell her Dinah is safe."

"All right," his wife replied.

"Then come next door. I'm going to need help. Start the autoclave. Phone both hospitals and tell them I'm going to stay here. Tell them I'm going to do what I can."

"From the sound," she said. "A good many won't make it either to Patrick or Ormund General."

"Yes, ma'am," said the boy, squatting beside the lacerated girl. "It already bees pretty bad in dat way," he said softly.

"All right," said the doctor. "Come along. Let's get her on her feet." Her pulse was better. "She can walk," he said firmly. "Let's move her next door."

They went out with her, across the porch, through the carport. The doctor opened the door to his clinic.

"Here," said the doctor. He opened the door to a treatment room. "Get her on this table."

"The girls are filling the tubs."

He looked up and saw his wife. She had tied her head in a green surgical cloth. It came to him like a strange shadow in front of his eyes that she had not worked in the clinic for seven years. The place was strange to her. When she had worked for him, during the toughest years, the clinic had been located in an old house. They had lived in another part of it.

He scrubbed rapidly and pulled on his gloves. "Take these scissors and cut her dress from here down and pull it aside," he said.

His wife took the scissors and followed instructions. A commotion occurred just outside in the corridor. The doctor nodded to his wife. She left the room. More casualties were arriving.

The doctor took a sponge. He began cleansing the wounds. The girl moaned. He took the syringe from the little pan of boiling instruments at his elbow, seated a needle, and drew it full of Novocain. He began on the girl's face, with a laceration that passed through the eyebrow. He took care to line up the two edges of the severed brow. "Wipe the blood away." He clamped a sponge and handed the clamp to the boy, who stood beside him. "Wipe the blood away with this," he said. "So I can see to stitch. Here, where I'm working."

The boy responded. "You," he said to the girl. "Lie on the floor."

"Me?"

"I don't want you to faint. Lie on the floor until you feel better. Then step outside and help my wife."

"She laid down," said the boy, sponging, wiping away the oozing blood.

The doctor worked quickly. When he had closed the gash over the eye he began on the cheek. He probed. The girl screamed.

"Glass," he said. She screamed again. His ears rang. "You'll have to be still," he said. "You've got glass in this one. We can't sew up glass into your face. Do you understand? I'm going to try to deaden it but there are other people waiting to be helped." She began moaning. He found the sliver and drew it out, beer bottle brown. He dropped it on the floor.

"The hospital is going to try to send an ambulance," his wife said behind him. "The ambulances are all out. Some, especially the funeral homes, are refusing calls."

"How about a taxi?"

"I called," she said. "Blue Top is going to try. They've lost four cabs."

"Four new air-conditioned ones," the doctor said. "Well." He threaded a fresh needle with black suture thread. "Prepare me some needles," he said. "Fill the syringe with Novocain."

"All right." She prepared the sutures, putting them in a line, in a great row just as she had been taught, long ago, by her husband.

"Have we more cases?"

"The clinic is full," she said. "The waiting room is full."

"Get them off their feet, the bad ones. Move the furniture. Get the bad ones next to the wall."

"Father Ned's here," she said. "He's helping."

She was gone then. A child was screaming in the corridor.

Conscious of the dragging of time, of others who were worse, the doctor nonetheless worked on, moving to the breast, feeling more and more alone. He had never felt so alone before in the entirety of his professional career. He also felt helpless. He felt hopeless. Both sensations began passing through him in emotional waves. It was like nausea.

The child was brought in next. "How old is she?"

"She seven, doctor," said the mother.

"Let's get her on the table," he said.

He pulled away the dirty towel. The left eye, he saw, was utterly destroyed.

"What did this?"

"I don't know. She come off the street. She saying somebody shot her. I was next door. Is she bad?"

There was nothing for it but to apply a pressure bandage. He worked as rapidly as he could. "When you can get downtown take her to a hospital. The eye will need some work. I can't do it here but it doesn't matter. She's going to have pain."

He shook a dozen APC tablets into a small envelope. "You can give her *half* of one of these now. This is powerful pain medicine. She can have another half in four hours. Half a tablet every four hours. No more than that. Because this is a *powerful* drug. Her pain ought to be a lot better in a few minutes."

He could already feel the child responding to the magic of sympathetic suggestion.

"How do you feel?"

"I feels a whole lot better," she said.

"Your mama is going to take you home and give you some powerful pain medicine. I'm going to give you a shot now. Have you had shots before?"

"Yes, sir."

"This is to keep you from getting a bad infection. It will also make you feel better. Can you count to ten?"

"Yes, sir."

The child counted. He raised her knee, turned her quickly sideways, and slipping aside her panties gave her a shot of penicillin in the buttock.

". . . nine, ten," said the child. "I feels a whole lot better."

"Get her home. Keep her still," he said. "If you have trouble call me. If you can get her to the hospital get her there, of course."

"I believe we couldn't make it, now, doctor," said the mother. "I have other childrens. Some of them are out —"

"Get home with her," he said.

"What I owe you?" said the woman.

"Just take her home."

"Thank you, doctor."

He crossed the hall and treated a woman with a gunshot wound. The slug had passed downward from behind, had missed the bone, and was lodged just beneath the skin to the left of her knee. He sliced quickly through to the coppered slug, a .32 caliber, and removed it with forceps. He gave her a shot of penicillin and dropped the disposable syringe in the waste can. His wife bandaged the leg.

"Can I have it?" the patient asked, eyeing the slug.

"Sure," the doctor replied. "Hold out your hand."

"I was thinking maybe they would need it as evidence?" she said, rolling the bit of metal in her hand.

"No," he said. "How did it happen?"

"She had went acrost the street and got a teevee out the store where the glass was busted. I tole her not to go," said the man with her. He was a big fellow with a touch of gray at the temples. "She got what she went for when she stepped out the door to steal," he said. "She come halfway acrost and it was lack she sorta stumbled and somebody else they snatched and grabbed the teevee away from her and she went down on her knees and I tole myself the next sheen come going hit her sure. So I run out and I got her back to the house and it was right then the first I knew she was shot. Somebody needs to whup her for crossing that street the first time."

"*She-it*," said the woman. She stuck her tongue out. Her man picked her up and shouldered his way into the hall with her.

"Boy thirteen. Broken leg," said the doctor's wife. "Simple fracture. The cast room?"

"All right," said the doctor. He was working automatically now. "How is Elizabeth Anne?"

"She's helping up front."

"Send her home. Can't you follow instructions?"

"George, these are her people too. She's helping."

"I don't want her hurt. I don't want her killed. What if it moves this way?"

The boy in the cast room was sobbing. "Crying won't help," the doctor said.

"I hurt," the boy said.

"How did you do this?"

"Somebody throwed a cinder block. From up high on a building."

"Why were you in the street?"

"They all in the street. Everybody in the street. The cops killed Hatcher. He was good. Hatcher was a buddy to everybody that knew him and, the cops, they cut him down in the street like a dog. Hatcher was kind to everybody. Everybody went in the street because of they memory of how good he was."

"That won't bring him back. It won't unbreak your leg," said the doctor.

"You just can't understand! You too old to dig it what I am driving at," the child said. "I don't mind this leg!"

He was feeling braver. "When this leg get all right I'll go back in the street again. Freedom *now*. Maybe you don't dig what I'm saying."

"Shut up," the doctor said.

"Maybe you don't —"

"I said shut up."

The boy lapsed into silence. The doctor applied the cast. "You'll lie right here. Later we'll get an x-ray. Meanwhile you'll lie here until we can move you. Are you hurting much?"

The boy shook his head. He closed his eyes. Tears welled from beneath his delicate lashes. "If you start hurting we can give you some medicine. All right?"

"Uncle Tom!" the boy hissed, his teeth clenched, his hands pressed stiffly at his sides. "Uncle Tom!"

The doctor's wife drew him away. Still the doctor heard the Parthian shot: "Motherfucken Uncle Tom!"

The cry, thought the doctor, of marginal man. Drifting, self-reared and self-instructed; self-decimated. He sees the enemy in every face, the man to whom every face is alien, even (perhaps especially) his very own.

Given time he could have told the boy a few things, the doctor thought, feeling a strange separation between himself and what was happening.

He saw himself as he had been in World War II, as a young man wearing captain's bars, an officer in the medical corps. He was given a few days' leave before he told his wife goodby and kissed his infant daughter. It was the last time he would see his father alive.

Then he was crossing the continent on the train, ordered to the Pacific theater of operation. He had found himself pretty well famished by the time the train stopped for a brief layover in Abilene, Texas.

Dismounting from the train as rapidly as he could the doctor had rushed into the Abilene terminal dining room only to be told that Negroes were not served.

"You might have time, I don't know," said the counterman. He was an older man, blue-eyed, leathery-faced. "There's a nigra restaurant — or maybe you'd call it a cafe. Anyhow if you could grab a taxi you might just make it there and git some grub before she pulls out," said he, nodding towards the train.

Out the doctor raced. He stepped into a cab, explained the situation, and was rattled across town to the fly-ridden nigger diner. There he gulped down a grease-drenched plate of "soul food." Greens, potatoes, pork chops, corn bread, stale coffee — back then into the waiting cab for the return trip to the terminal with the rancid taste of the squalid, run-down cafe lingering against his tongue like strange smoke.

He was in plenty of time. As it turned out the train was delayed. The cause of the delay, as it happened, was a contingent of German prisoners-of-war who, seated at the long counter of the terminal restaurant, were feasting.

It was a taste, a bitterness that he carried with him out of the Army and into private practice. It was a taste that returned to haunt him when Elizabeth Anne asked why she couldn't swing on the swings and slide down the slides in the city parks of Ormund City. *Given time he could tell these marginal men a few things . . .*

"Like those other children, Daddy?"

He always replied gruffly. "You just can't because we don't

have time." Then he lived with the look of reproach in the eyes of his own flesh from the third through the tenth year of her life.

When she was ten years old she came into the clinic in tears. A man had called her a nigger, a white man. He had told her she could not sit on the public bench while waiting for the bus. "Why, Daddy?"

He had to tell her then and again when she asked him why he could never exceed the speed limit when called out on emergencies. "Other doctors drive fast. All the other doctors drive fast to save lives."

The doctor: "Yes, but I am a Negro. The police might not understand my violation as well as they would understand the violation of a white physician. There's a difference."

Elizabeth Anne: "It's not right. It is not fair."

The doctor: "What is right and what is fair sometimes has nothing to do with what *is* and *is* will very often in your life be the word you must come to terms with if you expect to live and do well in this country."

She had nodded thoughtfully.

Now she was questioning him again.

"Are the hospitals sending us any help, Daddy?"

He looked at her, his flesh, a mature woman.

"Stop a moment, please? Drink this?" she was saying. "I made it."

He took the cup of coffee.

"Change your coat," she said. "Look at you all sweaty and bloody."

She drew him into the private office and pulled off the soiled smock, the drenched undershirt. She wet a cloth and wiped his face and his arms. She moved the cloth across his chest and handed him a fresh undershirt, a clean smock. "Drink your coffee," she said.

He swallowed a fifteen milligram dextro-amphetamine-sulphate spansule with his coffee, looked briefly at his watch, and calculated the timespan of his awareness. He would be good now until three A.M. or thereabouts, tomorrow, Monday morning, by which time he could risk another spansule and work straight through, if need be. Food was out of the question for him. There was no time to be spared.

He finally spoke to the chief resident at Ormund City General. The phones were giving trouble. The white man's voice, young and vibrant though it was, seemed to be spanning an enormous distance. It was as though the barrier were one of miles and centuries instead of mere minutes and city blocks. A phone never before had felt so strange to the doctor's hands. "I need help down here," he kept saying and all the while he was aware that in the mere telling, the mere pleading, time and blood and agony were being spilled in the corridors outside, just beyond the strangely still dignity of this sedately paneled office where he stood quietly talking, quietly pleading.

"We're covered up down here," the resident was saying. "I don't think there's a chance, doctor. Reports from the drivers indicate something worse than mere physical danger down there. The mob situation is apparently pathological and a white face, physician or otherwise —"

"I'm going to lose some people if I can't get them to you or get your help. I'm almost out of Novocain."

There was a pause, the more agonizing because children were crying and a woman shrieking, shrill with hysteria. Someone pounded on the office door, went away, returned, pounded again. "George!" The doctor's wife. "Daddy!" His daughter.

"We might help you there," the chief resident was saying. "Now just where are you located? Some of the Blue Tops have been having better luck. Negro drivers seem to stand a better chance. We put a Filipino intern on one of the wagons. Novocain? That address?"

The doctor gave the address. "I've already set one leg. I don't know how many more fractures I have. I could use some surgical plaster if you can spare it."

"Right away. I'll run right down to central supply. What else?"

"Gauze, sponges, disposable penicillin, suture thread —"

"I get the picture," said the other voice, eons distant, light years away. "I'll grab as much junk as possible. We'll hustle it out and hope for a cab. They come through sporadically. I can't promise you just when. Let me read this address back."

The doctor listened. "That's correct," he said. The pounding on the office door began again. A siren screamed in the street.

"You must be right in the heart of it."

"I am," said the doctor. Then he hung up, unlocked the door, and stepped into the corridor there to be greeted by the first of the burn victims, a senile woman, near to eighty as best he could judge. There was no time to find out her age, no opportunity to know her name. Ten minutes later she died on the treatment table. "Where?" his wife said, making a gesture.

"In the back room. No relatives?"

"None so far."

"Put her in the back room. Tell Father Ned."

"How did it happen?" the doctor asked.

[*226*]

"A dry cleaner's was fire-bombed. The fire moved to her rooming house," said his wife. "We're out of linens."

"Send Elizabeth Anne for our own."

"I have," she said.

"Try the hospital again. I forgot to mention linens," the doctor said. "If you can get them also see about something for burns."

Father Ned appeared. "Dead?" the priest asked.

The doctor nodded. "For the time being let's use the very back room."

"Yes," the priest replied. He lifted the worn body tenderly in his short, sturdy arms. A cry arose in the hallway. "They shooten! They gone kill us all!"

The next case was also a burn. A child. Then a man. Another child. An old woman. Then a sixteen-year-old girl with head wounds, gunshot.

"The circuits are all busy," said his wife. "Nothing works. I can't get the operator."

"Nevermind," said the doctor. "It probably doesn't matter anyhow."

"This one?"

"Dying," said the doctor. "Move her into the hallway. Ask Father Ned if he can find out who she is."

The doctor moved as though stepping into a dream, doing right and left those things he would never have dared attempt in the years of a lifetime's normal practice. It came to him from time to time as the minutes fled beneath his methodical fingers, as his back began to ache and his own perspiration time and again, stung into his eyes, almost blinding him, it came to him that should these people, his own people, any of them, decide afterwards to sue for malpractice, they could very probably take away from him everything he had earned and accumulated, everything he ever would earn in the future. Doing right and left those things the general practitioner should never dare, he thought grimly. Those things the general practitioner should never be called upon to do, he thought, in the dreamlike quiet, in the deathlike, twilight solitude and silence into which his consciousness, by the urge, dent and burden of sheer concentration, had eventually been pushed.

Motherfucken Uncle Tom. Even when the younger ones did not say it, he saw it. If they said it, he did not hear it or mind it. My people, he thought. The idea sickened him a little.

"Has it moved this way?" he asked once.

"It has come this way twice and has passed on," said the priest. "My own house has burned," he said.

"I'm very, very sorry," the doctor replied.

"The girl? The head wound?"

"She just passed," said the priest. "We moved her to the back room."

"Someone please clean the floor," the doctor said absently. "Don't let the treatment room floors get slick. I don't want to lose my footing. Please get me a change of shoes next door. Please keep the floors wiped!"

It was as though no one had noticed the blood before. Elizabeth Anne went on her knees, wiping the floors in the treatment rooms. An explosion boomed across the street.

"They got the paint store," said a voice. "That's one mother that is gonna burn-lawd-burn!"

"I believe it *is* going to come back this way. I believe it is coming," said the priest.

"Perhaps they realize we're a hospital," the doctor said absently. "Can you try to move some of the walking ones down to the church? They can't stay here if they can walk."

My home, my family, my clinic, my practice and I built it all for this, he thought. Christ have mercy. For this.

21

THE CONSUL

THE smell of smoke; the faint sound of fire sirens. He's drunk and he's run over a fire hydrant with an automobile and he looks to be about seven feet tall. All the English he pretends to know is something like "Me, Stavanger," pointing to that chest of his.

I'm trying to explain to the desk sergeant that Herr Lid —

The sergeant can't get "Leed" out of "Lid," in the first place and in the second place he realizes that it's a toss-up who's had the most sauce tonight, me or this Norwegian kid, and he keeps saying it like *lid*, stove lid or eyelid. Meanwhile, Ormund City is burning around our ears.

The station might be next. The poor cop has a drunk Norwegian sailor and the well-boozed Norwegian consul — me — and the wrecked car. Meanwhile the dispatch radio behind him keeps calling in one more fire, one more shooting, one more beating, one more looting, one more stoning, one mob breakout after another. Outside parked like a free exhibit from the last nine world wars is the mighty Riot Wagon, a $50,000 armored cross between what the Wells Fargo daddies push when they tranfer money between banks and what Jack

Frankenstein would want if he went up against George Wolf Man again.

The reason I know what "the thing" is happens to be because before we ever had this cotton-picking riot, the city fathers bought it and said aloud of it and in the local newspapers and on television that since we now own one of these, folks in and around Ormund City can forget riots. Well, there it sits. From time to time we look at it.

A big gray bitch with special lights, it can spray chemicals and it has gun ports and a loudspeaker and probably a toilet and a coffeemaker and hammocks for the crew. No crew around, however. There she sits.

Trouble is it has dawned on the cop here and the chief of police downtown and our mayor, Paco Perrone, and others, that riots and rioters, or *this* riot and *these* rioters anyway, don't follow the *rules*.

They don't stay put all in one place like well-mannered citrus trees so all you have to do is drive up in the tank and spray them with tear gas or vomit gas or Mace or one of the better, more sophisticated mob pacifiers — because this is Florida, folks, where up till tonight all your problems could be *controlled* anyhow — if not indeed solved — if some university ag prof could just find the right machine? The right bug spray?

It is suddenly dawning on Ormund City like dynamite's grandmaw — that any halfwit nigger with an $88 automobile, 10¢ worth of sulphur, and an 80¢ can of gasoline (the pop bottles are free) can make enough Molotov cocktails to burn down any building in Ormund City — any place, any time he chooses.

You want to spray him out of the notion? Why then all you

do is decide which one he is, then catch him, bring him down here handcuffed, stand him up in front of this $50,000 bitch and *spray* him. Simple as pie. Then watch him vomit. Everybody has their en-joys.

It was dawning on us. An armored spray truck — riot wagon — with a top speed of twenty-five miles-an-hour may be all right if you have standard garden variety rioters that grow on trees in stationary citrus groves, which as I say Florida *ought* to have because this other kind of rioter comes under the category of hitting below our orange juice belt. If a Floridian can't catch it and can't spray it and it won't stand still to be picked like a grapefruit, well?

"Me — Stavanger."

"What's he mean by that? He musta said that ten thousand damn times."

"That's the sardine capital," I explain. "Stavanger, Norway."

"Oh — but his name's *lid*. Do you speak his language?"

"Me? I'm just the Norwegian consul. Actually I'm —"

"Now your — ah, your name is?"

It keeps our cop busy trying to listen to the radio to words like "*Ormund City General, cut up pretty bad.*"

"*Somebody throwed lye from the top of that Jew store over on Magnolia? Yeah. He must of been looking up 'cause it hit Parker square in the eye so I'm takin Dan Edward to Ormund City General. Yeah — they got about ninety-five admissions over there in the emergency room already. It was a nigger, throwed the lye, that's right. Lye — you know — like they used to make soap with? Back in them good old days?*"

And: "*Good Christ — they're gonna burn it all down! That's Bug-Eye Joe's Liquor over next to Oregon? They took all the*"

*booze so now they done set the torch to the building. Yeah —
I'm sure. It's called Bug-Eye Joe's. I believe he's a white man
all right but his real name probably ain't Joe. Naw, wait a
minute. He's eyetalian, correction. He ain't a white man.*

"*I said he's eye-talian. Well — I imagine he would appreciate a phone call to be informed that what used to be his place of
business is about to have a new address. Tell him it is as of just
now located on charcoal alley . . .*"

The desk sergeant looks at me. He has Lid's seaman's papers
and passport spread out in front of him like perhaps he plans
to eat 'em if he can just figure where to begin.

"Me — Stavanger!"

"Okay. And now that we all know 'you Stavanger' how about
keeping your mouth shut for five minutes? I don't know," the
desk man says. "This here is so irregular."

"I was going to say my name is Allen Sappington." I put
out my hand to him. He shakes reluctantly, like a man who
suspects he may be committing himself in advance to a bargain
he knows nothing about. Anyhow we get past the handshake. "I
realize this must be a bad time for you," I am telling him.

"Well, get a hydrant busted and we are already low on water
trying to fight a hunerd and umteen fires. Now of course I
realize he is foreign to this country but tell me how they ever
give him a car in the first place when he can't even say '*pig*' in
the American language?"

"He probably has a Norwegian driver's license. Yes —" I
find it in the pile of things on the desk. "This probably entitles
him to drive a car. It's an international driver's license."

The cop nods, confused. He looks up at me. "The name they
gave me was a Mister Wade and you say you're —?"

"Wade was my wife's uncle. He died about three months ago. Wade, of Wade Shipping Company."

"Down at the docks."

"Wade Shipping Company, down at the docks."

"But you ain't Mister Wade. And that's the name they give me downtown."

"No — I'm Allen Sappington —" The radio butts in:

"Corner of Oregon and Central — ah — we got four suspects. All handcuffed. Kneeling facing the wall. Three barefooted. One wearing shoes. Hell — I can't stay here all night. The next bastard around the corner might be a mob. Maybe they think this is back in Africa or something. I don't know where they think they are but if somebody would get over here and get these four and butter 'em while they're hot? No, by God we have not laid a stick on them. Well, somebody has to book 'em I know that but if you can get these — because they're busting out winders about two blocks up — looters, I think —"

"Now let's see here," he says. "Who are you?" He looks dazed.

"Allen Sappington. Let me explain."

"Actually they tole us not to speak the word riot on the radio. The correct technical term for it is 'crowd control,' and they have all been tole to call it that if it ever came to this to call it a crowd control problem. I'm the only man here, completely alone, and they might want that riot wagon out there or they might want to burn down this station, the niggers might. So I can't exactly guarantee your safety or his either because we have a crowd control problem on our hands. Now you're Mister Wade's *uncle?* Is that right?"

"Look," I says. "Wade died three months ago and they appointed me Norwegian consul in his place. We have about twenty-five ships a year from Norway. Back when this was a pitch pine port they might have two hundred out there in the bay all at once. Sailing ships. Lately business has dropped off."

"Twenty-five a year," he says. "I didn't know that."

"The point is that the consul for Ormund City doesn't have a whole lot of business to tend to — maybe fifteen cases a year. Or less."

"So you're the new man — the console."

"That's right. I'm Allen Sappington and my father-in-law is George Wade and I'm vice president of the Wade Shipping Company."

"Oh — I get it. Because you married his daughter."

He is no stranger to nepotism, give him that. *That* he understands.

"I see what you mean now," he says, nodding, lighting up. "So you're actually the consoler and not Mister Wade."

"That's right. Mister Wade is in heaven. He's been up there for three months which partially accounts for the reason you couldn't reach him."

"Nobody tole us that down here," he says, miserable again.

"Well, this is sometimes, if not always, how the police department of Ormund City finds out things," I say.

"Well, I have to explain to you that I'm what you might call kinda new on this job myself? Just learning. Trying to feel my way in and along? Now so you're the consoler. What's next?"

"You must turn Leed here over to me."

"Just like that?"

"Me —? Stavanger!"

"I must give you a written receipt for him."

"Well if this ain't the God damndest mess," he says sadly.

[*235*]

"You know he couldn't of busted a fireplug at a worse moment than what he done — did? And drunk as he is — was — how do I know can you *handle* him?"

"*Station Four? Albert? Station Four?*"

"Yeah, okay."

"*Is that you, Albert?*"

"This is me. Over."

"*Is — do you have the riot wagon?*"

"Ah — well, it's here. It's parked right outside where the somebitch always usually stays at —"

"*I mean can you see it?*"

"Well if you'll wait a minute I'll look. Over."

"*Okay — go look. Because — ah — the mayor's here. And there is a rumor besides that the crowd control vehicle has been stolen by the other side and the mayor is slightly out of his mind that if it's — the mayor says if the rumor is right we would need at least an anti-tank gun. So check and — ah — take a look and see if the riot wag — I mean the crowd control vehicle is — if it's still there. Over?*"

"I'll see."

Albert walks to the window and looks. He walks back to the desk and sits down. He reaches for the radio. "It's here."

"Check again. Take a double check? Over."

He looks at me. "Ain't that the riot wagon?"

"Beyond a doubt."

"I just looked twice and I have a witness here, Mister Wade. Over."

"Who?"

"Mister Wade Shipping Company here about that fireplug sailor. The Norwegian consoler. Over."

"*Hold on — over.*"

"I don't aim to go nowhere. Over. Hell." He sighs. "Wisht I was home."

"The riot — ah the crowd control vehicle is definitely there?"

"Well, me and this sailor and Mister Wade, the Norwegian consoler can *all* see it."

"Hold on — ah — so the vehicle is there. And you're Albert at Station Four?"

"Yes, sir, by God. I am."

"Ah — the mayor says — ah — somebody just checked. What's the sailor say his name is?"

"I couldn't pronounce it, for God sake. I can spell it. Claims by his papers to be G-u-d-l-i-e-v L-i-d. Godlive Lid is about all I can get out of it. Godlive is slightly drunk, or tipsy. You know — he's that *fireplug* sailor? Over."

"Hold — ah — the mayor, somebody says that consul, old Mister Wade. Is the consul what you might say a very much older looking — an old man?"

"No. Over."

"Because the information we have here is that one died about — ah — sometime back the mayor says. So anybody else would have to be an imposter if he was claiming he was Wade."

"Sappington," I say. "Allen Sappington."

"I mean Sappington, that's what I mean," says our policeman.

"Are you Station Four?"

"Yes — this here is Albert."

"Well hold that Wade guy in custody — ah — because now there was two Wades and we just checked and the live one is home. We just phoned him. He's in bed watching teevee. And the one that was consul — ah — the mayor says he's dead."

[237]

"He's already explained he's Allen Sappington. The vice president of Wade Shipping Company that married the other one's daughter and he's the new thang-a-bob for this here fire-hydrant-sailor-problem."

"Tell Mayor Perrone I'm Allen Sappington," I say.

"He says tell —"

"*Hold.*"

"Me — Stavanger! Airmoon Seedy — um — Airmoon Seedy — boolshit!"

Which is, I would say, par for the course. Gudliev is getting a little fed up, what with the sirens and the smoke and such. Just another Sunday outing in good old chicken plucken, grapefruit picken, nigger rioten Airmoon Seedy. Only instead of hearing the darkies singing by the moonlight Gudliev is caught in a crowd control exercise. I keep wondering if he has any idea how restless the natives of Airmoon Seedy are. Besides that, what will he tell the folks back home in Stavanger? Putting a hand on his arm, I shake my head. He looks at me. The gaze of an ox somebody just slapped between the ears with a five-pound sledgehammer. "Ja," he says. "Ja."

The radio spits out a warning roar.

"*Station Four? Albert? Check Mister Sappington's identification — ah — this rumor we got was pretty strong that the crowd problem vehicle was, that the niggers had — has he got a driver's license?*"

I take out my billfold and hand our policeman my driver's license.

"Yeah — he's Allen Sappington, okay. He's twenty —"

"*Over, Four. Albert?*"

"Yeah, this is me. Over. He's twenty-eight years old."

"*The mayor would like — ah — the mayor would like to*

speak to Mister Sappington. Okay, Mister Mayor. Just talk right in here. Press the button."

"Sappington, this is the mayor, Sam Perrone, can you hear me?"

"Tell him I can hear him," I say.

"He can hear you, Mayor."

"I ah — you understand that we are having some crowd control problems —"

No sooner said than something explodes two doors up the street. I miss the rest of Mayor Perrone's message. The cop and Gudliev and I suddenly find ourselves looking out the window. Flames shoot out of a building three doors up. An automobile — maybe eighty bucks worth — scratches off. It comes zooming down Flagler, right in front of the station, fox tails flying.

"That's the sign painters," our policeman says. "They give it a cocktail didn't they? It's gallons and gallons of paint stored inside over there."

As he says this something else explodes. A roaring ball of yellow fire boils out of the place. "Vel, vel," says Gudliev. "Vel, vel!" He takes out a Pall Mall and a windproof lighter, and, as though reminded of something, he lights his weed.

"Mister Sappington? Four — station Four do you read me? Over? Over?"

The sergeant walks back to his desk and sits down.

"Excuse the interruption but that sign painting place two or three doors up? Well it's a total. I mean a complete total. It just taken a cocktail."

"Another fire — mark it on the map, Frank. Two doors from Station Four. No — we can't risk a firetruck! Just stick a pin there! Mister Sappington. He still there?"

"Yessir. He's still here and so is the fireplug sailor. By the way Mister Mayor Perrone if I could just ask you something along that line —"

"*Over God damn it let me talk to Mister Sappington? As the Norwegian consul after all and I think the world of your daddy-in-law and Wade Shipping Company and since you are in a way as it were a city official — can he hear me?*"

"It would be a lot simpler if he would call me on the phone," I say.

"He can hear you but he said why not phone him?"

"*God damn it please — just listen? My point is that Allen this crowd control thing is getting serious and we've got a report that they are going to burn that station you're in now so of course we can't pull Albert out of there since he will have to stay at the radio and do what he can from there, if they decide to burn it, but we feel you ought to come on out, you and the sailor, whatever he is, the both of you. So feel free to leave — ah — but the other thing is that we need the crowd control vehicle? Over here at downtown station in city hall? You know where that is? And — ah — I want to ask you, Allen, if you, as a private citizen, if you possibly think you could drive it over this way for us if it wouldn't be too much trouble? We need that vehicle to get me to a certain place where we hope I will be able to meet with other certain leaders on the other side to see what can be done? Have I met you somewhere? Have you military experience?*"

"Tell him we are both in Rotary," I say. "And I was a naval officer."

Now's the time to tell the Lord Mayor Paco Perrone *adios*, to grab Stavanger and haul ass — for the *hill*, as I believe there is or was one hill in Florida maybe 360 feet high.

"*Over?*"

"Excuse me?" I reach for the mike. The cop lets me have his chair.

"Not a-tall," says our friendly policeman, as he gets up and politely moves. "Want a Coca-Cola?"

"Not now, thanks," I say. I sit down. The radio has said *over* about seventeen times, meanwhile.

"Okay," I say. "This is Allen Sappington. I was a Navy officer. If you're commandeering me to drive that tank maybe you better code name me. How about Red Rover or something? Over?"

"*If you would just go outside and get in it —*"

"Can I bring along my ward? Because the only problem I have besides how to keep myself from getting barbecued on the hoof, besides also getting my wife's new automobile burned up, and so forth, is this seven-hundred-pound Norwegian. As consul I happen to be responsible for him and he looks like he really needs a drink. I think he is low on gas. So with your permission, Paco, maybe we could stop off at a liquor store? There are lots of them open — I mean wide open, windows and all — or on fire and I for one hate to see nine hundred thousand dollars worth of perfectly good booze go up in flames if there is any alternative."

"*Uh — well — since you're the consul — ah — Allen — it's okay to bring along anybody only it is pretty God damned important that you get on over here with that riot — ah — that crowd control. Yeah, good idea. Now on you're 'Red Rover.' Okay? Over?*"

"All right. Fine. Over."

"*You coming, Red Rover?*"

"Yeah, Red Rover and Stavanger will leave just as soon as I write your desk man a receipt for Stavanger. Over."

"*Red Rover, as mayor I want you to know I appreciate the example of leadership and citizenship that you are setting. Just come on with it please. Drives like an ordinary truck. Can you drive a truck?*"

"Be right there," I say. I stand up, ready to leave. The desk man sits back down.

"Thanks," says he. "You taken the riot wagon?"

"Yeah. Looks like I'm stuck. They volunteered me."

"That's too bad," says our policeman. Obviously he hates to see the last of us. "I shore as hell wouldn't wanna have to cross town in it myself. Not tonight. One cocktail and —" He made a perfect imitation of what it would be like, with his hands and mouth. A regular fish fry.

"Thanks for the encouragement," I say.

"Yours," he says. "Keys are in it, I think. Gas tank's supposed to be full. It holds fifty-one gallons."

"*Station Four, has Red Rover left? Over.*"

"Red *who?*"

"*Is this you Albert? Over?*"

"It is. Yessir."

"*Has Red Rover —*"

"They mean me," I says. "Red Rover, that's my new name."

"Ohhhhh. Yeah, Chief. He's just a-leaving. The consoler's wrote me a receipt for Lid on that fireplug-sailor-deal, that thang-a-bob and he's leavin right now."

"Come on Popeye," I say. I motion to Lid. We go out into the lot where the wagon is. I get in and he gets in and of course there is no earthly way to tell what switch to grab first.

I can't find the ignition. Then I can't find the starter. But finally I get it put together, ignition and starter. Then I can't find the headlights. When I am just about to give up the whole peanut jar, having sprayed vomit gas and honked the horn and blown the siren — things nobody dare do if he expects to sneak across town quietly and alive, I *find* the goddamn lights. They could light up the entire city. Visible all the way to Cuba. They are that bright. I slip her into gear and off we trundle, out of the lot and into the street and past the burning sign painter's shop. The fire gives a little burp as we pass, a pyrotechnic or volcanic hello from paintland, so I yank the siren a good one, in salute. Then we get the radio going. Gudliev does — which is a clue that maybe he is good for something after all. My first clue. He turns it on and hands me the mike.

"This is Red Rover," I say. "We're headed up through Central. Over."

"*Good luck, Red!*" It is our cop back at the desk. Station Four.

About then comes a shower of rocks. I shift into second and find third and after giving her everything she has I discover by the speedometer that nineteen m.p.h. is top speed.

Maybe we go four more blocks when our lights suddenly pick up a car stopped where a spur track crosses Central. All around it like maggots is a mob — more niggers than you can imagine could gather all in one place and the car is the center of attraction. They are smashing it.

When we get closer my impulse is to show good sense and drive around it but curiosity somehow beats better judgment to the draw. I stop like a fool, slide open the window, and yell to a guy on the ground.

"What is it?"

"Sah?"

"That car. What's happening?"

"Wellum. I hear tells dey got two white peoples? Dey cotch a couple of 'em. Man and a woman?"

"So what's happening?"

"Wellum. Dey say dey beatin on him trying to kill him and dey, well, dey you know fixin to — er, rah — you know, dat's what some of 'em say. I ain't went clost enough yet to be fer sarten what dey really is doin but I hear her hollerin. Listen right close you kin hear her maken dem wile screams? He must of put up a pretty good fight, what dey say, but dey got him down. You de po-lice or de garbage pickup or what you is?"

"Mostly," I says.

"Somebody don't do somethin dey show gonna be *two* dead white peoples, mister. What dey saying."

What happens then happens in my stomach. I cut the engine. Nobody seems to notice. I cut the lights. I hear her scream again. Stavanger hears it too. I open my door and get out. He comes out after me. We walk. I hear myself shouting: "Let's save them! Let's have help here! Move aside there!" My legs are shaking, my mouth is shaking. The woman screams again and with that Stavanger takes off like a scalded dog and it comes to me that as long as the two of us stay together I might have a Chinaman's chance but without Lid I'm a dead duck so I take off, following him straight through the mob. Meanwhile he's roaring bloody murder. He is bull-roaring mad and just as we reach the automobile the crowd parts, like dark water.

Stavanger wades in and I can glimpse him under the street lights, arms like pistons, feet just as busy. He is kicking, punching and yelling, bawling like an ox. Then the white man, the first victim is picked up. Stavanger and a couple of darktown citizens bring him to me and we stand holding the bloody, hard-muscled victim like frozen idiots while Stavanger dives over the top of the car. Christ, he doesn't think about going around it. He dives and scrambles over it. The others, onlookers passive till now, suddenly stir; they wade in too. It is all over in a minute. We have the guy, we have the gal. Her clothes are in rags and she's screaming, hoarse and raped. Stavanger picks up the girl like a loaf of bread. He runs like hell for the wagon. A big black buck helps me drag the guy. We get to the wagon.

"Anybody wants a ride can have one," I say.

The big nigger declines the offer. I start the wagon and we pull slowly past the car. The doors are open and the windshield is broken completely out. Some bright little bastard is busily trying to set the gas tank on fire.

Meanwhile the chief and the mayor keep hollering for Red Rover. Finally I shut the son of a bitch off and we pass on out of Central and hit the boulevard. Here by the river the smell of smoke and the sound of sirens lies far, far behind. I cross traffic and make it to the bridge and across then to the island at a steady, exhilarating nineteen miles an hour. The gal is weeping.

Up we pull to the emergency entrance. The interns must decide we *are* a garbage truck. They keep hollering and trying to wave us back, but I shut the engine. We take the man out first and then the girl. She is a real looker. A young, beautiful, half-naked brunette.

"Were you raped?" the intern says.

"Yes," she says. "But don't bother with me. Rann's got glass in his eyes."

"She was raped," says the intern.

"I can walk," she is saying. But down she goes, on a stretcher.

We enter the hospital with them; Stavanger and myself.

"You relatives?" a nurse asks.

"No," I say.

"Then you'll have to —"

"I'm just leaving," I say.

"Would you please move that thing? What is it?" says an intern.

"It's a crowd control vehicle," I say. "It races down the road at nineteen miles an hour, it cost Ormund City $50,000, and the gas tank holds fifty-one gallons."

"Then you came *through* the riot? The girl and the fellow, were they caught in it?"

"Yes," I says.

"Jesus," he says. "Man, are we having a night!"

"Anybody killed?"

"Two fatalities here so far. How many elsewhere I don't know. First one was much earlier. He was one the police nailed. Most of the time if we get them alive we can keep them alive. It would amaze you how far medicine has come. And now, if you don't mind moving that *thing*. The big guy — is he German? He's bloodied up pretty bad. Want we should bandage him a little? Looks like he's been fighting a brick wall."

"Well, you know Germans," I say.

Looking at Stavanger I see for the first time how badly he's beat up. I see how much it cost him to wade into them the way he did. As for me I'm only short a button or two.

"Maybe we better admit him and stitch him up a little bit," says the intern.

"Might as well," I hear myself saying. "He's a sailor and will need to be returned to his ship. These are his papers." I hand Lid's papers to the intern.

"Fine," says the intern. "Germans are something, aren't they? He saved the gal?"

I nod. "The man, is he —"

"I believe he's all right. He only *looks* bad. If you'll just move your bus now I believe we have another ambulance."

I go outside and climb into the wagon and start it. My hands are sticky. Finally I get a cigarette lit. I try to smoke it. Blood is drying on the steering wheel. It comes to me that maybe anytime you have just one fool to holler "Let's go!" there will be other fools who will follow, who will even pass the first one sometimes, and take the lead.

I back the wagon up to let a Blue Top cab and an ambulance move in to the emergency entrance. Doors open, stretchers are brought. People, black and white alike, lie down on the stretchers. There is a fireman and a policeman. The fireman can walk. The policeman goes in on a stretcher. I see blood on his face.

From behind the Blue Top comes a man with pencil and pad in hand. I'm just thinking he must be a reporter. He heads straight for me. I open the door.

"This the riot wagon?"

"Crowd control," I correct him.

"Seen any action?"

"Cruises at nineteen miles per hour. Cost fifty gees, and is useless."

"What's your name, sir?"

"I don't want my name in the paper," I tell him. "Since I work for the city. Might knock me out of a job."

"I dig," says the kid.

"If they sold this wagon — where would I get a job?"

"Oh well — we're not interested in this story anyhow. The

downtown brass is not anxious to portray Ormund City as a place where people riot in the streets. I'm mainly keeping tab on the emergency room. I have to figure some way to keep my reported number of casualties down to fifty. They want a fifty-person limit."

"How do you plan to manage that?" I ask.

"Well, the intensive care room will only hold twenty-five but in an emergency like this they can rearrange things and get up to fifty under intensive care. In other words anybody likely to die. They can take fifty of those. People merely admitted or treated or released don't go on the intensive care list. Except for the white girl of course, and the white guy. He may be blinded. I'm waiting on him to see. That's the real story. Otherwise it will be just fifty injuries and maybe three to five fatalities, no more than that. Keeps the thing within reasonable bounds, you know? Also makes me want to vomit."

"How's that?" I say.

"Playing it down. Deliberately suppressing news. Like that handcuff shooting. I wrote that story. They wouldn't let me tie that in."

"I don't understand."

"Oh, well. It was just a back page story, a handcuff shooting a couple or maybe three weeks ago. Cop shot down a kid. Kid was a Negro and was handcuffed to another Negro suspect. Both kids jumped out of the patrol car enroute from one jail to another. So this cop, he draws his gun. He gets the Negroes cornered in a blind alley. He shoots this one kid in the belly. Kills him. Seventeen-year-old Negro."

"I didn't notice it in the paper," I say. "I didn't read about it."

"That and beating that Negro yesterday and killing the

Hatcher boy, that got this whole shebang started," says the reporter. "That plus rumors, some guy named Watridge all beat to hell, and *that* we can't print. So —" He shrugs.

"The police *are* the cause?"

"Mostly. That's right. But the cause goes back a hell of a long, long distance. Because, well it's the *memory* of Negroes who have lived in Central and the Woodyard for generations," the young reporter says. He shrugs again, and slowly walks away.

And I set off for police headquarters.

22

COUSIN ALABAM

Cynthia had an errand, she had said, and she had left Lake Maas early. Cutler had left soon after. "An appointment," he had explained.

The grocer had mentioned dinner. "Just the three of us," he had said.

"Let's see how my time works out," Cutler had said, in his usual guarded way.

The grocer had nodded and closed his eyes. A few minutes later he himself had decided to return to the city. He had strolled up the lakeside to his mobile home trailer. Members could have tents or house trailers or cottages on the grounds for a modest fee.

There the grocer had taken a shower, shaved, and put on fresh slacks and a sport shirt, all the while thinking of Cynthia and Rann. Cynthia had picked out the shirt for him, a sinuous pattern of greens, strange shades of blue with flecks of yellow on a dark background. The grocer could not be certain the shirt fitted his personality. He draped a white silk tie and a palm beach jacket over his arm, stepped outside into the sodden, bruising heat, and locked the house trailer. He got into his white Continental convertible.

Just outside the barrier gate he had turned on the radio breaking into the new, curious sort of interview just becoming popular in Ormund City. One reporter is at the scene. The announcer at the station is talking to the reporter by phone. The dialogue being broadcast is punctuated by curious "beeps" that let every listener know what the score is. The grocer had begun using the technique with some of Kutrate's radio advertising. The disc jockey would, for example, phone a housewife, apparently at random, and ask her which Kutrate specials or products most attracted or pleased her that day. The "housewife" was carefully coached in advance, of course. In fact she also worked at the radio station. Now, using the method which reminded the grocer of his own radio spots, the reporter was describing some sort of riot — a civil commotion. The announcer was saying that the wire services had reported that much the same thing was going on in Cincinnati today ". . . after late night clashes yesterday between police and Negroes," the announcer said.

The telephoning reporter, none too calm by contrast, was saying that what he deemed to be about five hundred Negroes, many of them teen-agers, were advancing on a line of about twenty riot-helmeted police. The police wore white helmets, said the reporter. They carried sidearms. They held M-1 carbines at the ready, with fixed bayonets. The police would advance in one direction, not far apparently from where the reporter was phoning, and the mob, which was divided in two segments, would instantly melt, racing pell-mell away from the officers while from behind the unfortunate police, poor devils, under strict orders not to shoot, received a hail of sticks, bottles, bricks, and other debris, even including lengths of iron pipe, said the reporter:

Ah — the situation for the police is kinda hopeless (beep).

They have the choice whether to fire or not and they don't (beep) want to use these weapons because so far they have (beep) orders not to. So the crowd surges back and forth here, always coming at them from behind and what these men can do besides either open fire or get the dickens out of here I don't know . . . (beep).

"And the cause of it," the calm announcer is saying, "is the slaying of a young Negro this afternoon, James Hatcher, by a rookie patrolman. Hatcher was a robbery suspect, wasn't he?"

Ken — ah — I think (beep) you have to say that's the excuse for what's going on down here. Dozens of rumors and fights plus the Hatcher shooting before so many witnesses certainly set it off (beep).

"Where did the shooting occur?"

In front of a sort of a cafe, Poor Boston's. The police (beep) had a call. They spotted Hatcher fleeing from the scene. When they finally stopped him (beep) to question him they reportedly found stolen merchandise on him, in his possession, and just then the suspect broke and ran. It was quite a chase. Finally (beep) they had to shoot or risk losing their prisoner. You can get quite a few different versions, but that's the word from the mayor's office and when Mayor Paco Perrone makes a statement based (beep) on this report from the detective squad you better believe it's the straight scoop . . . (beep) The police here, I think have almost decided to withdraw and perhaps cordon off this area. Quite a few plate glass (beep) windows down here on Central have been smashed. I'm going to

*hang up, Ken and see what the police have decided. I'll phone
you right back (beep).*

"That's Dero Whitson in the center of the disturbance.
We'll be hearing from Dero again shortly. What we have all
been saying couldn't happen in Ormund City has happened.
How about that? Motorists are requested, by the way, not to
venture into the Central and Woodyard districts. Please stay
away? All right? We're going to speak to: Mayor Perrone
again now in a few minutes. Meanwhile here's more music from
your Sun Coast City headquarters for music and news! Let's
hear Little Linda Lottie's 'Lemme Love Ya Baby?' Time: five
eleven in the afternoon. Temperature here in the Sun Coast
City, ninety-six . . . degrees!"

The music began to fade up. The grocer reached for the
switch. He silenced the radio. In his mind's eye, for the moment,
he could visualize nothing beyond the measure and location of
the Central Kutrate store.

Driving on homeward then, automatically, like a man in a
dream, stopping in the carport, and walking into the empty
kitchen, into the desolate loneliness of a house such as he had
never as a child or even as a young man expected to possess, his
tongue had slowly begun to feel large for his mouth. He had
thought first of taking a drink; then of not taking one. Of
turning on the television set on the kitchen counter, then of
leaving it off — as it was. Finally he had taken a glass from the
cabinet and drawn a little tapwater and rinsed his mouth.

Then reaching for the phone he made a quick succession of
calls to the mayor, the sheriff, the chief of police and finally,
the publisher of the *Ormund City Times*. There had been no
problem, for the time being, no problem getting through to
people. Yet the more he phoned and the more he talked the

deeper Alabam Webster had felt himself sinking, the more his spirit floundered, the more confused he became. He heard himself speaking to people who should have been able to help him. It was as though they replied in another tongue, a foreign language.

None had the faintest notion where the Central Kutrate was located. None knew if it were burning. The lone Negro watchman who slept in the store had strict orders never to answer a phone. He could call out but he could not be reached. There was no record at headquarters of his having called, so far.

No news, the grocer kept thinking. Might be good news. He said it several times. Each time the voice at the other end agreed with him. The other voice promised to be in touch with him right away if and when any news of the Central Kutrate's condition, danger or damage should be encountered.

The grocer finally abandoned the phone. He rinsed his mouth again, spat in the sink, and paced slowly back and forth over the yellow Spanish tiles in the kitchen. Lose the high markup store, the poor who paid more for their eats than the wiser, more mobile rich, lose Central, lose all, thought the grocer. *All* . . .

The phone rang. He hesitated, then answered it. It was the mayor. "Somebody threw a gasoline bomb," Paco Perrone was saying. "It hit your store's roof but there wasn't much damage. Somebody, we don't know who, because it wasn't any of our people. Somebody got up there and put it out. You must have friends down there," Paco said.

"I do," said the grocer. "Any windows broken? Any looting?"

"That I don't know. The one fire bomb. That's all we've heard. Excuse me." And the mayor was off the line.

"Perrone? Perrone?" When the grocer had put the phone

down he could not bring himself to turn on the radio. He went upstairs, however, and walked out to the bedroom balcony and gazed at the central city lying across the shimmering bay. He could hear sirens. His breath came a bit short. Finding it more and more difficult to breathe, he stepped back into the carpeted room and stretched full length on the bed. It came to him that he should try to call Cynthia. Then it came to him that she probably should not be called. Doubtless she was home and safe. Doubtless she or Rann or both of them would be phoning him shortly. Certainly they would realize how essential the preservation of the Central Kutrate was? Or would they?

Could they appreciate, really, the extremely delicate maneuver, the essential timing, the astute merchandising? Hell yes, hadn't he talked to both of them all about it? But would they instinctively know, for example, how important *Monday* was in the grocery business?

Could they have any idea what the cost could be if a truly mammoth store were forced to stay closed on a Monday? Worse still, the cost — he shuddered — were such a store to be looted and destroyed by fire?

Of course, he decided, they couldn't. They would be calling him any minute now about going to dinner and he would have to decline. A groan came out of him.

Now this, he thought. Now this, God help. He got up slowly, wearily. Then on a sudden impulse he knelt beside the bed, folded his knobby hands, and began to pray.

He paused.

"God if it be thy will I might — I will give up Lake Maas? I am praying, I am pleading in the name of Jesus Christ for everything I have slaved to build my whole life long that it shall not be destroyed? Amen."

Having finally proffered the ultimate sacrifice, prayer exhausted him.

Dazed, fearful, sick at heart, Alabam Webster stood up at long last. Lean and trembling, half blind without his glasses, reeling like a drunk, he gazed wildly about him. He found his glasses on the bed, picked them up and threw them down again. His throat was painfully raw. His armpits had begun stinging. He was sweating.

Stepping into the bathroom he again drew a glass of water. He managed a few swallows, each a painful effort, for the grocer's esophagus as had happened his whole life long in every time of crisis, was in painful spasm.

Suddenly then, the phone rang.

He answered it. "Hello —?"

"Purchase Walker speaking," said an odd but strangely familiar voice. "Mister Webster?"

"Yes."

"I understand you facing — *are* facing a little problem, that you got a little problem . . ."

23

THE PUBLISHER

Beneath his calm there ran a current of tension which had suddenly now in the course of a single Sunday afternoon knotted up, inflamed and come to a head, like a dreadful boil.

"Ask Dave to step in here a minute," he told his secretary, the woman who had worked for his father. His father had been called "the old man," or "the boss." He was "the kid."

Dave entered. "What now?"

"What we said on the editorial page and in the news sections last week — what we said couldn't happen here has happened."

"Do tell," Dave said. "The God damned city is about to be burned and bombed off the map — *is* being burned and bombed off in fact — and you want me to stand here and discuss last week's news for Christ's sake? Are you some kind of nut?"

"You can sit down," the publisher said.

Dave sat down. "That's what we said last week. Last week we were bragging. Up until today we had every reason to brag. Right up until the middle of this afternoon. I'm assuming you have something on your mind because whether you realize it or not I'm a very busy man. This is a very busy time."

"Dave, what's the lead editorial tomorrow morning?"

"I'll think of something," the editor said.

"There are some points I believe we should make. I've been thinking."

"Thank God somebody has. Shoot," said Dave.

The publisher frowned. He swung sideways in his swivel chair.

"The Negroes on the spot. Those who saw the shooting say it was unjustified. Now any killing of this kind has to be investigated, of course. But the first point I believe we have to make is this. How else can police fight increased crime if they are not permitted to use force in apprehending suspects who resist or flee?"

"Uh-huh," said Dave. "Shoot 'em dead and then bring 'em to trial. I already have scads of extraneous parallels. There was a pope, for example, Formosus by name. He bet on the wrong horse, so to speak, and after he was dead and buried his successor had him removed from the tomb and dressed in his papal robes and tried in a court of law. The prosecutor told Formosus to speak up if he was not guilty. When he didn't speak up they cut off the fingers he'd used to bless this and that and then threw his body into the Tiber. So what you suggest is not without legal precedent. How about an editorial on Formosus? How would that grab you, kid? 'The courts should bring James Hatcher to trial, says the *Ormund City Times*.'"

"Dave, *please?*"

"Uh-huh," said Dave. But now he was noncommital. "All right. Get on with it."

"Next we have to pinpoint the problem in community leadership. Why the breakdown in communications between the responsible Negro leaders and this lawless, younger element."

"They are not all that young, some of them," Dave said. "But go on."

"Point: Our colored residents are just as inconvenienced by this as the whites. Our colored population has been placed in more danger — far greater danger."

"Very good obvious point," said Dave.

"Now I think we have to boldface my *main* point. I want this one in boldface, Dave."

"You want it in the lead editorial, boldface. Okay, now what is it that's so important to you at this moment when we're trying to find out how many corpses there are thus far? While we're trying to get a body count? We also have two reporters in the hospital, in beds, besides one we sent there for the story. We may lose others."

"Dave —"

"Okay, kid. You're getting more and more like your old man. God damn it you're terrible."

"Dave, we have to say in boldface that after examining the facts, we — the *Ormund City Times* — are satisfied. The record shows that Ormund City is no worse than the average American city, and that racially it fares better than most."

"Yes," Dave said. "When you lie, it is always best to print it in boldface. Otherwise it might get overlooked. That's the worst possible fate for a lie. But we've got to say it. Otherwise we'd have to really *look* at the record. We'd have to report the son of a bitch in depth and really see how rotten we are. We'd have to face up to so much that it would be a question of whether this newspaper could survive it."

"That's not a fair statement," the publisher said, knowing that it was fair.

"Yeah, you're right. It isn't fair. Because it's getting so a true statement is no longer a fair statement. All over the God damned U.S.A. it's coming to that. Well, that's a *wonderful* excuse. We're no *worse* than the rest. In fact we get along with our niggers better than most. That's a beaut. You know I've lived a long time. I've grown up, I've been educated on newspapers. Newspapers have been my bread and meat since I landed my first paper route? That's too many years ago to think about — now especially. And you know something, kid? I really believe in the press. I really believe in freedom of the press. I'm giving my life for that belief, corny as it sounds. And *this* situation raises a pretty awful problem for me. The race war — and kid, it is a war, let's try to face it — *the race war* brings us face to face with the *responsibility* of the press. We have freedom. We also have a heavy responsibility."

"Yes, and as business organizations we're fighting for survival, don't forget," the publisher said. "Look at the big newspapers that have folded. Good newspapers."

"Yeah," said Dave. "And look at the little newspapers that are opening up shop every day and showing a profit because they know how to shut up and when to — oh, well. Hell with it."

"Dave, about the shooting? What do you think really happened?"

"You don't want to know, kid. You've seen the report from the detectives. You know we've toned down and smoothed up and ironed out what the Negro eyewitnesses say. I wish you could have talked to the dead boy's mother. I had that pleasure about five minutes ago."

"What was he like, really? Wasn't he a thug?"

"No," said Dave. "I don't believe he was. I think Hatcher ran because he was so afraid of being picked up and dragged downtown and fingerprinted, thereby shaming his family's good name and reputation. Because you see he really hadn't done a God damned thing but stop and attempt to help an old man with a broken head."

"He *hadn't* just committed a burglary?"

"Holy Christ," said Dave. "He was in church all morning with a girl he planned to marry! Guess how many witnesses saw him in church?"

"No police record?"

"The only record he had was for being a goòd guy who loved children, a guy who worked hard when he could get work, a guy who was down there in the middle of Central really trying." Dave shook his head. "If only he *had* been a hood!"

"Then you discount the detectives' report."

"The detectives report what the police tell them. No policeman, not even a rookie in Ormund City, is going to walk in and say he's sorry he made a mistake. He was hasty. He misjudged. It doesn't sound nice. It looks awful, and besides, it would only get him fired. It might also land him in jail. Worse still it would indicate that something is dreadfully sick about the entire department. the entire city, even this nation. We might have to admit to prejudice or fear. Or worse still, hysteria."

"You're right, Dave."

"Yes, God damn it, I am. And I would give the whole world to be wrong. I'm just grateful that you're not leaving it up to me, kid. Because it helps me to let you be the son of a bitch. To have you make the decisions, to have you forcing me to print a lie — in boldface. Then the matter's out of my hands. I can go home to my wife and kids and not sleep at night. I can blame you and the advertisers. I can sneak back in now and then and strike little blows for freedom behind your back On page seventeen."

The publisher sighed. "I've interrupted you long enough,"

he said. "The point is, to repeat, that the record will show that Ormund City is no worse than the average American city, and that in race relations it fares better than most."

"I'll get it in there, even if I have to make some other hapless, helpless bastard write it. I might have to get Charley to write it. I wouldn't like to puke right into that new typewriter we bought me."

"Thanks, Dave," said the publisher. "Thanks a million."

24

GUDLIEV

As he went back aboard ship the cargo handlers, all of them blacks, hardly noticed him. It seemed strange that they could be here working, shouting, laughing as usual. Yet here they were.

Going below, Gudliev walked lightly down the passageway to the little cabin he shared with Gunnar. His shipmate lay in the lower bunk. He was reading as usual. Gunnar was an old man, well entered upon his thirties. Gunnar's sap was down, as the saying is, so much so that he rarely ached and yearned for shore. He had children and a wife in Norway, besides. So his need and his desire was not nearly so much as Gudliev's.

"Well, well. I am back," Gudliev said. What a relief to find someone to speak to, how peaceful to be in the tiny cabin again, speaking his mother tongue.

Gunnar laid the book aside and sat up, swinging his legs down, touching his feet to the deck. Gunnar was lean and lithe and a good seaman. He hailed from Oslo. He spoke with a Danish brogue.

"So I see. The viking is back," said Gunnar. "From what others say returning to ship, there is trouble ashore."

"Aye," Gudliev replied. "Accurately told." He sat down in the gray steel chair beside the desk they used when writing letters home. He regarded the bandages on his hands.

"Has the viking burned his hands ashore?" Gunnar said.

"Nay," said Gudliev. "I was in fighting. Not very much of it, but enough. With fists and feet I fought and we were able to save two of them. Otherwise those would have found their death I believe."

"Fighting ashore. In a strange nation, Gudliev? That could be serious."

"I was in trouble with the police," Gudliev said casually. "But they brought me back here, as you see."

"You saved two of them? How many are dying?"

"I think none, or few. I don't know. So much was said. There was so much coming and going and waiting. It was a nice thing for me that I was full-drunk. Otherwise I might have worried too much."

"You were drunk, besides."

"Yes, at first. The waitress goes shirtless."

"So I hear."

"One forgets all else," said Gudliev. "One drinks beer. One drinks brandywine. Time is nothing. She takes your crowns. She drops them into the music box. Her teats shake like little figs when she dances. I must send her a few crowns to repair her automobile. Or perhaps I have given her enough already. It's a problem I have been puzzling in my head."

"Have you money *left* in your purse, my young friend?"

"Not much, if any," Gudliev admitted. He began pulling off the tape and unwrapping the bandages. Presently he came to stains of blood.

"Here," said Gunnar. "Wrap them back, my boy!"

"The doctors at the hospital were kind," Gudliev said.

"And they knew what they were doing," said Gunnar, wrapping the bandages again, applying the tape, seeing after Gudliev as though he, Gunnar, were father of the household. "Don't pull them off again. We'll have a look day-after-tomorrow. Have you much pain?"

"Nay," Gudliev replied. "I feel as fit as ever. I can do my work."

"And to think you saved two of them. The white bigots were lynching them, I suppose? And in you flew with your fists and feet, my boy. The U.S.A. is a very sad case when a lad from Norway must teach them lessons." Gunnar shook his head. "A very sad nation and here in the U.S.A. I have uncles and cousins."

"So have I," said Gudliev. "Who hasn't?"

"But you saved two of the poor bastards. The whites were murdering them . . ."

"Not exactly," said Gudliev. "It was they, the black ones, who were murdering whites. There was a girl and a fellow. The blacks had captured their car. They were killing him and screwing her. The American stopped the armored truck. He got out — the woman was screaming."

"Father-god," Gunnar said softly.

"In my brain I saw my sisters. There were shrieks for help. Something exploded in me. It may be that I went berserk. The blacks themselves pitched in for me, one or two of them. It was a quick fight. I leaped over the automobile. I was a madman. A black was mating her, in the very act. The others held electric torches, screaming, jeering, watching and waiting their turn."

"Then you fought . . . on the *other* side," Gunnar said.

"We saved the woman, that's all I know," said Gudliev.

"You struck *blacks,* in anger?"

"By God, yes! Be a son of a bitch and go to the devil if I didn't! The bastards are savages, cannibals, smut faces!"

"My poor boy, those white master-racists ashore have brainwashed you. Truly, I fear it."

"Nay, by Christ. Son of a bitch and go to the devil —! Gunnar, *I was there.* The blacks were desecrating automobiles any man of Norway would give his legs to own. Gunnar, they are unholy savages. They respect nothing —"

"You had no right to interfere," Gunnar said. "Even if the blacks should get two of them on the other side what difference could it make to you? Don't you know it's centuries now that these poor black wretches have been beaten and raped and hanged and exploited by their colonial masters?"

"You have explained all that to me before, many thousand times, Gunnar. But, I warn you, if you speak to me about it again let me tell you that it will be the last word between us when both shall have a mouth with teeth up front."

"That's as it may be," Gunnar said, somewhat shaken and ruffled, to be sure.

"You may *live* to speak to me a second time but the tooth doctor will have done repairs on you meanwhile, and the jaw doctor perhaps, and perhaps the head doctor as well," Gudliev said. "I'm not so thick as to be unable to draw my own opinions, old man! Those bastards are black savages. How would you take it if you finally worked and saved every öre, every pfennig for thirty years and finally owned a car — *of your own* — and then *they* battered the life of it with cobblestones? Eh? What of that? How long have *you* dreamed of owning a car? How often have you told me those fairy dreams, eh? Taking the old lady and the kiddies for a drive in the mountains? Ho! A horde of black trolls jumps into the roadway with stones and clubs. Poof! Five minutes and the dream of your lifetime is a rubble of junk? And if that weren't enough then they set *fire* to it?"

"What attracted you was the automobile?" Gunnar looked a bit relieved.

"Of course! How could I know what it was screaming. It could have been a squalling pig for all I cared. But when I *saw* those monsters, those black, bastardly devils killing a fine new automobile! Gunnar, it was like a flame in my nuts. Fire shot up my spine bones like smoke leaving a chimney!"

"Aye?" said Gunnar. He had stretched out, but now he sat up again and swung down his thin legs in the usual way. "If they would treat a car that way then no matter what has gone before, I — perhaps even I can't forgive them. I — perhaps I would have fought myself. I don't know," he mused. "Still —"

"And as there was no saving the car," said Gudliev, a bit piously, perhaps, "as it was clear the poor automobile was beyond saving —" He let a note of sadness creep into his voice. "We had to be satisfied with carting off the dying man and the woman."

"Did it matter that they were white? I mean would you have defended black folk the same way? No — excuse me. It's not a fair question," Gunnar said. "Forget I posed it."

"No, by God and go to the devil, son of a bitch!" Gudliev exploded. "Let me pose *you* a question. If your old mother were being mauled by a bear, if five Lapps were raping your sister, your automobile was afire, and your father was thirsty for a bottle of beer, what would you do? Stroll to the grocery? It may be as it perhaps is that great Danish-talking bastards who live in Oslo and have such fine ways about them, weighing questions, making grand judgments, solving every problem in the world but their own, it may be as they are wiser than we Stavanger folk. It may be as we haven't so much time and money for beer halls and newspapers! But when we're called upon, be sure Mister Kingtongue, Mister Finemouth, be sure that Stavanger-folk answer with fists and feet. Then if there's talk to be done the mouthing can be tended afterwards, between such as remain standing and able! Well, shall we talk Stavanger-style Goldmouth? Eh — your royal highness?" Gudliev glowered at his friend. "Come on get up!"

"Leave off! Shove it, fishhead! Leave thinking to people with brains," Gunnar muttered, though somewhat timidly. "You're due on watch in ten minutes," he added.

"That's accurate," Gudliev said.

"Well, save this for another time? Shall we?" Gunnar said. And he sighed, as if to say *Look, what a burden!* And then: "You were born a bumpkin, Gudliev, but a finer shipmate no man could wish. Now relieve the watch and stop drinking ashore so much? Take a friend's advice."

Gudliev was rapidly changing to work clothes. "Aye," said Gudliev. His hands were aching, as though each finger had its own tiny pounding heart.

"Did you screw any glad girls?"

"Aye," said Gudliev. A couple."

"Tell Uncle Gunnar about it."

"Another time," said Gudliev coolly. He limped out but he went swiftly up the ladder, without touching the chains.

25

GYP

So a man said you want something to work with and I says
yeah. He gimme a short piece of iron pipe.

"This be about your size," he says.

So I took it and I walked over to a car wrecked by the curb
and I hit and busted out the windshield and then went around
the other windows busting them and he says that's a real good
job you doing and I tell him I say thanks for the pipe and he
saying sure, just had one extra and thought somebody might
need and enjoy having it. Then he set the gas tank on fire and
after that he got us a drink from a busted open store. I had
some beer and he had some gin and a crowd of peoples come
from the other direction and we went and joined in with them
and some started singing and passed beer around. And it was
real fun. Like Christmastime and better.

Then a car came. They had some cocktails in the car and we
all walked up to the drugstore and the boys started lighting the
cocktails and throwing them, bumming the drugstore, throwing
the bums against the walls and through the windows until
finally it got to burning real swell and we started to feeling
satisfied. I stepped across the street and taken me a brick and

busted out the window of the dry cleaning-shoeshine place. Somebody said why did I do that and I said well I never liked them esso bitches very much. That they always trying to short change you if you don't watch them and somebody else said was that right and I said hell yes so they got up another cocktail and pretty soon the cleaners was going almost as good as the drugstore and I ran and caught up with the crowd and we busted another place and got some more beer and whiskey and one real big guy he got several boxes of cheese and he started passing out the cheese, cutting it up in squares and passing it out so we would have something to eat and it was real good cheese and made me feel a whole lot better after I got something on my stomach. Next they bummed another loan company. It burned real swell, better than the shoeshine-cleaners.

We were all having fun and I was hoping and wishing that it would never be over, that it would go on and on this way like a lovely dream forever, with people dancing and singing and drinking and eating . . .

26

COUSIN ALABAM

Maybe you better get down low. Hide on the floor," said
the Blue Top driver. He had begun to turn through back
alleys and side streets, all the while working the vehicle closer
and closer in towards the Central and Woodyard districts.

"Whatever you say. I'll ride in the trunk. Would that be
safer?" Alabam Webster's throat had begun to feel as if he had
swallowed gunpowder. His tongue felt swollen.

"Nawsir, Mister Alabams," the little black driver was saying. "I don't b'lieve you gonna be no safer did you git in de
trunk. For say they do succeed and stop us and was to set us
afire in de gas tank like they has been doing, maybe hit might
turn out so I might not have no chance to get the trunk unlocked and opened?"

"The floor's fine, just fine," said the grocer. Down he went,
on all-fours like a dog.

The cab was moving faster now, suddenly picking up speed.

"I might haves to buss the speed limits a little bit now," the
driver was saying. "No tellin' what we liable to find frum now
on in."

As though for emphasis the cab suddenly lurched around a

corner. "Can't make it dat way," the driver was saying to himself. "Lawd, lawd! Let's see about dis here." Again the cab lurched, this time in the opposite direction, skidding and running on sand for a time, then back to hard, rough pavement. Suddenly the brakes were stomped. The grocer braced himself. The gears ground into reverse, the cab shot backwards.

"What's wrong! What's wrong?" the grocer called.

The cab wheeled in another direction and was soon going smoothly again. Something flickered against the car seat. Looking up the grocer glimpsed a flaming building. The tires crackled over broken glass.

"See we got the niggers and the police both to dodge," the little driver explained. "One or another of 'em bees just about everywhere you turn and look."

"I know you wouldn't let anyone stop us," the grocer said. Alabam Webster felt a headache coming. A pain had begun behind his nostril and was reaching, groping its way into his left eye. "Mister Purchase Walker said you were his best driver."

"He did say that?"

"Yessir, he sure did. Said you were the best man he had on his payrolls," the grocer lied, so saying because he himself so desperately wanted to believe that the Negro cab company owner had really said something of the sort. In reality all Walker had said was that he hoped to get a cab through to the 312 Club. He was sure, Walker had said, that he could get a Blue Top out to the grocer's Bayside home. No trouble there, he had said. The question was whether any driver could break through the cordon and make it down to the Three-Twelve. The risk was one the grocer would have to take — getting down into Central and getting out of Central afterwards. That is, if he wanted his store saved.

The grocer had wondered if it would not be simpler for Walker to come over to Bayside. The Negro had laughed, saying: "I think you better come down here." He hadn't left the grocer much choice.

"Very well," Alabam Webster had said, "send a cab." The Negro had not even bothered to say goodbye. Ten minutes later the Blue Top had whipped into the Bayside driveway. The grocer had gotten in the back seat wondering whether he were wise or foolish. At least he was responding to the only person who had offered concrete help, concrete support and concrete information.

"Your store is not burned or looted yet. There may be a possibility of saving it, but you must come down here at once," Purchase Walker had said.

"How close are we?" the grocer asked. Seemingly preoccupied with his driving the little Negro made no reply. "And now another thing," the grocer continued. "I want you to know Alabam Webster is never ungrateful for a favor. You get me there safe, I'm going to make you a nice present. Something above the amount of your regular fare."

"Don't worry about that, Mister Alabams," the little driver said.

"A week's free groceries from the Central Kutrate? How's that sound?"

"You don't have to do that," the driver said. "Mister Walker take care of me."

"But I want to show my appreciation. A week's free groceries?"

"Well — ah, that would be real nice. If they just don't burn that store down, because you know they *might* of already burnt it down. God-lawd look how dey bustin dat winder!"

The grocer heard soft waterfall crashes. "Here come a gang totin cases of whiskey. Set low now."

Ourfatherwhoartinheavenhallowedbethynamethykingdom comethywillbedoneonearthasitisinheavengiveusthisdayourdaily breadandforgiveusourtrespassesasweforgivethosewhotrespass againstusleadusnotintotemptationbutdeliverusfromevilforthine isthekingdomthepowerandthegloryforeverandeveramenour fatherwhoartinheavenhallowedbethynamethykingdomcome thywillbedoneonearthasitisinheavengiveusthisdayourdaily bread . . .

"Now we getting somewhere!" said the little driver, interrupting the tumult of the grocer's prayer-saying.

"What?" cried Alabam Webster. He had dropped his glasses. He was groping for them, and the floor was suddenly rancid as it had not seemed before, rank with flaccid aromas — cigarettes, chewing gum, niggers, sand, a cigar butt — ashes. His hands found the floor increasingly unsanitary and unhealthy. The cab lurched suddenly sideways again. His Panama hat was knocked off. Before he could recover it the cab seemed to leap, crashing over a series of bumps that caused the hat to be crushed, ruined. Another corner was rounded. The cab stopped.

"We here," the driver was saying. He opened the back door. "We here, Mister Alabams," he said.

The grocer pulled himself up awkwardly. He crawled out of the cab. He paused, brushing his clothes. "Are those firecrackers or — ?"

"I b'lieve they probably bees guns," said the driver. "They shoot back and forth that way now and then. We got by before they started up. What you do you wait and when you hear 'em about to stop that's the time when you cross through. What you have to do is hit that *pause.* You come through on that. That's why we had to patrol ourselves back and forth that way. Till they quit."

"I see," the grocer said. He was trembling.

"Some peoples on top of buildings that ain't been burnt yet? They shoots down into the street. Sorta plinkin around you know."

Another cascade of breaking glass — plate glass and about two thousand dollars worth of it by the sound — echoed from the nearby street.

"Right this way, in here," the driver was saying. "They naturally don't bother none of Mr. *Walker's* clubs or property."

"So this is safe?"

"Have no fear," said the little driver. "Mister Walker haves you in the hollow of his hand!" He opened the alley door and went ahead of the grocer down a carpeted hall illuminated by indirect blue lighting. The driver took off his uniform cap. He stopped before a wide mahogany door. He drew a deep breath and knocked lightly. The door was opened by a slender colored girl in an orange miniskirt. When she smiled her bright teeth and her beauty reminded the grocer of Cynthia. Vaguely, he wondered where Cynthia might be this instant, what she might be doing and thinking.

"This way, Mister Webster," said the young woman. "Follow me."

She swung past the grocer, going ahead of him across the azures and beiges of a large oriental rug, past a French antique table. Wall sconces lit the anteroom. A large painting in an ornate gold frame was hung on the wall to the right. It depicted a babe in arms being fed by a mother. Beside both, a little girl in a Dutch cap was peering fondly at the infant. A French clock was ticking on the mantel.

"The smell of smoke is not so bad in here like it is outdoors," the girl was saying in her musical voice. The grocer, who had not been aware of it till then, just as suddenly smelled it. Smoke and destruction. "If you will have a seat. I know Mister Walker is expecting you." She walked out and the grocer was left alone. On the left wall, opposite, there was another painting larger than the first. A court scene from old timey days. French or English, he decided. Young men in knee britches, young women in full dresses and wearing wigs piled high on their heads, eating and drinking, having a picnic, sitting together on the grass, walking arm and arm under the trees, and beyond them was a garden full of fancy statues.

The door at the far end of the room opened. "This way please," the girl called to the grocer. Another thought of Cynthia, a second pang of sinking remorse as the grocer followed the slender Negress into what obviously was the wealthy Negro's office. There was a desk, but the Negro himself was seated in a chair. He made no move to get up. He was reading, turning pages in a loose-leaf notebook. He took off his glasses.

"Have a seat, Mister Cousin Alabam," the Negro said. He wore dark slacks and a red smoking jacket with black lapels.

"You're Mister Walker?" the grocer heard himself saying. He felt strange without his glasses. The metal rims, the bifocal lenses, had always afforded him such a sense of confidence and protection that without them he felt rather naked. "I didn't expect anyone so young," said the grocer.

The Negro had slipped off his own glasses, heavy horn-rims. He touched the frames to his mouth and seemed to smile. "Of course I know *you* from your pictures," he said.

He's too young, the grocer was thinking.

"Your many civic charities and activities," the Negro was saying. "So I've seen *your* picture many times in the newspapers. Nobody takes my picture. I don't like to be photographed."

"Well, I've known who Purchase Walker was for so long. A leader and a fine businessman," the grocer said. He wiped his palms on the knees of his trousers.

"Rough trip?" the Negro asked.

"Not so bad, thanks," the grocer said, and: "I've known about you a long time."

"And now you see me in person," the Negro said. "And you need help, don't you, Mister Webster?"

"Call me Cousin Alabam if you want to," the grocer said. He ventured a smile. Purchase Walker seemed not to notice.

"Cigar? Brandy? Coffee?"

"Look, I'm —"

"I understand," the Negro said.

"There's a hell of a riot going," the grocer said. "Like you said on the phone —"

The Negro nodded. "We got a whale of a hell of a lot of trouble out there. And you, Mister Webster, you've got 78,000 square feet of supermarket. Modern, automated, brand new. Right here in the middle of all this trouble. Am I correct? Your Central Kutrate employs 312 persons full and part-time?"

A twisting shift of undercurrent in the conversation made the grocer wary.

"Yes," said Alabam Webster. "The store is — quite obviously, ah, it represents a considerable investment. Naturally I want to protect it if I can." How could this nigger know the square footage? The number of employees? Alabam Webster, suddenly on his guard, felt his knees go slightly numb. "If I can," he repeated slowly.

The Negro was smiling. "For fun let's assume I did a little research on your operation? Let's assume that I found out that between the two stores, Bayside and Central — Bayside being your fancy one, that between the two of them, Cousin Baby, you grossed just over thirty million bucks last year? Take it a step further, let's assume that I also know your markup is sixteen to twenty percent on groceries; twenty to twenty-four percent on fish; a shade less on center cuts. A shade more on lunch meats and bacon. Central Kutrate moves 35,000 bakery units a week — loaves of bread and such; three thousand cartons of milk."

"How did you come by those figures?"

"*Central* Kutrate, now in the *middle* of this riot, grosses between sixty-five hundred and seven thousand a week on sundries. You average 116 items a week as loss leaders — items sold at cost, or at less than retail. Central is far and away the more profitable store, compared to Bayside."

"Well," said Alabam Webster. "Well God damn."

"Play it cool, Cousin Baby. Don't take it hard. Because I haven't got started good. Because I want you to know, to be sure before we really *start* this little discussion that I know everything? From the age at which you quit wetting your pants to the time each morning you flush the john. How much you smoke, where you were this afternoon."

"So you've tried to do a job on me, Mister Walker?" The grocer felt himself beginning to bristle. "Why?"

"And while we're in the meat department." The Negro slipped on his glasses and consulted the notebook. "Last week Central Kutrate sold twenty tons of poultry. You sold seventy-five beeves. End cuts, I mean."

Alabam Webster gasped.

"Because the *fresh* centercuts, the *good* stuff, *that* all goes to the Bayside store, to white customers. The end cuts all come down here to be sold in Central. It so happens your end cuts operation, your nigger meat department, is more profitable than the operation over on Bayside. So it's sort of like the whiskey trade. More profit on the cheap half pint than on the imported fifth of Scotch."

"You have tried to do a job on me," the grocer said hoarsely. "Why?"

The Negro slapped the desk so hard the grocer nearly fainted. "You got the nerve to ask why? Let me tell you something — I don't care if they burn and loot and *dynamite* that God damned Central store of yours. Makes not a particle of difference to me what they do to it and I could wave my hand, *move my finger*, and your Central Kutrate is just one more burnt down place of business. All I have to do is pass the word and you're *out* of business down here permanently. Forever."

Purchase Walker was selecting a cigar. He found one, smelled it, trimmed it, and stuck it between his teeth. Looking thoughtfully in the grocer's direction he let the lighter flame burn a moment longer than necessary. "See?" Slowly, carefully, he warmed the cigar before he lit it. "See?" he said, laughing, suddenly shouting a raucous, arrogant laugh in the grocer's direction. "I know how many trucks of *cardboard* you sell a day. How many bags of ice your ice makers turn out; how many barrels of ashes they haul off from your incinerators." The Negro laughed again.

The grocer stood up in a white fury, clenching and unclenching his hands. "No!" he screamed. "No!" Then he sat slowly, slowly down again. "What right-minded employee —" Swiftly he calculated the malice of his trusted employees, his department heads, wondering who would peddle secrets to strangers. For a fleeting instant he recalled an insult scrawled in pencil, and crudely illustrated. He had found it on the wall of the employees' toilet, the men's toilet, in the Bayside store. "Cousin Alabam's mother —" the inscription had begun. The grocer had ordered the walls cleaned, painted over, and checked daily thenceforth for such childish, abusive attacks.

"Bacon — 30,000 pounds a week," the Negro was chanting. "Man, that's fifteen tons of bacon you sell in six days. Or take this one — 700 smoked hams, *last week*. A ton of lamb; three tons of pork sausage. Tell me how you do it?"

"Word of mouth is the best advertising," the grocer said wearily. "How did you get this information?"

"Four women on your staff fulltime sending out flowers and cards to every funeral and wedding. Sending a gift from Cousin Alabam to every new colored baby born in that sixty-seven bed roachtrap that passes for the nigger hospital. All of this loving attention from their Cousin Alabam."

"I came here because I thought you could help me," the grocer said. He felt dazed. "While we sit here Central is being smashed, looted — every building . . ."

"Not *my* buildings, Baby. I've lost some cabs, but no buildings. And not as many cabs —"

"And taxicabs," the grocer said. "I suppose I must have lost some cabs myself . . ."

"That you have. That you have. We got that much in common. But not one of my *buildings*, Cousin Baby. You dig? And nothing I have that means *big* dough."

"Smashing, looting," the grocer said. "Shooting . . ."

"Look," said the Negro suddenly. "I've been *out* there. Before you came, I walked around. This is my neighborhood and year after year you know what I've seen and witnessed? It's gone to seed. Shoddier every month. Just now tonight I saw my people talking in the streets, eating, and drinking. Children singing."

"Guns," said the grocer. "Gasoline bombs." He was trembling again. "Molotov cocktails . . ."

"This town has never appeared to me as beautiful before as it looks tonight, with the fires burning and the people outdoors. Sure some are getting hurt. Some are getting arrested. A few have died. But that happens every day *anyhow*."

"I need that store, Mister Walker," said Alabam Webster.

"Sure you do, because it's located *here*. For you and the rest of the whites who come in here and take the money out, back to Bayside, this is your colonial possession."

"You profit too," the grocer said. "You promised help."

"No Cousin. I *offered* it. For a price of course. You want the price tag, Cousin Baby?"

Cousin Alabam stared at the Negro. "I'll have you prosecuted," he said. "You got nothing but a few statistics . . ."

"Spoiled meat," the Negro said.

"What —?"

"Meat, dressed up with chemicals, marked down, disguised. You never *heard* of rotten meat? Diseased meat? Meat you wouldn't *touch*, much less eat, Cousin Baby?"

"All right. If you *can* help me," the grocer said hoarsely again. "You, the vice king, with your numbers rackets and whore houses. All right. What's your offer?"

"That's much better," the nigger said. "Much, *much* better."

"Let's get down to business," the grocer said. "You're offering me help."

"But don't rush. I'm in no hurry. Nobody's going to take

away all *my* nice little black and tan chicks. Nor a game we call bolita. Nobody can burn that up and destroy it. What I have can be moved out of the way of destruction. I mean who's going to burn *all* my girls or wreck *all* my cabs? But 78,000 square feet of building? What a target, Mister Webster!"

"I came here," the grocer gasped. "Only because I thought you might want to use your influence with the nigra community — to save my store."

"You can call me Purchase."

"Because I know you have influence. You're a very successful young businessman, Purchase. You're what I'd call a real Christian at heart. I can tell by just looking at you. A Christian — and I mean it in the best sense of the word." The grocer forced a smile, knowing how ghastly he must look. He forced a smile of warmest Christian sincerity, nonetheless.

The Negro grinned, puffed at the cigar, and tipped a length of gray ash into the crystal ashtray at his elbow. He tapped the notebook with his index finger. "Wrong, Cousin Baby, dead wrong. You're here because you tried the sheriff, you tried the police, you tried the mayor. You even had the mayor call the colored preachers for you, including my own preacher, Father Ned Matthews. The mayor even tried the governor of this God damn *state*. He got you nowhere. *None* of them got you anywhere . . . One cocktail has already hit your store roof. Somebody — maybe one of your friends? Me —? Somebody snuffed *that* one out — right?"

"Then — then it was your organization . . . then you'd exploit . . . you'd take advantage of this situation! No, I *know* why you did it. I know why you're helping me. You might want a favor from me some day! And besides, I *know* you're a Christian," the grocer said, groping his way, trying to smile through a dawning realization that this big black son of a bitch was actually enjoying himself. Small tides of anger began rinsing Alabam Webster. His smile came harder and harder. "Either you won't help me or you can't help me," Alabam Webster was saying. And at last he quit trying to smile. "I'm not here to bargain or make deals. I merely —"

"You *need* that store. Admit it!"

The grocer nodded. It was so true. He surrendered.

"What's the deal?" he said, and felt instantly better.

"I'm going to pay you twenty thousand cash for your taxi license — company, cabs, equipment. You're going to sign the bill of sale and the receipt for the money. Ton-Ton will notarize the contracts."

The grocer nodded. Wounded but not dead, he was thinking. Hurt, by God, but not killed.

Caught by a nigger. A nigger, by God.

"All right. It's robbery, but bring the papers," he heard himself saying. "I'll sell. I'll sign."

27

LEROY

It was a sporting goods store. Leaping through the broken window Leroy found a wild west style 30–30 carbine, brand new, and the price tag was still hanging on it.

Snatching up the gun, he began rummaging along the ammunition shelves. In all there were five boxes of 30-30 shells, 100 rounds. He picked up a skinning knife with a fine hand-tooled scabbard. While slipping the knife on his belt he looked around him. In the spilled and looted jumble of merchandise there were many, many items of value. Nice field glasses. Several fine archery sets, but the place was on fire and he was in a hurry. Leroy stuck the shell boxes inside his shirt, taking care to button it. Then he leaped back through the window and sprinted across the street to the alley. Darkness made running easier. He climbed the warehouse ladder effortlessly, cradling the gun, smelling the good smell of oil and new metal. Once on the roof he unbuttoned his shirt. Riding like they did the boxes made him look pregnant, all pooched out in front. The notion amused him. Like some knocked up chick, ready to throw one any day now, he thought. Pregnant with bullets, that's what. The thought was a tingling in his arms. Hot damn!

Carefully laying out his ammunition he opened a box, took

out a shell and levered open the carbine's chamber. The mechanism made an abrupt, impressive sound. He felt the weapon with frustrated fingers. Sure as hell this mother ain't *single* shot, he thought. Then he found what he wanted. The magazine loaded from the side. Shoving in one shell after another he loaded the rifle until the tubular magazine would hold no more. And now he approached the edge of the roof. There was a wall on his left. Leaning against it, Leroy peered into the street.

The cop was still there at the intersection, by the corner near a mailbox. The carbine was still propped on his hip. Nearby, in a police car blocking the intersection, sat another cop. The cherrytop on the cruiser was revolving. The cop in the street holding the carbine wore a white helmet with a strap that passed under his fat chin. The cop in the patrol car was hatless. He sat slouched there with the car door open. He was talking to the other one, and smoking a cigarette. While Leroy watched the hatless one flipped the cigarette to the sidewalk. *Which one? Who comes first?* Leroy wondered, and his belly swelled. He got a good, powerful feeling, all watery and wonderful inside him, like a mixture of love and fear, like falling down from a high place. It gave him a throb. His nerves seemed suddenly strummed, like guitar strings; then a change came and the feeling was different. It was suddenly like walking in a big important cafeteria and seeing everything in the food line, everything to choose from and pockets full of folding money. Reach for the pies, load the whole tray with nothing but pies and go sit at a table. Still Leroy can't begin. Fork in hand but Leroy can't start to eat because he keeps on thinking and wondering which to eat first. The enjoyment slides down, buttering his ribs, and going on down, between his legs, and finally he takes the first bite . . .

Riot cop, Leroy decided. He levered a shell into the chamber.

The sound, just right — *wonderful!* Still the cop didn't budge. Stock still he stood, and so close, almost in touching distance, he seemed, and in the same place as before. Birdlike, and not expecting a thing.

Framing the man above the sights Leroy jerked the carbine's trigger. No soap, a miss.

The cop looked around suddenly as though wondering where the sound came from and uncertain what to do; wondering if the sound could have anything to do with him, not wanting, maybe, to believe it did. He kept looking around, like a bird. Shoot at a bird with a b.b. gun. Watch it fly up and settle back on the wire in the same place, because maybe it can't connect you and that bead that just barely missed it.

Aiming again Leroy remembered what somebody once told him about *squeezing* the trigger. Squeezing that God damn trigger and holding on target so you really don't know yourself *when* that gun will go off, remembering:

"By the time that gun kicks, if you shooting a *big* rifle, the bullet has already gone? So the kick don't have nothing to do with it if you miss or hit. It's the trigger *pull*, see?"

Leroy took a practice aim. Then, lowering the gun, he levered another shell into the chamber. Taking aim again, he was careful now to touch the trigger with the mere tip of his finger. Slowly, gently, patiently — he began to squeeze. His finger tingled. The rifle jerked savagely against his shoulder. Simultaneously the cop sprawled backwards. His helmet rolled away. His carbine hit the street with a clatter. He was screaming, hollering for help and the other cop, who had been sitting in the car with the door open, leaped out. He was leaning over the wounded man. Leroy levered in another round. Carefully, he squeezed the trigger again. Down went the second cop, jerking down crossways of the first one, his arms flailing. The first cop screamed again and then moved, crawling from under the second one, dragging himself like a sick rat. He moved on all fours to the police car. He reached the door. Slowly he hauled himself into the front seat.

Gonna use the radio. Call help, Leroy thought.

Sure enough there was a siren. Kneeling, Leroy shoved the ammunition boxes back inside his shirt. He buttoned it carefully. Crossing the warehouse roof he climbed nimbly down into the alley and set off running. Down streets and back streets, through alleys and sandy lanes; he knew these trails like his tongue. Meanwhile the sirens fell away far behind him. Shooting opened up from back where he had been. The cops would be shooting out every window above that motherly intersection. It was their way. They started shooting and they imagined somebody was shooting back because there was no telling, the way shots echoed, where a shot or noise came from. And while they stayed in one place shooting the way they did, it was no trick for a sniper to move far away to another position, to another roof, to another target . . .

Where spur tracks crossed a street ahead Leroy bore left, running lightly, the ammo boxes jogging against his belly. The rifle carried easily in his slender hand. He saw a crowd in the midst of the intersection, a mass of Negroes smashing a car and hollering. There was a fight going. A woman was screaming bloody murder. The cries put a cold claw in Leroy's gut. He swung left, giving the scene wide berth, running and running on and on, yet her screams seemed to stay with him, somehow hanging on his insides like bats, roosting upside down.

"Christ, they killen somebody. Christ they got to be," he whispered.

The cries went down on him, deep down, and made him uneasy.

He found the rusty fire access ladder in the dark sandy corridor between two warehouses. He climbed again, and swiftly crossing the broad roof, he found another spot. There was a fine view of Central in two directions. A firetruck passed beneath him, sirens growling full blast. He wasted four shells, firing wildly. "Wasting shells; cool it," he told himself.

He laid out the ammo boxes, neatly as before. Then, leaving his gun behind for the moment, he descended swiftly to the alley and ran to the corner. Central was deserted.

He ran across the street, took a brick from the sidewalk, and calmly smashed out a window. It was the Merrytimes Liquor Store. The glass cascaded, splintering to the sidewalk. Leroy leaped through the opening, knocking aside cardboard displays. Catlike, he bounded to the rear of the store.

He opened the refrigerator. He took out a cold six-pack of Miller's. Next he walked calmly back and forth, ranging the neatly dusted shelves.

Finally he settled on a pint of apricot brandy and a fifth of White Horse Scotch.

With hands full of beer and booze he leaped back through the shattered window into the contrasting warmth of the street, only now realizing how cool the air-conditioned store had been.

Sprinting across the wide, warm street he climbed the rust gritted ladder, with the six-pack under one arm, and the bottles tucked inside his shirt.

He opened a beer and picked up the rifle. "Better *re*-load," he said aloud.

He squatted. He put the beer can aside and reloaded.

Afterwards he stood for what seemed a long while, holding

the rifle in the crook of his arm, and drinking beer. He watched the street below. Far down toward Magnolia immense lights appeared. An engine roared. As the vehicle came closer Leroy recognized the riot wagon. On it came, droning like a bus. As it passed Leroy threw the beer can. It hit the roof of the wagon and bounced in the street, rolling toward the gutter.

"Why waste bullets?" Squatting down to open the brandy he recalled the woman's screams. He took a couple of swallows. He felt the brandy drain down to his deep insides. If he drank enough would he start feeling good again? He wondered.

A car was passing up Central, a police cruiser. Letting it get gone a ways, Leroy opened fire. The car swerved. Then, with a burst of sudden speed, it skittered and squealed, rounding a corner, roaring away. Leroy laughed.

Having me a gazz, he thought. Hot damn Mama see me now. Hot damn!

He swigged half the sweet brandy before opening a second beer. And finally he sat down with his back to the wall. The urge began to grow like a swelling. He put the gun aside and uncovered himself to the night air, to the sirens and the yells and the flames and gunfire rat-tatting; to intervals of stark silence; and his swelling grew. Leroy sat naked in the world and presently his hands moved and found the growth of his desire swollen and hard and with hardly a thought for what he did, he began. With his back to the wall he began, and visions came at him, slowly at first, and then faster . . .

The riotcop and rifle. Death and womanscream.

Darkness . . .

28

CUTLER

LUCKY for you it was your eyelid," the doctor was saying.

"Lucky for me," Cutler said. "Yeah, I got covered up with luck." He grunted.

He could feel the doctor's breath.

"Several eyes have been severely damaged. Some people have lost their eyes tonight. Count your blessings."

"Yeah," Cutler said. "Are you about through?"

"Just about," said the doctor. "I think you're lucky you got out alive." He was suturing the lid. Cutler's face was numb. "Hell, you didn't even lose teeth."

"I want to see my girl," Cutler said.

"Just hold still please," said the doctor. "I'd say you were *awful* lucky."

Let the bastard talk then, Cutler decided.

"I'm wondering why you ever drove down there with your girl in the first place."

"We knew there was a riot going on and we decided we'd like to see what it's like to get raped and have the shit beat out of us," Cutler said.

The nurse laughed. "God," she said. "God help!"

"You're going to have a lot of swelling," the doctor said. "This will need to be looked after." He was bandaging the eye. "You sure got lucky."

"Where's my girl?"

"She's upstairs. I'll find out where," the nurse said.

"Okay," said the doctor. "Let's shift you over to the cart. She can wheel you away."

"Thanks," said Cutler.

"I'll bill you. Don't worry," the doctor replied. "I'm not going to all this trouble just out of the kindness of my heart. No sir. I'm in this racket to get rich. Is the next customer black or white?"

"Take your choice," the nurse said.

"Okay, bring me a black one," the doctor said. "Variety is the spice of life. And *you* take it easy," he called after Cutler.

"I can walk," Cutler was saying.

"Lie still," said the nurse. "Cracked ribs, split ear, broken nose, busted hands. Sure you can walk. You realize how lucky you are you didn't lose teeth? You know how many teeth have gone in the wastebasket tonight?"

"I want my girl," Cutler said.

"That's where we're going."

The cart was pushed into an elevator. The doors closed.

"She's up on nine. I'm probably not supposed to be doing this, you know."

"If you'll just let me stand up I'll show you I can walk," Cutler said.

"Shut up," the nurse said pleasantly. She laid her hand gently against his cheek. Her cool touch relaxed him. The elevator hummed to a stop. The doors opened. They were in the corridors again.

"Nine-oh-seven?" the nurse asked.

"Right down there. Is that a male patient?"

"He wants to see his girl."

"Oh. Cynthia."

"Right," Cutler said.

"He's the one that was with her."

"He's the one," said the nurse. She touched Cutler's cheek again.

"She's been asking for him. It's a ward. You may get some gripes — but I doubt it. Did you get permission?"

"No," Cutler said.

"Go ahead then. As long as you don't ask and get a negative in advance. If anybody says anything we didn't have this conversation."

"Right," said Cutler's nurse. They were moving again. A door opened. "Six beds, all full," said the nurse.

"Which one is Cynthia?"

"Here."

"Visitor to see you."

"Rann?"

"Hi, kid. What was it like?"

"Not too bad. And you?"

"I haven't heard a word aside from how lucky I am."

"What about your eye?"

"Just sliced his lid. No eye damage," said the nurse.

"It happened, then?" Cutler said. "They . . ."

"Yes, but they aren't going to put it in the papers. Isn't that nice?"

"Yes, it's nice of them," Cutler said. "Nice . . ."

"Does it matter — I mean . . ."

"Well if you're asking if I'm happy about it. If you mean wouldn't I like to kill about fifty of them, it matters. But if you mean in the other sense . . . spiritually, physically, esthetically . . ."

"That's what I mean," Cynthia said.

"Don't be silly. We're getting out of here. We're cutting out. I can walk. Can you?"

"I think so. I'm pretty sore."

"You're both talking foolishness," the nurse said. "You can't get *released* tonight."

"Shut up," Cutler said. "You need our beds."

"True," said the nurse.

"We're going to the airport if you can walk," Cutler said.

"What about luggage?"

"No luggage," Cutler said.

"In bloody clothes?"

"Maybe we'll have to stop by my apartment and grab clothes."

"That's better," Cynthia said. "The airport, and then where?"

"Tennessee. To meet my folks, to visit the glorious ruins and remains of the clan Cutler. I might need some of their pull, for a steady job."

"Those alcoholic sisters," Cynthia said.

"The whole horrible outfit," Cutler said. "That's going to be our honeymoon. Somewhere along the way maybe we'll even get married."

"This guy's full of good ideas, isn't he," the nurse said.

"Yes," Cynthia said. "He can be one brilliant son of a bitch when he tries to be."

"Shhhhh! Other patients!"

"Well, if they heard me they know the truth about Rann Cutler. If they didn't it's their hard luck," Cynthia said.

"I'm going to show you I can walk," Cutler was saying.

[293]

"First let's go see about getting you *released*, okay cowboy?" the nurse said. "And we'll take care of you too, Cynthia. I think you better get on that plane while he's still in the notion. I get off work in about forty minutes. I'll drive you."

"We can make it —" Cutler began. The cool hand covered his mouth. "Shut up. I want to help, I can help, and I'm going to!"

"Thanks," Cynthia said. "That's lovely of you." She was weeping.

"I'm hoping to get a man someday myself," said the nurse. "Maybe *I'll* need help. Besides, I like driving to the airport. Almost makes you feel you might be going somewhere yourself someday. We'll send for you in a minute," she said.

"Thanks again," Cynthia said. "'Bye, Rann."

The cart was moving again. In the elevator the nurse touched his cheek.

"Sure you can walk?"

"Try me," said Cutler. "I might need some help with Cynthia, though."

"You'll have it, honey. You'll have it," she promised. "Now let's get you released out of this madhouse."

29

THE CONSUL

When I reach the station Paco Perrone, the mayor, asks what, if anything, he can do for me in return for bringing him the riot wagon, and by the way haven't we met somewhere before and I say: "Paco, we both belong to Rotary," and he says, "Oh, yeah, that's right, we do. Now you *need* anything?" And I tell him I might appreciate a ride home and one telephone call? My wife might be wondering about me and her car by now.

Paco allows my sense of humor to sail straight over his slightly balding young head.

He goes pacing back and forth beside me like a second-string fullback trying to get Coach to send him in the game, Paco Perrone is not about to hear me. Not really.

"Fine," says Paco Perrone, the mayor. "Good," he says.

"And I wouldn't mind getting my wife's car back, Paco."

That one stops him. "*Car?* What car?" says Paco, as though he never heard the word. "What car?" Paco frowns.

"I drove down to Station Four this afternoon in my capacity as Norwegian consul of Ormund City. I took my wife's car — a brand new baby blue Buick loaded down with all the extras the dealer, the manufacturer, and my wife could think to hang on it. It's pale baby blue."

"Oh," says Paco. "*That* car." He looks at me then like he's seeing me again for the first time. It's coming to me gradually that perhaps Italians are the only people in the world who can pull this stuff consistently. It takes — hell it *requires* an Italian to really pull this off, I'm thinking. And Paco: "You mean you want *us* to get your car from Station Four? *Now?* Ah — uh. Well. I see and well if things clear up a little by *tomorrow* maybe we *can* but for the time being .. ." He lets the idea slide deeper and deeper into the back of that vacuum cleaner bag a biologist might term "Paco's brain." "Okay?" he says.

"Oh, well," I say. "It's just her brand new automobile."

With this Paco explodes. Hearty, nervous, political laughter.

Then he turns deadly serious. Our fullback is really going into the game. "Then I'll take you with me," he's saying. "You can drive the crowd control wagon."

"Now I don't mind driving the God damn tank," I'm saying. (Somewhere along the bus line the idea of giving me a ride home has become outmoded as I'm rapidly discovering.) "But goddammit where the hell are we going?"

Fleetingly I think about throwing in what the policeman at Station Four said about just one Molotov cocktail, what it would do for the wagon, but you don't do that to a fullback putting on his helmet. You don't tell him he has no protection.

"That's right," says Paco. A strange look, a spaghetti-inspired Roman shadow, begins creeping over the mayor's shady Italian features. Paco looks, eyeballing me.

Paco discovers me, again! He is Columbus discovering the New World, for the third time.

I'm expecting Paco, any minute, to ask me my name, rank

and serial number and suggest that maybe we've seen each other some place before? But his town's on fire, after all and he has started to tremble and he looks like "well, we all have to die sometime or other." Or maybe: "We, who are about to die, salute you!" I can't quite decide which it is with Paco. He's true-blue though. I have to admire him.

"Didn't *you* grow up in Ormund?" says Paco.

"Who, me?" I say.

"Well, yeah," says Paco. "Didn't you?"

"Well, yes," I say. "Yes, by God, now you mention it. So I did. Did you?"

"You know the little nigger Episcopal Mission Church on the corner—well near the corner of Woodyard where it runs into Central?"

"Well, I think I could find it," I say.

"Christ," says Paco. "Jesus Christ we *can't* miss it. There's a Jew store and a drugstore and a dry cleaner's across the street burning, on fire. It's a brick church. Red brick."

"In that case," I'm saying, "it would be hard to miss."

"Christ, we can't miss it. Any idiot could find it. You wouldn't mind helpen me pick up Father Ned and a nigger named Boston Humes at the clinic and taken them a place Father Ned can show us. It's back of the 312 Black and Tan. Would you mind, Allen?" He gives me his "We are both in Rotary, after all," look.

"I suppose not," I say. "But I would like to have one phone call. I got married a few years back and she has not heard from me lately, like all day today. She's probably worried sick out of her head about her car."

"In that case I'll see if we can get a line clear. Wouldn't you think so?" Paco is asking the chief of police.

"Sure," says the chief in a distracted voice. "I think that's very reasonable. Sound thinking. By the way a white woman was raped."

"What's wrong with the phones?" I ask Paco. Meanwhile the chief has grabbed a phone and is trying to get my wife on the line, trying to get an operator, a dial tone — anything. It's like watching an ape trying to operate an electric canopener.

And Paco: "See, everybody away from here has seen it on teevee and heard it on the radio so they're all trying to call and see if Grandmaw or Aunt Lucy or Cousin Edna is dead or something. So you got all that incoming."

"Right. Right," says the chief, nodding.

"And meanwhile Brother Dan and Sister Sue and seventeen thousand niggers are trying to call Chicago and St. Louis to tell their cousin's half brother by marriage either, one, that they are all right or, two, that the house just burned and the store is on fire, two kids are in the hospital. Multiply this by *thousands?* Get the picture?"

"Right," says the chief. "The circuits overload. Blooey — just when you need 'em, no phones. Just like wartime conditions in a country under attack and being invaded."

"Right," says Paco. "Only what we are calling this is a very mild — *very* mild — crowd control problem. And we are going to solve it tonight. Right now. That's our purpose for going down here right away. I b'lieve Chief's got your wife on the wire, buddy?"

I take the phone.

"Where the hell have *you* been all evening?" I say. "Drunk again!"

"God damn you can't you ever quit clowning?" she says. She's been crying. "Is the chief correct when he tells me that *you*, Charley Brown, *you* are going to take the mayor of this misbegotten sandpile down to some church and elsewhere in the Woodyard?"

"Yes, I've been volunteered."

"Where's my car?" she says. "I wonder why I insisted you drive mine in the first place. The chief says it's over in the middle of the God damned riot."

"It is. Right where Daddy left it. Parked beside Po-lice Fo-ah!"

"That's the station they're threatening every five minutes to burn," she says. "I've been watching the tube what with you gone and the baby's asleep and Fred's eating cereal and *reading*. He's gassed because the usual Sunday programs are all fouled up — canceled."

"Did he ask about me?"

"Yeah. One time I think he said 'Where's Daddy?' and I told him to shut up or I'd belt him in the mouth."

"How did he take it?"

"Very reasonably. He shut up. No more daddy questions from Fred. His real hang-up is the teevee. It's a real one for him. So what are you going to do? Get your fool self killed?"

"Probably. Paco is so sincere. I can't resist him. We're both Rotarians and all that . . ."

"Did you get the sailor turned loose?"

"Yes. He's back on his ship by now, I guess."

She was quiet for what seemed a long while. "You okay?" I ask.

"I can't ask you not to do it," she says. "If you weren't such a lousy God damned wonderful fool I could probably ask you not to do it. But you're such a son of a bitch. Is the city all fresh out of policemen?"

"Just about," I say. "Firemen too."

"All right. Do your duty. How's that?"

"Coming from you, old girl, that's pretty swell, I'd say."

"Just don't come hollering and bleeding and blaming Mommy when they bring you back here feet first. Okay?"

"Okay." Another silence. "Either I'll bring my shield or be lying on it."

"You want to say 'hi' to Freddy?"

I think about it seriously.

"Tell Fred Daddy said hi."

"Sure. That's better," she says. "The only news I have is pretty out-of-date stuff. For better or worse I love you. So much it hurts. And you're a son of a bitch to risk everything I have in this world — not to mention my new car — you're a terrible bastard to hazard our life together, everything, more than half of me by doing this thing. But I can't tell you not to go. So I'm going to hang this God damned thing up and I will expect you when I see you. God help me I'm going to stay here and keep house. Maybe I'll see you on the tube. This has about cured me of teevee."

"If a camera comes my way, sweet lady, be sure I'll wave."

"I'm hanging up now," says she. She hangs up.

"Very well, gentlemen," say I. "Shall we set off?"

Paco picks up a sawed-off automatic shotgun and three boxes of riot loads.

"Might as well," Paco says. "Now is about as bad a time as any, I guess, he, he, he! We'll want to go right on through at top speed," says Paco.

I hear him load shells into the shotgun, one after another. Five in all, and the hair on my neck wakes up.

Paco is saying goodbye and he'll be talking to headquarters

by radio. Don't worry about a thing, he's saying. Once more he's the portrait of Sunny Italy.

And out we go. We climb in the riot wagon and shut the doors.

"Christ, what a natural for a Molotov cocktail," Paco observes. "What's top speed?"

"Nineteen. You mean *you* don't know?"

"Ninety — good, we may need it," says Paco. "We may need every ounce of it. The situation is much, much worse. Fire-trucks can't get through. We've tried to cordon off the area. Containment. What I'm going to tell this leader, Purchase Walker, is the stark truth. Law and order must be restored. That's my whole pitch. Law and order. How do you think that will sound? Allen? Law and order?"

"It will sound great," I tell him. And after a pause: "If we get there." I can already see fires flaring down in Central.

"Is *this* top speed?" says Paco.

"This is it," I say.

A couple of bricks or stones bounce off my side of the wagon.

"Where's that coming from?" says Paco.

Something new begins hitting the wagon.

"That's rifle fire," I tell him.

He's quiet then. We trundle slowly toward our destination.

"This must be the church," I say. Shots knock holes in the silence.

30

SON OF CONSOLATION

GYP

SOMEBODY said the riot wagon was pulling in behind the 312 Club, so some of us took out running that direction and sure enough it was there. It was in the alley back of the 312. There was a crowd already piled up in there like potatoes and the lights on the wagon were so bright you couldn't bear to look straight at them or they would make you blind as God. The wagon stopped.

A Blue Top rolled up next and a man got out. His head was bandaged and I didn't know him at first. Then I saw it was Poor Boston.

"Hey Boston!" I hollered at him. He come backing out of the cab and straightened up. He looked at me.

"Who is it?"

"Gyp," I says. "You done forgot me already? What you doing?"

"They got a meeting inside. Purchase and the mayor and Father Ned," he says. "They sent after me to come."

The riot wagon engine shut down. The bright lights went off and the door to the wagon opened and a couple of whities climbed down. The crowd clapped their hands. Maybe they thought it was hot stuff for a couple of white crackers to come down here, I don't know. A lot of them were drunk as me and they clapped and pretty soon everybody was clapping all together like marching so I started clapping because if you can't shut 'em up you better join 'em. Ain't making no money, so I might as well clap, I thought.

Boston just stood still like maybe he wasn't sure what he better do. Like he was bewildered and didn't know where he was.

BOSTON

Gyp standing there clapping her hands and I don't see no sign of Leroy. And I have to guess it's the mayor coming out of that truck. It ain't any way to be *sure* of anything and then the door to the 312 building opens and out walks Purchase and raises his hands up over his head like the referee at a prize fight.

They see Purchase and they stop clapping, so I think well maybe they was clapping for Purchase to come outside. Maybe *that's* why they was clapping. And then I looked at Gyp again and she looked just the same, like nothing had happened, like Hatcher had never been born, that was how she looked.

"All right!" says Purchase, loud as he can yell. "Now what we have, we have the mayor down here. So we are gonna get these fires put out and we are gonna get these streets cleaned up and we are gonna cool it because our point has been made. So let's cool it, *now*."

"Hell, *no!*" somebody hollers.

"Listen to me! I got Father Ned inside, in this building behind me here and in front of me here you see the mayor and with him another gentleman. They all came down here to work this thing out and give us what we have wanted for so long, for all these years . . ."

"Freedom now!" some kid yells just beside me. Can't be more than twelve. "Freedom now!" he squeaks again.

"Shut your face, kid," I says.

"Father Ned has something to say," Purchase went on and with that he stood aside and the priest come out the door and he stood there for a long time. And I thought he looked mighty tacky and shaggy standing that way, hunched over, but finally he said something. Finally the words began to come through and to reach me, tired as I was and hurt as I was. His words started getting to me and it was strange. And under that bandage my head felt like somebody had poured hot grease on me and burned my skullbone crisp as parched corn. It was like the hurt had remained in it, caught in a tight spiderweb of heat and flame and I thought maybe something has broke my stitches. Perhaps my wound has started to leak again and bleed because I could feel how it was tight and swelled. But when I did put up my fingers to feel the bandage was dry and I wondered if my imagination had finally broke down and started running away with my mind. I said to myself *everything* has begun to break down on me. I felt dizzy again.

FATHER NED

And they started hearing me and the words came one after another. It was no trouble once I got going and when the quiet settled over them, restless though they were, I knew the worst was over. I knew I was changed and I did not know why, but I knew something had happened.

"The peace that passes all understanding," I said. "The love that is living in our hearts," I said.

Then Boston came forward out of the crowd. We both stood aside and then followed the mayor into the building.

31

THE WOODYARD

The rubbish is swept away. Pieces are pulled together and the dead lie buried in the walled cemetery where Big Cuba was laid to rest. Hatcher lies buried and his was a big funeral with many people coming to pay their final respects. And Hatcher thus goes to the grave a martyr. And Gyp is back in the street and Leroy stands first at one corner and then another wearing the shoes which look like fifty dollar shoes. The world passes Leroy like a slow wind and he lets his mind and his thought roll back and come forward, back and forth over that trail of memory.

Father Ned will sometimes be seen, the incessant priest, moving as though brought back to vibrant life by the blood letting and the bone shattering, by that catharsis of explosions and fires and that pin-puncture rip of bullets popping the air. What the priest says and what he does seems to have less effect than his presence, for it has come to be said of him that when others were hiding and fearful it was Father Ned who walked the streets. It was Father Ned who tended the wounded, who comforted mourners, and who afterwards spoke on his people's behalf in the councils of the city: Father Ned.

The doctor is more withdrawn. What he sees and thinks is not revealed. The clinic has a soiled odor that will not be cleansed away. No amount of scrubbing removes the odor — is it the doctor's obsession, his imagination, that the hallway and the treatment rooms will never again smell clean?

Painters frequent the clinic, dressed in white coveralls, wearing white caps. Empty paint cans are a cluster on the lawn. Nothing, the doctor confides, nothing he does can remove the strange stench. Of course it isn't blood. No, he says. It's more the odor of unwashed feet. The doctor's wife wakes in the deep midst of still tropical nights. She wakes sobbing and dreaming. She dreams of fires. A siren sets her shuddering, rocking back and forth, arms clutched across her abdomen. Nothing seems to calm her.

Purchase Walker goes his way as before. He joins the church and is confirmed by the bishop. Ton-Ton bears his son out of wedlock. Purchase leads his people, but in strange ways for it comes to be rumored that he drinks chicken blood and that on Fridays he walks out on the roof garden above the Black and Tan. He goes there alone and in darkness and seems either to pray for forgiveness or to converse with someone. Rumors vary, but all agree that when Purchase Walker gets drunk on rum, he howls. Now and again he howls like a murdered dog. And people fear him.

As Fate must have it, Poor Boston takes over Papa John's, by what arrangement or non-arrangement with Watridge no one knows, for Watridge disappeared and Dimple Morton too. Dimple has left the police force and has drifted on, on South, perhaps.

Like a graven image Poor Boston sits solid as stone behind the cash register. Nothing is added but a couple of pool tables that provide the click of balls, that familiar resultant murmur and click, and that sudden commotion when the balls are racked up anew and sorted, dropping against the felt and sounding on the solid slate beneath.

Boston makes no effort to fix up or to change anything. He has the wisdom. Boston even leaves in place the burnt out, bonewhite neon sign that Watridge in his white man's vanity installed on the front of Papa John's. Boston leaves that glass mark of Watridge's folly hang weathering where it is, washed by tropical rains and glazed by a tropical sun and shaded by the crowding, mysterious trees.

Boston attends sessions of the new Bi-racial Committee. Taking his place about the table at city hall he hears talk of parks, of summer youth programs, of imminent police reform. The words slide like a slow river, meandering harmlessly across his mind. Concepts drift like water hyacinths on the dark surface of the River Meade, now seen, now disappeared; and all of this fated, he knows, for the salt tides of forgetful forgiveness.

Before such a meeting is half over he has folded his hands. His lids become heavy, and finally he dozes. As the meeting ends the mayor wakes Boston with a gentle touch on the shoulder.

The old man rouses. He looks up. As recognition gradually glides into his features Poor Boston invariably gets to his feet; invariably sighs, stifles a yawn and tells the mayor: "Thank you. I surely had a nice time."

And then, after saying further polite farewells, he goes home, back across town to the Woodyard.